I0742983

To my Tribe,

Thank you for indulging me the space and time to weave this tale.

Contents

Prologue

♥

San Marcos, Guatemala

San Marcos, Guatemala

I sat in the departure lounge at San Marcos airport caught in my daytime musings.

Out of the corner of my eye I catch the distinctive cerulean blue Kingman plane descending towards the runway. I leaned forward and craned my neck to get a better view. The older gentleman sitting opposite me flashed an inquiring look.

"My husband is the pilot," I said, beaming with pride.

"You must be proud of him." His Texan drawl was unmistakable.

"Every day," I said, with what I knew would be a dreamy look on my face. Nolan did that to me.

Excited, I stood up and walked towards the wall of viewing windows so I could watch Nolan perform — this was his stage, and I was always in awe. He was a skilled airman, always cool under pressure, and the display before my eyes was a testament to his skill.

I loved watching him land a plane, whether it was from a distance or sitting next to him in the cockpit.

As I continued to observe, the plane deployed its landing gear.

His plane barely touched down on the landing strip when I see what looks like a flash.

A split second later, Nolan's plane exploded right before my eyes.

I let out a piercing scream; horrified. I immediately wanted to run towards the metal debris scattering along the narrow runway.

I needed to do something, anything, to help my boys. The Texan, who watched the horrific scene unfold, grabbed me from behind just as I launched myself towards the door.

"Where the hell do you think you're going?" he yelled over the commotion ensuing in the departure lounge as he turned me around to face him.

"I need to get to my husband and sons. They are all on that plane," I wailed, looking straight past him to the horrors on the tarmac.

With his eyebrows raised and his mouth ajar, he looked at me with an undisguised alarm on his face.

"I'm sorry, darling, it's not safe out there. Please stay inside," he begged as he held both my arms in a vice-like grip.

"Let me go! Who do you think you are?" I screamed and shouted, all the while trying to shake him off.

As soon as he loosened his hold, I disentangled myself and flung open the double glass doors leading straight onto the tarmac at this small airport.

I was swiftly overcome by the smoke and the heat.

Instantly, noxious smoke filled the departure lounge as I retreated back inside.

Just as quickly as I had opened the doors, the other waiting passengers quickly shut them. I looked at the burning wreck, powerless to do anything, as hopelessness moved through me like an invisible chill.

Emergency vehicles were on the tarmac within seconds, as the insalubrious fumes of jet fuel permeated the air and several fires raged.

The ambulances couldn't get close enough to the main body of the plane, but the firefighters braved the smoke and the unrelenting heat from the fires which, even from the safe haven of the departure lounge, was still suffocating and unbearable.

It felt like hours, but after a few minutes of watching the horrendous scene before me, I felt a trembling but gentle hand on my back.

"Can I call someone for you, darling?" the concerned Texan asked me in a most gentle manner.

He was standing right next to me, but he sounded far away, as if I was underwater. I might as well have been. I was drowning in a sea of anguish. Shaking my head, I ruffled through my handbag for my phone while blinded by the tears streaming down my face.

With trembling hands, I placed the most difficult call I had ever made.

Coughing and spluttering from a combination of smoke inhalation and crying, I finally managed to speak.

"Dad, you need to get here! They are gone!" The composure I had mustered to place the call was lost and my voice broke. As if the first time I said those words, made this living nightmare truer than it already was.

"Who is gone, sweetheart? What's going on? Can you go somewhere quieter? I can hardly hear you." Confusion laced his tone.

"Nolan's plane has crashed!" I shouted into the phone; my voice hoarse, my soul shattered, my heart broken.

"What! Where?" he asked in disbelief.

"Right here on the runway at San Marcos Airport. There are fires burning everywhere. My heart is breaking. I can feel it." The fight left me and my body sagged. My knees weakened and suddenly I was kneeling on the departure lounge concrete floor, sobbing.

"No. I'm on my way to you now. Where are the twins today? I'll send your mother for them." He spoke, now panic stricken.

"On the plane with Nolan," I cried out.

"What! This can't be happening. Can't Nolan land a goddamn plane! What is wrong with him!" he bellowed down the phone.

"Dad, stop, please." I couldn't tell what was louder, my father's booming voice in my ear, or the uncontrollable roaring fires outside.

He stopped the panic and hysteria, just long enough to talk to me. "Listen to me, I'll be there as soon as I can, sweetheart. You're not alone."

Chapter One

♥

Michael

Istanbul, Türkiye

I had spent many years learning all about the business side of media and publishing. At only thirty-six years old, I had helped increase the family business, my great grandfather's legacy's worth by some billions, something my father spoke of with pride. However, when there was a story which called to me, I chased it relentlessly.

I was a photojournalist and I loved it. Over the last ten years, I had fewer and fewer opportunities to be in the field, as I was acutely aware of where my responsibilities lay. Now I was finally back in the field to cover a story about prison conditions here in Istanbul. I was to meet my source at the Long Bar in the Raffles Hotel, where I also had a suite upstairs. The irony was that *he* was a Prison Warden.

I didn't wait long for him to arrive. Despite the ill-fitting suit he wore, he carried himself with pride and an air of authority.

"It's good to finally meet the man behind the camera," he said, shaking my hand vigorously.

"The pleasure's all mine, Mr Zehra," I added, sizing him up, wondering how helpful he would be.

"Please call me Kaan. We are friends now. So let's drink."

"Not when I'm working, Kaan, but please order whatever you like. It's on me." I had never been much of a drinker, especially when I was working, and this story was much too important to discuss over a fog of alcohol.

"We can't meet in a bar and not drink, but no matter, more shots for me," he said, jovially as he beckoned the bartender towards us.

After he ordered and downed three shots of Macallan, he spoke with an unexpected confounding air of seriousness. "What you're trying to do is admirable, but how are the prison conditions in Istanbul any of your concern? You're far away from home and no one else in the world cares about this subject matter of yours."

"This is where you're mistaken, Kaan. If the world knew what your inmates are facing, they would care. This story will help you to help your inmates. That is what you want, right?"

"They all think I have the power in that prison, but my hands are tied. I have my own puppet masters, and I don't even know who they are." With the air of authority now gone; he was a humble man.

He had a lot to say, and the alcohol fuelled his vim. The problem was, I was not the type of journalist who jots down notes, and nods his head. Photographs are my reporting medium.

"I hear you, Kaan. Will you take this camera inside the prison with you and use it? I need the world to see how much people are suffering there. I believe sharing the story with the world this way is what must be done to drive the change you need."

With apprehension, and a visible tremor, he tentatively held out his hand to take the camera.

I've been doing this long enough to quickly recognise human emotion. Kaan was worried and afraid. I schooled my features, as I didn't want to give Kaan the impression that this could be a negotiation. He could be trusted. He had been the source for several other pieces we had run in one of our other publications.

After some minutes of silence, Kaan eventually spoke up. "Only because it's you. I trust you. I have heard only good things from our mutual friend — your colleague — and I saw the work you did in Yemen. Your pictures are enough to make a grown man weep."

"You saw those? That was a tough story to cover. It was very difficult and extremely dangerous, but it needed to be done. That is exactly what I want to do here. All you have to do is work with me to make that happen."

More silence, but I could tell he was convinced. All I had to do was wait for him to reconcile with his decision.

"I'll do it, but this could land me in some trouble. What I need is this drink to drown my sorrows at home after it's all done," he said, gesturing towards his glass.

"You want an eighteen-year-old bottle of Macallan?" I had known this story would come at some price.

I hadn't anticipated the price would only be a bottle of top shelf whisky. I was both surprised and appreciative. I made sure not to show pleasure at such a small price to pay for access to a story detailing one of the biggest but little known human rights abuses of my generation.

As he looked at me sheepishly, I glanced around and noticed *her* sitting in the restaurant. I had been in here for the better part of thirty minutes. How could I have missed her? She was looking straight at me, or was she? I couldn't tell.

She was elegant, polished, and poised. The most beautiful woman who had the saddest eyes I'd ever seen. She was looking past me and straight at my Nikon camera with a longing in her eyes, as if she had finally found what she had lost. This had never happened to me before.

"I'll send you a case. Kaan, it was a pleasure meeting you, but if you'll please excuse me, I see someone I need to speak to," I said as I shook his hand.

Walking away from the bar, I hurriedly moved towards her table. I had to speak to her before any other man did. A woman as beguiling wouldn't be sitting alone for much longer.

It had been a while since I'd approached a woman. I was somewhat jaded and out of practice, but something about her made me want to know her. She was stunning, but something else was pulling me towards her, and I needed to know what it was.

As if she sensed my presence, she looked up as I neared her table, and when our eyes met, I couldn't help the smile on my face. She smiled too, albeit half heartedly, with her perfectly groomed eyebrows raised in a silent question.

After all the talking I had been doing with Kaan, I had become speechless. "Hi," I said, as I swallowed thickly.

"Hi?" she answered by way of a question.

"I'm Michael Masterson, and I was hoping to talk to you." I had never been so inarticulate in my life.

"Michael? Have we met before?" She was soft spoken, and her hypnotic voice drew me in. She looked at me intently, as if she was trying to remember me.

"If we had, we would certainly remember each other. May I sit?"

Before she had a chance to refuse, I sat down, and she continued to look at me, puzzled.

I couldn't tear my gaze away from her pouty pink lips, and when I eventually did, our eyes locked. I needed to know her and whatever secrets she was keeping. She looked me over, and her unique hazel eyes rested on my face warily. I suddenly remembered how dishevelled I looked as nights of sleeplessness and tension had taken a toll on me. I hadn't shaved in the week since I'd been here. I always tried to make sure I looked like someone befitting to be my father's right hand. The business even had a small department of image consultants whose sole purpose was to curate the right impression. As the emerging face of Worldwide Media, image was everything, but not today, as I was not in Istanbul in that capacity. Just when I happened upon the first woman of interest to me in a long time.

"You can sit, but not for too long. I'm expecting my colleagues to join me." She was polite yet detached, but I'd never shied away from a challenge. I didn't know how much time I had, but I needed to make an impression; a good one.

"What's your name?" I asked, still stumbling, and she looked at me with what seemed like questions in her eyes. The unique flecks of gold in them were a distraction.

"Are you in the habit of asking strange women their names?" she asked me with a shadow of a smile on her face, but still unable to disguise the look of disapproval as she took in my unkempt, ruffled look.

"You're hardly strange, and no, I never ask names." As soon as I said that I instantly regretted how cavalier I must have sounded.

"Hmm, that's direct and very good to know. If you would excuse me, please, I need to be ready for a business meeting." The wariness in her eyes looked more like disdain.

"No, that didn't come out right. Honestly, I'm a little nervous and it seems I'm not really selling myself well here." She laughed softly, and I was hooked. I really needed to know her, and hear her laugh again.

"It's not what you're saying that's not selling you, Mr Masterson," she said as she raised a single eyebrow.

"Everything else is easily rectifiable, I assure you." I went with the charm offensive, as nothing else was working in my favour.

"I'm Sofia. Sofia Kingman," she said, again with a chuckle.

"Sofia, how do I get in touch? I want us to continue this conversation." She sized me up with some interest.

"As I said, I am here for work, and my colleagues have now arrived. If you could excuse me, please," she said with finality.

She wasn't interested. I'd been dismissed. I was a little disheartened, but mildly amused. Rejection was new to me.

As I walked away from her table and looked over at her colleagues, I tried to catch the vaguely familiar logo on one of their work folders. I missed it, but I had her name and that would have to do for now. The rejection stung, but getting to know her would be my next mission.

For the first time in a long time, I wanted a woman, not just for what she could offer me in my bed, but for her story. I needed to know who she was, why there was a haunting sadness in her eyes, and to understand the reason for the glassy-eyed stare, and if given permission, I wanted to see her and photograph her in any way she would let me.

Chapter Two

Sofia

Michael Masterson was his name and seeing him holding his camera dragged me back to that place I always avoided, especially in public. It had been nearly two years since I lost my family at San Marcos, and I felt even more absent than ever. That camera reminded me of a time in my life when I was alive and full of vitality, and I realised how much I wanted to live and feel again. I wasn't sure how, but I was sure it involved the scruffy Michael Masterson and his Nikon.

After trying and failing to concentrate on the conversations around me at dinner, I excused myself to my luxurious twenty-seventh floor suite at the Raffles with sweeping views looking out over the Bosphorus. With a pounding in my chest and sweaty palms, I was wearing a hole in the carpet as I paced nervously. All I could think about was the rumpled man who had left an impression on me. I finally mustered the courage to contact the Concierge to find out about him and to request his room details. I'd never been so bold.

As I waited for them to answer the phone, I couldn't believe I was making this call. I tried to stay calm, practicing the deep breathing my yoga instructor insisted on.

"Good evening, Ms Kingman. How can I help you today?" the almost robotic voice of the Concierge answered.

"Hi, I need some information on one of the guests, umm, Micheal. Michael Masterson..."

"Ms Kingman, I'm going to have to stop you there. It's against hotel policy to provide guest information. I'm sure you can appreciate that." She was no longer robotic, rather she had become firm but still polite in a customer service way.

Exasperated, I tried a different angle. "I understand. Perhaps you could transfer this call to his room, please."

"Hmm, let me see." This was progress, and I couldn't believe the excitement bubbling at the surface. I still wasn't sure what I would say to him. "Thank you for waiting, but that guest isn't taking any phone calls."

"Seriously?" I sighed. *Who was this man?*

"I'm sorry. They have a 'do not disturb' on their account."

Disappointed, I hung up.

With my hands shaking, and my internal heat sky high, I turned to the internet and typed his name and the word "photographer" into the search bar. Immediately, he came up on The Worldwide Chronicle website. I broke out into a sweat, and as the adrenaline coursed through my veins, I could hear the loud beat of my heart in my ears. He looked very different and something dead and buried within me came alive. Without the scraggly beard and unruly hair, with brown eyes and a jaw, which looked like it had been carved from stone, he was handsome, very handsome.

What had he done to me in such a small amount of time?

In my state, I cared little for current affairs, but the Worldwide Chronicle was an old institution with reliable, objective news and storytelling. There was no telephone number listed. However, there was an email address that I decided would have to do. So, I set about composing what I hoped would be a redeeming email. My shaking hands were not helping, but somehow, I typed a short and to the point email.

> Sofia Kingman — *Dear Michael, firstly please forgive my rude and abrupt behaviour when we met at the Long Bar. I was not myself and I have not been for a long time. If you are still in Istanbul, I would like to see you again and apologise in person. See you soon? Sofia.*

He had written back. As if he had been waiting to hear from me, he didn't take long to respond. I was surprised, as no one emailed anymore, or did they? I was thrilled, but nervous. The palpitations I felt in my chest had to be the first time I have felt alive in two years. Just seeing his name in my inbox was enough to put a grin on my face.

Why him? I wondered. I had stopped feeling anything, especially for anyone, after San Marcos.

> Michael Masterson — *Dear Sofia, I always make it a point to accept apologies in person and never via email. I like to see and hear the sincerity in every apology I receive. So yes, let's meet at the scene of the crime at 8pm tomorrow. But while I imagine how you will look when you are grovelling, answer me this — why have you not been yourself — for a long time? Michael.*

I let out a sound, and it sounded like a giggle.

Was I giggling? I had become giddy, giddy with excitement and nervousness.

Was I really going to see him again?

He had asked a very important question. Perhaps the most important one, and I was trying to craft a response when my phone ringing interrupted me. I looked over at it; it was Ross Kingman, my father and my boss, and I let it ring out. I'd finished work for the day, and he could wait until morning. Just as I was about to continue writing to Michael, it rang again.

What could be so important? I decided to answer it as he would worry if I didn't.

"Hi Dad, did you forget the time difference?" I giggled, still excited about hearing from Michael.

He couldn't keep the edge out of his voice when he spoke to me. "Sofia, you need to come home. I have some difficult news."

"What is it? Is Mum okay?" I asked in a panic.

"Your mother is fine. The Transport Safety Board has finalised its findings on Nolan's plane crash." He sighed.

"What did they say, Daddy? You don't sound right." I tried to keep my voice calm.

"Come home, sweetheart. We'll talk about it then." My father had always been a vault when he needed to be.

Nothing else mattered at that moment except to know what had Ross Kingman unsettled. I couldn't believe that after nearly two years, information about Nolan's plane had come to light.

The nervousness I felt when I had sent and received an email from Michael amplified. I had to get back home straight away. I stumbled around my hotel suite, picking up everything and trying to get it packed as quickly as I could. Despite my nervousness at my father's summons, the suite was devoid of all my belongings within minutes.

The brief conversation with my father had me leaving the Raffles in record time. A car took me to the airport, where everything suddenly became a blur. Fortunately, I'd been through enough terminals and departure gates in my life that it had all become muscle memory. I don't remember buying the ticket, checking in, passport control, or even boarding the plane.

I sat on the plane with fourteen long hours of flying time ahead of me. Long plane rides and my thoughts for company had become the norm over the last few years. The longer I was on the plane trying to imagine what news my father had, the more my head spun. The deep breathing wasn't helping, and when my thoughts flashed to the man with the scraggly beard and the unruly hair, I found an unexpected calm. I welcomed it, but I was puzzled, and suddenly felt guilty.

I didn't know why my husband and children died on that tarmac, but I found myself entertaining thoughts of another man. I missed my family with everything I was, and thinking about what news my father summoned me for to Los Angeles, had taken me back to the days and weeks after their deaths. My father's disdain for Nolan had become even more apparent. As a pilot himself, he believed Nolan's errors as a pilot caused the plane to crash land onto the tarmac, killing our sons too.

A little before lunchtime, the plane landed at LAX. Even though it had been a long flight, I went straight to Kingman Air Corporate Office, despite being a touch messy, airplane rumpled, and emotionally weary.

Over time, I had mastered the art of pretence, and I made sure to carry myself with as much dignity as I could. I put on my workplace facade and Penny, my father's executive assistant of seventeen years, immediately ushered me into his office.

"Sofia, you're here. I am so happy to see you." My father's voice boomed. He was a presence, and he owned any room he walked into.

"Dad let's cut the pleasantries, please. What happened to them?" I was slowly dying inside each second I was in his office, without knowing what the report said.

"Sofia, sit down, please," he said as calmly as he could, leading me to the tan Chesterfield in his office.

His top floor office was as masculine as him, with the six large windows overlooking the Los Angeles skyline serving to brighten the space. He sat down next to me, and held my hand, something he had only ever done when he needed to break difficult news to either my mother or me.

He inhaled deeply before he spoke. "There's no easy way to say this, but Nolan's plane was shot out of the sky."

I suddenly felt ill as the bile rose and my stomach churned. "What! How could that be?" I cried, my heart thumping, nearly jumping out of my chest.

"It's been a long time, darling, but does anything come to mind at all about the plane coming into land?" he asked me gently.

As soon as he asked, the memories of San Marcos came flooding back. The sight, the sounds and the horrendous smell. "I did see a flash as the landing gear touched down on the tarmac. I thought it was a spark caused by metal on tarmac, but who would want to kill my family?" I sobbed.

"This is what I have been asking myself, too. Sweetheart, did Nolan have any enemies you knew of?" The anguish in the room was palpable.

"Of course not. Nolan was a placid person." I finally defended him, as I should have done all along.

"He was in the Air Force for most of his life, Sofia," he countered.

"Yes! You're right, he was in the Air Force, and he knew how to fly, and to land, and everything else that comes in between. Shall we now put the matter of him crash landing the plane to bed! For months and months, you made me feel like rubbish, reminding me at every turn how pilot error killed my family." By now, I was sobbing uncontrollably; the workplace facade long forgotten.

"I'm sorry I said all those things. I was angry too. My grandsons had been snatched from me." He held me as I cried in his arms.

When I eventually stopped sobbing and composed myself, I looked into his tear-filled eyes and asked the question in my mind as a sudden spike of anxiety shot through me.

"Who would go after a retired fighter pilot?"

I was trying to remember anything Nolan could have mentioned, but it was impossible that Nolan would have brought something like this to himself, and to our children.

"Let me call my man; he is a private investigator who can look into this for us."

I agreed with him instantly. I had to know who had murdered my family and why. "Daddy, you should have put your investigator onto this months ago."

"Hindsight is twenty-twenty, and we didn't have all the facts. We'll get to the bottom of this now. I'm sorry about everything you've been through, sweetheart. You shouldn't be alone. Go to the house and be with your mother. I'll join you as soon as I wrap up here."

Suddenly, I was wrapped up in the warm cocoon of his sincerity, but all I wanted was to go to my own home, somewhere safe and familiar.

"I am a grown woman, and I don't need to scuttle to Mum every time my feelings are hurt," I insisted.

My mother, with all her manners and good upbringing, had been gracious towards Nolan, but had never liked him for me. I suspected she believed Nolan wasn't good enough. The fact that when we married, he had fifteen years on my then twenty-three hadn't helped either.

"This is more than hurt feelings. This is finding out some truly devastating news."

I still couldn't bring myself to go to my parents' home. I wanted my own space, to be with my thoughts and take in everything I'd just learned.

"Dad, I need a copy of the report."

"Sure, I'll have Penny email it to you straight away."

"I'll be at my apartment, and I'll see Mum tomorrow." My lips twitched, and my eyes welled up as thoughts of how my mother had been cold to me over the last few months crossed my mind.

"You need to let your mother in," he spoke convincingly. I was anything but convinced.

When my family died, my mother had been grief stricken. The loss of the boys had affected her too. As time went on, she had seemed happier and had returned to shopping and lunching with her socialite friends while I remained stuck in my bottomless well of grief.

"Not now, not today. I need to process this news. Besides, Mum has been on a different planet ever since this happened."

"She was hurt. We had never experienced a loss so profound, and she turned inward." He would rush to her defence, he had always been loyal to my mother.

"I was hurt too; I still am. My children are gone, and I miss them every single day. As my mother, she should have been my comfort." I sighed.

"Take some time to see her this weekend. You have a lot to talk about. I'll call Thomas. He'll drive you home," he said, as he kept my hand in his.

"No need, I'll walk. I need some air," I muttered, as I kissed his cheek and left his office to make the seven minute walk to my home.

As soon as I walked out of Kingman Air Corporate Offices, the heavens opened up, pelting me with rain. It had been weeks since it rained, but no amount of rain could wash away the filthy horror of learning that my family had been murdered. As I walked I let the tears fall freely down my face all the way home. I arrived at my apartment building, soaking wet, from both the rain and my tears. Thankfully, the doorman was new and didn't know me well enough to make small talk.

My private elevator had me in my penthouse within seconds and straight into my double height foyer. I walked farther into the open concept great room adorned with oversized windows, which on a beautiful day would let the light in. The great room housed a spacious living area, a dining space, and the surprising farmhouse style kitchen, complete with an apron sink thirty-four storeys high in a contemporary penthouse. It should have felt good to be home, but I felt desolate.

In my daze, I ran a bath, poured some bath salts and sat in it, staring out at Los Angeles, relieved that Nolan's skill or lack thereof hadn't played a role in the loss of my family. As I sat in my four thousand square feet of solitude, I realised the crash was beyond his control. I had to know who and why would destroy my family in this most violent way.

First, I needed to apologise yet again to Michael Masterson for the missed connection in Istanbul. Why he came to my mind then, when I needed comfort, I dared not think about. I hadn't let him know I left the country, as I had left in a hurry.

> Sofia Masterson — *Dear Michael, again I must apologise for my extremely rude behaviour. Leaving like that is not who I am and there is a very good reason. I really wish one day you would let me explain myself. I am now back at home in LA — Where do you live? Meet soon? Sofia.*

This time, the response wasn't instant, and in the few hours it took to receive word back from him, I began to worry that whatever chance we had to connect was gone. At two o'clock in the morning while I had been tossing and turning, he eventually responded, and the pounding in my chest started again.

> Michael Masterson — *I don't know you yet, but I am in terrible danger of becoming a fool for you. I still want to meet and hear that apology. The longer it takes, the more fascinated I become. I leave Istanbul tonight, and travel to Johannesburg. Yes, one day we will meet. Michael.*

As soon as I heard from him, I made a decision. This had been playing on my mind for a while and had to be kismet. I immediately sent a message to Bradley, my assistant, for us to meet at my apartment in the morning, while I set about putting my plan into place.

I didn't sleep much the night before. At eight o'clock, Brad came off my elevator and into my penthouse.

"Hi," he said, with a scowl on his face as he handed me a coffee cup with my favourite cappuccino and our breakfast muffins.

"Brad, a little more enthusiasm wouldn't be amiss," I said brightly as I led him from the foyer and into the kitchen.

"I'm trying, but a work meeting at eight on a Saturday morning. Not even Thomas Edison had that kind of work ethic." He sighed dramatically, shaking his head.

"Thomas Edison? You'll need to explain, as I'm a little slow this morning." I inhaled deeply as I savoured the cappuccino.

"Yes, he secured more than two thousand patents in his lifetime."

Brad had always been good at making me smile, even when the world had seemed like it was closing in. I had hired him as my assistant during my first week on the job, and he proved himself to be the best choice many times over, sometimes blurring the lines between assistant and friend.

"Right. Because you pulled out that all important factoid at eight on a Saturday morning, you're exactly right for what I want to do here today." I smiled brightly, trying to win him over.

"If I work like Edison, can we be done by one? I've met someone and we have afternoon plans."

"Met someone? Who?" I asked, curious and intrigued. *I had met someone too.*

"Work first, boss, then I will tell you everything." His single-mindedness, when we needed to work, always kept us both focused.

We wolfed down our breakfast, and I led him into my home office. The only room yet to be decorated in my apartment, a shrine to my lost family. Their photographs were on every surface, and the boys' art framed and on the walls.

"I want to go to South Africa because I want Kingman Air to establish a presence there." I said, with the conviction I felt.

"South Africa?" he asked, with an expression on his face I couldn't quite read.

"Well, yes, as well as the whole of Southern Africa," I pressed.

"That's a hard region to get into, Sofia. It's tightly held. Shep had me look into it when you were working away once, and he put it in the too hard pile."

"You might be wrong. I've been studying all night. Let me show you," I said with enthusiasm as I pulled up information from my laptop and projected it onto my double desktop screens.

"Wow, this is a lot of work. Between your arrival yesterday and now, when exactly did you have time to do all this?" he asked, as he pulled the office chair closer to the desk.

"I didn't sleep much. This is an exciting project."

"It is?" he questioned in disbelief.

Brad and I spent all morning working on a proposal to present to my father on my plans for South Africa. By midday, it was finalised, and I sent it off to him.

"I see why you want to expand the business to Southern Africa as a region. It's good business, but why do *you* have to be the one to do it? You'll be gone for weeks, maybe even months," Brad asked, as he readied himself to leave.

"You're right. It's good for the airline," I said and hoped he would stop trying to understand why I needed to be there.

"I see you're not going to tell me. Is there something to tell?"

"Nothing, but *you* need to tell me about this new someone you've met."

I wasn't ready to tell Brad, or anyone, that I was going on a wild goose chase for a perfect stranger.

Chapter Three

♥

Sofia

First thing on Monday morning, I went to see my father to find out his thoughts about the proposal. He would have read it on Sunday, while I was out with my mother, who I had eventually spent the day with. Our time together was short, but it had been special. It would take time to repair our fractured bonds, but the day spent together had been a good gateway to that.

I went to his office and launched into convincing him about going to Africa.

"Dad, as you saw from my proposal, their airlines are in shambles, due to fuel shortages, an ageing fleet, and rumours about general mismanagement. I think if we play our cards right, there's plenty of money to be made."

He remained quiet, as he studied me until he eventually spoke. "I read your proposal. It's compelling. I've never heard you talk about money before. You normally enjoy the chase, never the fruit of all your hard work, but I'll be sending Shep this time."

"There's no need to send Shep. I can go. In fact I want to go." I sounded a little too enthusiastic compared to my normally composed self.

"Hold on, Sofia. Your own research shows that the business development would be in five, possibly six, countries; that's a lot of work, and you've just finished up in Türkiye, where you've done very well by the way. You need a break, a holiday or something."

"I've put a lot of work into that proposal, and if I didn't think I was capable of it, I wouldn't have brought it to you. Besides, Africa has lots of places to holiday. I can take a break while I'm there."

With his salt and pepper hair, my father looked very distinguished. He had been a good mentor since the day he invited me to work with him, and promised me that my business degree would be put to good use.

After studying at Berkeley, I worked for a boutique interior design firm for a year. I had never been challenged, but that was where I had fallen in love with interiors and honed my photography skills.

"I know you're capable, and you're passionate, and the best exec in this company, but I think you're trying to escape from something. Is it the finding from the Transport Board which has made you want to do this?" He asked, with tenderness in his eyes.

He had always been perceptive, only this time he was wrong. I wasn't running away, rather I was trying to run towards something else.

"This has nothing to do with that. I want this for Kingman, and I know I can deliver."

"Your mother won't forgive me for this. She loved spending time with you yesterday, and she wants you in LA more. You could start taking photos again."

"I love what I do here at Kingman. I can't be here shopping and lunching all the time with her, " I said, and he chuckled softly.

I wouldn't talk about taking photographs, not today, and not now. I needed to maintain my workplace composure.

"Why work so hard if you can't enjoy the fruits of all your hard work? You're a wealthy woman. You haven't touched your trust fund or the inheritance from your grandfather. I gave you a jet, but you choose to travel commercially. The only extravagance you seem to have is your penthouse, which you've slept in only five nights this year."

He made a lot of sense, but I had my mind made up. I needed to be in South Africa, and I had to be there soon. Even though I had never lived in the penthouse with Nolan and the boys, it reminded me of everything I didn't have.

"Dad, will you let me go, please? When I come back, I'll go out with Mum, close down Rodeo Drive, shop 'til I drop, and spend Grandpa's millions. I'll even take a trip all around the world in my jet."

He was no longer chuckling, but now laughing a full throaty laugh. "I can't say no to that. Although something tells me you have too much sense to do any of that. I want you to be happy, and you haven't been for a long time," he said, with sincerity.

"I'm trying to be happy, but it's a process. I won't let you down in South Africa. Will you keep me updated on what your investigator finds out?" I asked, blinking back tears.

"Of course I will. Go ahead for as long as it takes and let Kingman Air be part of the Southern African Fleet. One last question — what's motivating you about Southern Africa?"

He caught me off guard. "Hmm, there's a lot of money to be made." *Now I was speaking his language.*

He nodded silently in what I've learned over the years was acknowledgement, and not agreement.

Returning to my office, I felt lighter on my feet that even in my current emotional state he had trusted me enough to oversee this new challenge.

I arrived at my suite of offices, where Bradley was anxiously waiting for my return.

"Brad, it's happening! I am heading to South Africa, and I want to leave in six hours. Let's make that happen." I couldn't hide my excitement, and I could never pretend around Brad. He knew when I was overcome with grief and having bad days, and when I had the few good days, he was right there with me.

"Congratulations! You've worked hard on this. Where would you like to start, and I'll arrange that straight away."

I didn't miss a beat. "Johannesburg."

"That's very precise. Consider it done," he said, with an eyebrow raised in question. *How much longer could I keep this from Brad?*

I ignored his questioning glance. "Oh, and I'll be taking my jet this time."

He nearly whooped with joy. "Finally! I get to tell a pilot to file a flight plan. Do you still have any anti-Malaria tablets left after that trip to India? You will need to take them again while visiting this region."

"Yes, Mummy." I chuckled as I walked into my office to pick up some things.

The flight was quick, or perhaps it was the anticipation of what lay ahead. This was worlds away from the flight I had taken only days earlier. Not only was I in the comfort of the Bombardier Global Dad had gifted me the year before, but I was hopeful and full of excitement.

On arrival in Johannesburg, a car was waiting to take me to The Westcliff. An easy twenty minutes, and in that time, I was bold and sent Michael another message.

> *Sofia Kingman — I hope you're free tonight. I'm in Johannesburg, and I can meet at the Flames Restaurant for dinner at 8 o'clock. See you soon, Sofia.*

When I arrived at the Westcliff, I was relieved and grateful to Bradley. I had stayed in a lot of the Four Seasons, but none as extraordinary as this one. It was in the middle of the city, yet so serene and tranquil, as it was perched on a hillside with tree top views as far as the eye could see. My suite was modern, yet so warm and inviting. Exquisite African fabrics juxtaposed with modern contemporary décor adorn the suite; it was tasteful.

I could see myself getting a lot of work done here and calling the place home for as long as I needed to.

I stepped out onto the terrace off the bedroom and the panoramic views of the city and beyond took my breath away. I hadn't paid much attention to my surroundings in a long time, but I felt something new and invigorating being here. Perhaps it was my long-awaited dinner with Michael, the anticipation of what was to come, or perhaps the African spirit, which I had always heard about. Whatever it was, I felt alive again, and I revelled in that feeling.

After enjoying the views, I allowed myself time to enjoy the soaking tub and got ready for dinner. I made an extra effort to try and look like my unburdened, carefree self. It had been years since I'd dressed up for a date. Thankfully, the day I spent with my mother was bearing fruit, as we had gone shopping, and I had allowed her to indulge in one of her favourite hobbies — dressing me up.

I decided my usual severe ballerina chignon needed to go, and opted for a low, loose knot for my long brown hair. I kept my lips subtle as I had gone for bold eye makeup. I didn't want it to be obvious that I had been planning this outfit for days, so I chose a plum lace camisole and a casual but smart figure-hugging skirt, which although showcasing my long legs was still a classy length. I'd always been self conscious about my larger than average breasts and tiny waist, but as I looked in the mirror, I loved the reflection looking back at me. After checking myself in the mirror for the umpteenth time, I made my way to the restaurant. The simple walk to the Flames was beautiful, and the whimsical cobblestones paths gave the impression of being in a small English village.

Chapter Four

♥

Michael

I wouldn't allow myself one scintilla of excitement at seeing Sofia again. I'd already been in this situation with her before and she had left me waiting for hours.

After she had emailed me the first time, I waited for her response, but it never arrived. I had assumed I would receive the response the next day as we had arranged. Then she didn't arrive at the Long Bar. To say I was disappointed was an understatement.

I had looked her up, and there was little information about her on the internet, only a generic company profile on the Kingman Air website and a few photographs. She didn't have a social media presence, which seemed odd as she was young, beautiful, and photogenic. It made her that much more intriguing. Like me, she worked for her father, and I wondered if this was for love or for money.

I did come across a wedding announcement, but she didn't have a ring on her finger when we met. Was she married? Weddings got cancelled all the time, this I was painfully aware of. I could have found out all manner of information about her, but I really wanted to hear it from her, so I decided to bide my time.

I ordered a car to the Flames Restaurant from the Houghton, where I had a suite, which was only a short drive away. I arrived early, just to be certain I didn't miss her as she was proving to be quite elusive.

At eight o'clock, she entered the restaurant. She was just as breathtaking as I remembered. Her perfect hourglass figure and the subtle sway of her hips had me wondering how I could be a gentleman around her. I put on my friendly but approachable face, as I was still unsure about her marital status. I didn't want to be caught in another dalliance with a married woman, as that, from previous experience, never ends well.

I stood up to greet her as she came closer to the table, I could tell she was feigning confidence. Perhaps, she was nervous, or maybe there is a story there. I would wait and see.

"Sofia, how are you?" I greeted her with a kiss.

She froze, but was gracious enough to let me kiss her on the cheek.

"Michael, it's good to finally see you, and do this — I mean, have dinner." She smiled, but visibly exhaled.

She was uneasy, and I decided to make her as comfortable as possible in my company. I wondered how a woman as gorgeous as she was, and so accomplished, was as nervous as she was. I started to wonder if she was married after all.

"I've been looking forward to seeing you again since the last time. Thanks for getting in touch." I couldn't resist letting my eyes openly run up and down her enticing body.

"Yes, I am not very friendly at the best of times." Her smile didn't quite reach her eyes, and her voice was shaky.

Why was she so nervous?

"You seem friendly now, so I guess I'm in luck."

As soon as our table was ready, we were seated in a quiet position on the terrace in the warm summer evening.

"How come you picked this restaurant? I actually have been here before, and they have one of the best desserts in the whole city. "

"Is that a fact? I'm going to have to try it. I'm staying here; it seemed like an easy and safe choice," she said with a wider smile. She had no idea the effect it had on me.

"That makes sense, but what brings you to Johannesburg? I can't believe it, but we are in the same city at the same time again. This has to be a sign." I heard the excitement in my own voice, and inwardly cringed, hoping I wasn't coming on too strong.

"Work," she answered simply.

I looked at her expectantly, but she didn't elaborate. I supposed working for an airline was top secret and she didn't want to share anything proprietary. I circled back to the job question and got her talking.

"I work for an airline, my father's, and we want to establish a presence in this part of the world. I am here to make that happen," she said, smiling nervously as she gingerly picked up her glass of water and quickly replaced it without having a drink.

"That sounds like a huge responsibility, and a huge commitment. Will it just be you working here on this project?" I coaxed her gently.

Not only was she incredibly sexy, but her father trusted her business acumen.

I had read up on Kingman Air and its successes. It was the largest and most profitable privately owned airline in the world. I was impressed that she was a big part of that. I, however, had stopped short of finding out everything about her.

"Yes, just me here, but I have a great team behind the scenes."

"That's impressive. You know, when I first met you in Istanbul, I thought you had intelligent eyes, but I would never have guessed that you hold down such a challenging job. Is your work easy?"

She chuckled softly, becoming at ease in my company. "Intelligent eyes, huh? I don't know about that. Does that line usually get you far Mr Masterson?" she asked as she licked her lips.

"I don't know. This time, is it getting me far?" I tried to lure something, anything, from her.

"It depends on where you're trying to get to."

Was she finally flirting with me? She's a difficult read.

"As far as you'll let me. I want to get to know you in every way possible." *Was that too direct? I had been out of practice for too long.*

She raised her eyebrows in what looked like bewilderment, cleared her throat, and answered a question I had forgotten I had asked.

"The job isn't particularly easy, but I love it. It keeps me busy, and my mind occupied. What do you do?"

"Well, as you found my email address on the Worldwide Chronicle Website, you should know that I am with Worldwide Media." I wondered what else she had found out about me.

"As a photographer? The first time we met, you had a camera, and I assumed you took photographs."

Either she wanted me to say exactly who I was and what I did at Worldwide Media, or she hadn't found out much.

"Yes, I take photos. I'm a photojournalist, amongst other things." I felt a twinge of guilt as I told that lie of omission. If she didn't know who I was, and what I did at the Chronicle, there was no need to tell her; not tonight while she was walking on eggshells.

She didn't need to be more overwhelmed than she already seemed to be.

When I told her that I was a photojournalist, she seemed to sit up and pay attention. She came alive when talking about my work and trying to find out as much as she could. I was disappointed she was more interested in my work than in me. If I hadn't known any better,

I would think she was a reporter or an investigator, or even involved in corporate espionage.

"So, in Istanbul, were you working on a story?"

"Yes, I was. I'm still working on it."

"How are you working on a story in Istanbul while you're in Johannesburg? Can you talk about it or is it a secret?" she asked in a conspiratorial tone.

"As long as you don't tell," I whispered, indulging her playfulness.

"If you think I could be your secret keeper, then please do, and I promise I won't tell," she said as she crossed her heart and giggled.

The more we talked, the more I realised that I wanted to tell her all my secrets, and even get to hear all of hers.

"The story in Istanbul is about the prison conditions and the human rights abuses going on there. The story is difficult to research with more complex layers than I had ever realised," I confessed.

"Oh, no. That's huge, and so important. But how does a photojournalist even get that kind of access? Drone shots?" she probed.

Why hadn't I thought of using drones?

"That's where it became tricky, and I was losing my mind trying to figure it out. I even thought about becoming a prisoner myself."

"What! That's dedication. Your employer probably would've fired you, or promoted you. It's hard to be sure." She giggled at her own joke, and I couldn't help the grin on my face.

"I found a different way. It's all in hand now. Besides, my employer doesn't micromanage me much." I chuckled softly, as I thought of my father. I wondered if this was the time to be honest and tell her what I really did at Worldwide Media.

"I'm glad you quickly discounted that idea. That would have been so dangerous. So what's the story here?"

"There's a power crisis."

"Power? As in political power?"

"Yes, that too. Although I'm talking about electricity."

"Oh, I don't think I understand, but I can't wait to see your coverage on it."

I had to change the subject, so I asked her what I had been dying to ask all evening.

"So, do you have family?"

She appeared thrown off balance as I tried to steer the conversation away from me.

"I do; my parents. No siblings."

There was a pregnant pause as I waited for her to continue.

"I did have my own family, for a while anyway. A husband, two children, twin boys, but they all died in a plane crash twenty months ago."

I couldn't help the audible gasp that left me.

Understanding dawned on me as I tried to hide the horror and disbelief which must have been written all over my face. This was why she was so melancholy, so full of trepidation at just a conversation, and so uncertain of herself. She had been dealing with a monumental loss, and I had to tread lightly. I was not equipped to deal with what she was going through; I didn't think anyone truly was, but I still wanted to know her, peel her layers until I got to know the real her, who I was certain was buried underneath a mountain of grief.

"Now I've lost you. Did my sob story put you off your dessert?" She tried to infuse some humour into what I could tell was the heaviest conversation anyone could ever have with a near stranger.

"No, I'm just taking it in, and wondering how you are still walking around after the most tragic thing that could happen to anyone happened to you three times over, but in one fell swoop. I am so sorry to hear that you lost your family. How are you?"

Her eyes suddenly glazed over. This was not how I had anticipated dinner would go.

"Thanks for asking, and I feel like I could tell you how I am feeling because you are so easy to talk to, but I would rather not turn this into a therapy session."

"No, this isn't a therapy session. We are two adults having dinner and talking, and I have asked you how you are, because I really want to know," I pressed gently.

"You're not journalising me, are you?" She was now trying to put *me* at ease.

"That's not a real word, and no, I'm not. If I were, I would be taking pictures."

She smiled weakly. "I'm still waiting for it to get easier. If you really want to know something, today is the first day I have felt alive in a really long time."

Her declaration took my breath away, and I could feel the thudding in my chest. I suspected if one looked closely, my pounding heart was visible, even from across the table where she sat. Sofia Kingman might already own me.

"In what way?" I probed, willing her to say what I hoped she would.

"I've only been here for a few hours, but I think being in Africa is a balm, a little like a tonic for my broken heart, and perhaps looking forward to seeing you again has had that effect on me."

Another grin appeared on my face. I needed to hear her say that, as I, too, was feeling optimistic about being with her.

"Well, I am glad I had a hand in that," I said as I exhaled deeply and smiled at her.

We steered away from the heavy topics after that, focusing on the lightest of small talk, but my mind kept veering to how strong she was, to live through the heartbreak she was living through. It must have taken some courage to approach me as she had done.

Dinner ended much quicker than I had anticipated, even after insisting we both order the spongy Malva pudding with its apricot jam and cream to make our time together last even longer.

"Wow, this dessert has rocked my world. I wouldn't have tried it otherwise."

"I love it too, and I have loved it since I first had it when I was a child."

"You came here often as a child?" she asked, visibly interested.

After telling me about what had happened to her family, her demeanor changed. She seemed to relax, and she was smiling more. She even reached out and touched my hand, albeit for a second, and quickly withdrew it before I could catch hers in mine.

I didn't know her at all, but if this was the real her coming through, for seconds at a time, I wanted to be there when she was free from the pain and grief she was suffering through.

"I spent many summers here. Perhaps the best summers any child could ever dream of."

She didn't press the issue, but at mentioning being a child, she retreated into her shell slightly. I needed to remember she was fragile.

Once we were finished, and the bill was settled, I looked at her and spoke quietly. "May I walk you to your room?"

"I would be terribly disappointed if I had to walk there on my own," she countered, with what I saw as an attempt at bravado.

I longed to tell her to be herself with me, and not try hard to be someone she was not. We walked together, close enough to smell her shampoo, and I couldn't tell if it was fruity or floral. Whatever it was, I wanted to drown in it. I put my hand on the small of her back. I was pushing it, but I needed to touch her, any part of her.

When we arrived at her suite, she stepped away from me and put some space between us, nearly three feet. She was too far to touch and I was crushed. Her relaxed demeanor from dinner was now gone. She had become tense and rigid, it was clear I was not welcome inside. I expected that, and I respect it.

"Sofia," I spoke softly as we were in the corridor outside her door.

"Hmm." She smiled, looking at my shirt where I had the top two buttons undone.

"I would like to see you again soon. We still have a lot to talk about." I looked at her, but she didn't look at me.

"I would love that, too. How long are you here for?"

"I am never one hundred percent certain as there is always fluidity in the stories I cover. I can stay in one place if I have a reason to."

"Do you have any reason to stay long this time, Michael?" She licked her lips. This time she made eye contact and maintained it. She was gorgeous.

"I don't know. Do I?"

"Only you can know that answer," she said, in a breathy voice.

She was sending mixed signals. I didn't want to control her, but I needed to take control. I knew exactly what I wanted, and it was her.

"I would like to see you again. How do I get in touch with you? We can't keep sending each other text messages, masquerading as emails."

"Hmm, by telephone I suppose."

I gave her my number, which she programmed into her phone, and she called me immediately.

"Call me. I hope that will be soon." I kissed her on her cheek and left her standing in the doorway of her suite.

Chapter Five

♥

Sofia

The parting after dinner had been quite abrupt. I wasn't surprised, but I wasn't ready to let Michael in, anywhere. Dinner had been perfect, and Michael was different. Unlike a lot of my friends and colleagues, he hadn't known me prior to the plane crash. He didn't seem judgemental, nor was he trying to read into my words. He took me at face value, and I loved that.

As I sat with him at dinner, I realised how attractive he was, not in the ruggedly handsome, world-weary way Nolan had been. Michael looked angelic with refined features which had been hidden well underneath the beard when we first met. I also became aware that I compared everything about him to Nolan. That was unsettling, until I realised with dismay how very much in love with Nolan I still was. I was wracked with guilt at spending time with another man. In all these months, it had never occurred to me that I might want to move on. I had never allowed myself to see past my grief and imagine being with anyone else. I didn't think I would be calling him after all. I had to settle these unresolved feelings for me to even try to be in his company.

I was attracted to Michael, and he was attracted to me, but I still carried a torch for Nolan.

I was up at six the next morning and used the well-equipped gym at The Westcliff. I booked myself in at the spa for some treatments the next day as it would be Saturday and I wanted to treat myself. After the gym, a quick shower, and some breakfast, I got started with some work. The information Brad had sent to me about the airlines and the competition was all-encompassing.

By midday, I had made some phone calls and set up some meetings with key personnel within the local aviation industry. The local flag carrier was in some financial trouble, and there was talk of a takeover. Kingman Air wouldn't be getting involved in the takeover, rather we were looking to establish our own routes in the region adjacent to the local carrier. "The sky is large enough for more than one carrier," my father always said, which was why we had always been welcome in all regions we ventured into. We didn't engage in any hostile takeovers, as this would serve to put our customers, planes, and pilots in jeopardy.

As I was thinking about pilot and plane jeopardy, I started to wonder if this might have been the reason why Nolan's plane was downed in Guatemala.

Had our presence there offended anyone, I wondered. *Was Nolan in some type of disquiet with someone, or had he been concealing something sinister from me?*

I had always believed Nolan lived a whole lifetime before we met, but he had always been so open with me.

Could he have been in so deep with someone that they had wanted to kill him, and our children had become collateral damage?

I made one more call to an old friend from school. Alex McVeigh had always lived on the fringe, even in school no one really knew him, but he and I had formed an unlikely friendship. He was rough around the edges, and I had always been so well put together. He had never confirmed nor denied if he worked for or was involved somehow with any intelligence organisation, but that was my general feeling, and I knew better than to push him for answers.

When I called him and told him all that had happened and what the findings were from the investigation incident report, he was disappointed I hadn't called him sooner.

Having Alex on side and investigating this matter put a smile on my face. He would work hard to find the answers I desperately needed.

As soon as I hung up from Alex, I heard a knock at my door. I hadn't ordered room service, and housekeeping had already cleaned my suite around me while I had been working, so I couldn't imagine who it would be.

When I walked over to the door, opened it, and saw Michael, I was surprised. I didn't know what to make of his unannounced visit, but I remembered my manners and let him in. I showed him into the living section of my suite and sat down on the sofa opposite him.

"This is a surprise," I said.

"A good one, I hope?"

"Do you always drop by unannounced?"

"I'm sorry, I didn't mean to offend you. I'm usually well mannered, I promise." He was unfailingly polite which ordinarily would have been endearing.

"I'm sure you are, but a telephone would have worked just fine." I sounded rude, but I had become used to solitude, and even though secretly he might have been part of the reason I was here, I wasn't ready to have him dropping by whenever he wished.

"How's work?" he asked, circumventing my abruptness.

"Yes, I have set up meetings for Tuesday all day. Michael, what's going on here?" He hadn't come to see me for small talk; I sounded impatient, but I had to know.

"Tuesday meetings? Does this mean your weekend is open?" He seemed hopeful.

"All I have planned is a spa day tomorrow, and then I will venture further into the city."

"Okay. I had to see you again. I want to get to know you. I get the sense that our dinner date went well, and I came here to ask if you wanted to go somewhere with me?"

He had a sweet boyish look on his face and seemed excited. Now that I had got over the surprise of his unannounced visit and he was in my personal space, I noticed his body. Sitting on the opposite seat in the small space, dressed in a deep green v-neck t-shirt, which clung to him, it was hard not to notice his well-defined chest and toned forearms. His six foot two frame was well proportioned. He certainly didn't eat Malva puddings every day or whatever sweet treat they served wherever he travelled to. I suddenly became flushed and felt hot, I didn't know where to look when I heard him clear his throat.

Why was this happening now, I wondered.

"Somewhere?" I eventually asked. I had been caught staring.

"My friend owns a game reserve, and I was wondering, well, hoping that you would come with me."

"Where's this reserve?" Michael felt safe, and I liked him, but I was far from home, and this seemed so sudden.

"Not too far. It's a forty-five minute flight from here." He put on a convincing tone, but I still didn't feel quite ready to go anywhere with him. Moreso with the burgeoning sexual attraction which had taken me by surprise.

"Hmm." The temperature in the room suddenly felt even hotter. All I managed was a weak smile.

"You seem doubtful. Are you afraid of the lions and the leopards?"

"It's not the animals I fear, Michael."

"What, then? I would never harm you, in any way."

"I know I can trust you to not harm me, but my emotions are all over the place, and I don't understand them myself."

He moved and came to sit next to me. His masculine scent and a mix of his cologne filled my nostrils, and the familiar pounding in my chest started again.

"We can go together to the game reserve, as friends. No pressure, no expectations. I think you will like the place. They may have a spa, so you won't miss out on that," he said, softly.

Such a spontaneous thing was exactly what the old Sofia would have done when I still had a zest for life and was not weighed down by grief. Now my world was upside down and I wasn't even sure men and women could be friends, especially ones who were attracted to one another, like Michael and I clearly were.

I'd seen the way he kept gazing at me during dinner when he thought I wasn't looking. Now, even though he was trying very hard to maintain eye contact, his eyes kept running up and down my body.

"I don't understand why you're so kind and so accommodating, and why you haven't run a mile in the opposite direction."

"That's because, if you let me, I can be a good friend."

"You might just be a little charming. So, what time do we leave?" I laughed quietly.

"A little charming?" he asked, with a wounded tone.

"Just a little," I said as I gestured how little with my thumb and index finger.

"I can be back to pick you up in three hours. Is that enough time for you?"

"Three hours is perfect," I said as I laid my hand on his solid thigh, as if it was the most natural thing. I quickly moved it, but he had already noticed.

"Perfect. I'll see you then and thank you for agreeing to come with me. You're going to love it," he said, as he got up and made his way to the door.

I agreed to go on a trip with Michael, even after all the instructional monologues I had been having with myself since I met him. I was putting myself in a situation for which I wasn't quite ready for. After one date, I was going on a trip with a man — that had to be one for the record books.

I kept trying to convince myself this was a reconnaissance mission, to figure out flights and routes. I was lying to myself. There was a whole team for that role, and routes were certainly not at a game reserve.

I was going to the game reserve because I wanted to get to know Michael. He was magnetic, and I was curious. It didn't hurt that he was good to look at and I could breathe him in all day, if only it were possible.

I got myself ready and packed appropriately for a weekend in the bush with a man I barely knew. The flight would be short, but I was nervous about everything, who would do this and was I even safe with him. I supposed I was safe, we were "friends" after all.

Ha, it was clear to see we would never be friends, not with the way my hand had strayed onto his thigh, and we had both loved it.

Michael and I met outside The Westcliff and rode silently to a nearby airfield. We boarded a small Cessna Citation. I was relieved, as my father piloted one just like it personally. He had always assured me it was safe whenever I quizzed him about the night flights he took my mother on. I wondered if a private jet was all part of the package when visiting a game reserve. I shrugged off the question and got comfortable.

Once we were up in the air, I turned to Michael and caught him watching me. I gave him a small smile.

"Thank you for convincing me to do this. I haven't flown for leisure in a long time."

"Are you okay with flying, Sofia?" I didn't read minds, but this question had to be about Nolan and the boys.

"It has never crossed my mind not to be I work for an airline. I've been flying around the world ever since I can remember."

"I thought after all that's happened, you would be reticent when it comes to flying?" he asked, his brow furrowed.

"If I can be honest with you, it's not flying that I have a problem with. It's a lot of the simple things. One of the most significant to me is that I haven't been able to take a single photograph since it happened. I suppose that would be the unusual explanation for the keen interest in your job."

"You enjoyed taking photographs at some stage?"

"I did."

"But?" he coaxed gently.

"When my family died, I tried to find some comfort in anything, even in my long-time hobby of photography, but I couldn't bear to pick up my camera, as I had taken to photographing the boys all the time. Every mother does, but I took it to some obsessive levels."

"Obsessive? How?" he asked with interest and a devastating smile, which I shouldn't have noticed, not when I was talking about this.

"Even mealtimes were a photo op. I think I had at least five cameras, and that's not including my phone." I chuckled as I talked about that. "I had felt then, that if I couldn't capture the boys, there was no reason to take photos. It was after their deaths that I laid my camera down and I haven't picked it up since."

"What you've been through is unimaginable, but I can definitely help with that photography situation. Did you bring any of your cameras on this trip?" he asked with a kindness that melted me.

"No, I didn't. I don't know where they are."

I knew exactly what had happened to all my cameras, but I couldn't dare say it out loud to him, or could I?

"You don't? Did someone take them?" he asked, with genuine concern on his face as he pursed his perfectly shaped lips.

I sighed. "No, no one took them. Thirty-four days after burying what was left of my family, I returned to our family home, from my parents where I had been, but the lethargy I felt was overwhelming. Somehow, nine days later, after summoning reserves of energy, which I didn't think I still possessed, I managed to pack up all that was in our home. Save for photographs and some baby keepsakes, everything else was donated or sold, including all my cameras. I couldn't bear to look at them. They made me feel too much, and I didn't know what to do with such heavy feelings at that time."

With a heave of his chest, he exhaled the breath he had been holding as I spoke. "That was profound, but I'm guessing this part is a drop in the ocean of all you've been through. I'm so sorry."

He didn't waver as he looked deep into my eyes; I saw the sincerity in his.

"You're good. You put me on this plane, high in the sky, so you could get me talking, while I had nowhere to run or hide. I know you did," I said, as I smiled at him grateful and felt the tears welling up in my eyes.

"Since you've put it that way, I'm glad I did." He smiled, and this time my stomach flipped.

As we spoke in the confined quarters of the small plane, we both leaned into each other.

How was I trusting this stranger so quickly and so implicitly with all I had kept buried in the depths of my soul? I felt lighter baring this to the stranger who I had spoken to honestly more than anyone else close to me in a long time. It felt good speaking like this, and the comfort I got when he held my hand in his and looked at me was more priceless than the therapy I had since I lost them.

Shortly after that, we arrived at the reserve. Phillip and his wife Taryn met us at the lodge. A beautiful, thatched building served as a reception area, gift shop, and staff office. The gift shop was a true shopping destination in the African bush. It carried locally made décor pieces, artwork, and even furniture. The reception area showcased some of the minimalist contemporary furniture, made by local crafts-men and women, all of which wouldn't be out of place in any high end interiors magazine. I made a note to buy some furniture for my long neglected home office. In addition to the art, amazing wildlife photographs adorned the walls.

"This reserve has the big five." Taryn inched closer to me as she spoke.

"These photographs are stunning," I said, as I stared at them in wonder.

I was in awe of how the photographer had captured the beasts in their natural habitat, looking at ease as if posing for the photographs.

"Look at the small print in the bottom right corner."

Michael was the photographer.

"Wow, this is unbelievable. These are fantastic," I said as I ran my fingers across his name.

Was I subconsciously trying to touch him again?

"Yes, he is incredibly talented, and kind, too."

I chuckled. Taryn had an air of mischief about her.

"Did he bribe you to sing his praises?"

It was her turn to laugh. "Not at all. Phil did say things were very new between you two."

"Yes, we are friends."

"I've heard about that too, which is why I have put you in two separate chalets this way."

She guided me towards the western side of the gift shop where the chalets were located.

"Yours is this way. We didn't have any other ones free on the other side of the lodge, so I'm afraid you and *your friend* are next door to each other — how dreadful. He seems horrid, but don't worry, you can double lock the door from the inside, and the windows have locks, too." She smirked, and I decided immediately that I liked her.

Chapter Six

♥

Michael

Phil's reserve was luxurious. After he took over from his father, he had done a lot of work to modernise the savanna accommodation for his discerning guests from all over the world. There was even a wood fired hot tub off to one side of the chalet. I wondered if Sofia would want to try out the hot tub with me, as friends, of course. An outdoor shower was adjacent to the hot tub.

As it was almost sundown, I went out to find Sofia so we could go and watch the animals come down to drink. This was something I loved about being here at the reserve, and I hoped she would love it too. I walked towards her chalet but stopped when I got to the outdoor shower. I could see her naked body through the wooden slats. I should have walked away and returned to my chalet, but if I did, she would see me leave, and might think I was some kind of creeper. I had to make my presence known. I called out her name three or four times, and it wasn't until she turned off the shower that she saw me and screamed.

"Sofia, it's only me. I am sorry. I called out to you, but you didn't hear me," I said, facing away from her.

"So, you decided to barge into my outdoor bathroom, to what? Have your way with me? I knew you couldn't be trusted." She was flustered and jittery.

I handed her a robe, which she hurriedly donned. Try as I might, I couldn't look away.

"I didn't barge in; this is a shared space. Our two chalets share the pool as well as use of the outdoor shower. You, however, decided to be in *flagrant dilecto* as this is a communal space. Now, to answer your question, I didn't come here to have any kind of way with you. I came to invite you to come out to the viewing deck and watch the animals meander down to the watering hole. They do that at dusk, and I thought it might be something you would like to see."

"Yes, I would love to come to the viewing deck, but I prefer to do so with some clothes on."

I couldn't say I was upset at the recent developments. I finally got to see her in all her glory, even though it was a complete stroke of luck. The view wasn't disappointing. I could tell she put effort into looking the way she did. She was flustered, and I worked very hard not to smile and tell her exactly what was going through my mind when I saw her. I was hoping that would come later, for now I needed her to trust me. Once she was dressed, we made our way to the lodge and joined Themba, our guide, who drove us to the viewing deck two kilometres away.

"Thanks for bringing me out here tonight," she said, as she and I got out of the vehicle and made our way up the stairs to the elevated viewing deck.

"The best time to see the animals is at dusk and the sunrises are remarkable too. I also wanted to give you something you might need for the rest of our trip."

"Really, a gift. I love those," she murmured, chuckling.

I would be remembering that.

"It's not much, but I think you'll like it."

Once we got up the steps of the viewing deck, I handed her one of my newer cameras, something small but very powerful. When she shared with me about her old photography hobby, I realised we had something important in common. I wanted to share my passion with her, and hopefully bring us closer.

"Zfc, this is the perfect camera. Thank you so much." Spontaneously she threw her arms around me, and I held her close, breathing her in. She was soft in all the right places. I didn't want to let her go, but for now, I had to. It was the right thing to do.

"I'm glad you like it. It's perfect for you."

She was appreciative, but I saw what looked like apprehension on her face when I handed over the camera. This smaller Nikon was simple enough to use, and it was obvious she knew her way around a camera, as she looked at it and its intricacies. All that was missing was taking that first shot to bring her out of her photography hiatus.

I didn't press the issue of taking any photographs; she would do it in her own time. The last time she had taken any was when her family was still with her, and only she would know when she was ready to take the first picture.

"I'm sorry I overreacted about the shower incident. I don't have a problem with my nudity. At least, I don't think I do, but I just thought you were trying to ambush me. Even as I'm saying that I sound so ridiculous," she said, with a self deprecating look on her face.

"No, you don't. I'm a man, and I'm not blind. I am not wired like most, however. My default is respect, always. Besides, I have a very high regard for what you've told me about your life and what you are going through. I don't intend on bulldozing my way through your emotions, or even your body for that matter. You and I will both know when you're ready to be more than friends."

"I don't know if I will ever be ready. I feel so guilty being with you."

"But why would you feel guilty about spending time with a friend?" He cocked his head to the side.

"You're being deliberately obtuse. We might be friends now, but I imagine we'll be more than friends, and I think you know that too."

"So why are we playing at being friends when we both know that we both want to be more than friends. Why do we have to play games?"

She was going through the worst pain imaginable, and I wanted to be patient with her. My mind knew this, but why did I keep pushing her? I hadn't spent much time with her, but my heart and my treacherous body already knew I wanted more of her and from her.

I had to take a step back and give her some breathing room, but how much willpower would that take, and did I have it?

"Well, you told me I was your friend when you invited me here, so maybe I'm playing along. I just need to sort through some feelings about some things."

"Do you want to talk about those things?"

As she gently pushed me away with her words, she moved to stand closer, accidentally brushing her rounded breast against my bare arm. She didn't notice, but the thousands of nerve endings in my body did.

"I'll tell you eventually, if we become more than friends." This would have to be enough for now. I didn't want to push her away.

This was when Themba joined us on the viewing deck and pointed at something in the distance.

"Do you see the buffalo coming in from the far side?" He said, looking out onto the vast savanna.

"Yes, I see them," Sofia said excitedly, then regaled us with how maternal they were and how they were very much a herd animal.

"I see someone has watched *Battle at Kruger*."

"Of course. I watched it while I was waiting for you to return to the Westcliff for me after you invited me here. One always has to be prepared for all eventualities."

"Really, like a buffalo attack? How did you let your imagination run so wild?" I chuckled, as she gave me her dazzling smile.

I wondered where else her wild imagination had taken her.

After that, there was no more banter as the magnificence of the African wildlife became apparent. Wildebeest, warthogs, gazelles, and zebras came in formation to the watering hole. Hippos began bobbing their heads from the river. A herd of elephants sauntered to the banks of the river, as did the giraffes. It was a remarkable sight, and I was happy to share it with her and see the wonderment on her face. In the distance, we heard the unmistakable rumble of a pride of lions. However, we didn't have the luck of seeing them that evening.

"Wow, are you getting these shots? This is magnificent," she whispered, trying to look at the camera display.

"Yes, I am. Come closer and take a look." She leaned in closer to me peering at the display, and again parts of her softness brushed against me. Her feminine scent consumed me. I inhaled deeply to take her in. Like the animals I was looking at, my instincts were on high alert, only I couldn't behave like one of them.

"May I?" She asked softly.

She took the camera from me and worked it out confidently. "I love that setting sun on the horizon; it illuminates everything perfectly." She whispered, as she gazed at the camera display.

She brought it up closer to see, accidentally taking a photo of the dazzle of zebras. "Oops, I don't know how that happened."

"Beautiful," I said, as I gazed at her.

She turned to me and held my gaze. She was right; the sun setting behind us illuminated all the beauty she had. She smiled, then handed me the camera quietly.

After an hour of watching and waiting and watching some more, we eventually returned to the lodge. I had got some good shots, and I felt her eyes on me, although she didn't say much more after the animals had started coming down to drink.

The restaurants were clearing up, but we were able to order food and get it sent to my chalet.

She was surprisingly at ease in my living room, where we proceeded to eat. We shared a bottle of wine and talked about her first safari as a child. I told her about the summers I had spent at this reserve with Phil. Sitting close to each other, we looked through the photos I had taken. I kept my hands to myself, although her body was close and was screaming at me to hold her and bring her closer to me.

As the evening wore on, Sofia had become not backwards in coming forward, and she asked a question which I hadn't dared to think about in a long time.

"Why aren't you attached? Or even married, Michael? You seem like the perfect package." Again, she looked me up and down appreciatively. What was a man to do?

After taking a breath, I decided to be open and tell her the truth. "I agree. I am the perfect package."

She laughed, her first real laugh with me, and I loved how it sounded.

"I was engaged to be married some years ago. We were very much in love, or so I thought, until I realised, she preferred my brother. They got married six months after they told me how much in love they were."

"That's terrible; your own brother. Did she ever tell you why she didn't want you anymore?"

"As a matter of fact, she did. Her explanation was a hodgepodge of excuses. My commitment to my work seemed to be her biggest gripe, and to prove to everyone that all was well in my world, I even offered to take their wedding photographs," I said, with a shrug of my shoulders.

"Why would you put yourself through that torture?" she gasped.

"I was lying to myself that I didn't care, but it took me months, even years, to get over their betrayal."

"Are you over it now? I mean, really over it?"

"I'm not in love with my brother's wife, if that's what you're asking, but my relationship with my brother has never been quite the same."

"This must be a sore subject. We don't have to talk about it."

"I'm over the whole thing. They have two girls now who I absolutely love."

"So you don't harbour any hard feelings, and imagine the girls as yours, or how things could have been, if things had worked out between you and her?"

"Far from it. When my time comes to have children, it will be with someone who's in love with me and vice versa."

Her gold flecked gaze was intense as she took in what I was saying to her. "How did you get over that?"

"I threw myself into my work. I focused on making as much money as I could and for a while, I bedded everything with a pulse."

She swallowed audibly. I had to be honest. If she didn't know now, she would eventually, and I wanted her to hear it from me. It wasn't the best example of who I was as a man.

"You did?" she asked, as she folded her arms across her chest, while I fought hard not to stare at the glorious result of that move.

"I am very much over that phase, too. This happened some four years ago, and I am done with that life. Now who's journalising who?"

She chuckled softly. "Well, I'm sorry that happened to you. It sounds like the worst kind of duplicity."

"I've definitely moved on." I smiled as I said this.

"Moved on? Have you been serious with anyone since then?"

"I'm hoping to get to know you better, if you will let me."

At that moment, she chose to pick up her camera and stand up. "Will you walk me to my chalet? I think I'll call it a night." I couldn't read the expression on her face.

After telling myself to go dead slow with her, my heart had ruled over my head. I thought I could be open with her.

"Of course."

We walked in silence the short distance between our doors. As we were walking, her fingers grazed mine, and when I glanced at her, I saw what I thought was an expectant look.

Once we got to her door, I didn't think. I moved in closer and pulled her towards me, kissing her like the starving man I was. I had been dying to taste her lips since the day we first met. This was not what I had promised, but this very moment had been in the making the whole evening. As I tasted her over and over, I couldn't stop, and she didn't make me. She kissed me back, like I had never been kissed before. I don't think she noticed the little moans she was making, but they sent blood rushing right down to my groin. We kissed for what felt like hours until she took a step back for air.

"I'm not sorry, Sofia. I've wanted to do that since the very first time I saw you in Istanbul," I told her breathlessly.

"Don't be sorry. I loved everything about that kiss, but you should go," she said, placing her palm on my chest.

She was just as breathless as I was, as she stepped closer to me. She might have been saying goodnight, but she didn't seem ready to leave. Not yet.

Like me, she was just as affected. She was flushed and her hair was beautifully tousled. Her chest was heaving rapidly, and this had the effect of pushing her breasts out towards me. It took every ounce of self control to not take her back to my chalet. The relief I felt in knowing I wasn't alone in how I was feeling made me want to taste her lips over and over.

"Not until I kiss you again."

I knew I was pushing it, but I had to kiss her again and again. This time, I held her close, as her scent overpowered my senses, and I didn't want to let her go, ever. She plastered her body against mine, and I felt every curve and contour as I ran my hands over her back, her hips, and held both her cheeks in my hands.

How would I ever let her go tonight or ever? Tonight, I had to. Kissing was one thing, but I didn't want to pressure her into anything else that comes after.

"Good night, Sofia." Reluctantly, I stopped kissing her, as my hands lingered on her body.

Her pupils were dilated and her skin on her long neck was flushed. "Good night, Michael," she said as she slowly licked her lips and opened her chalet door.

I watched her shut it, and only after it was bolted from the inside did I walk back the short distance to my chalet.

Chapter Seven

♥

Sofia

I didn't know if it was the fact that I hadn't been kissed by a man in two years, or the fact that I hadn't been kissed like *that* before. Not even by Nolan, who had ravaged my body for years. Michael's kisses consumed me, and they made me want to yield to all he was.

I didn't know if it was the dopamine, oxytocin, and serotonin cocktail traversing my system, but I still heard the loud boom of my heart beating in my ears. I still tasted him on my lips, and I smelled him everywhere. I smelled myself too; I was so turned on and my body was letting me know. I knew right then that if I let it happen, I'd easily lose myself in him. My body hadn't felt this way in a long time, and I was desperate to surrender to him. However, I would feel guilty. I was not ready to be with him. I went to bed and for the first time, it wasn't Nolan's face I saw in my dreams, but Michael's.

I was up with the birds in the morning, and what a beautiful sunrise it was. The topography of the land was enhanced by the beautiful colours. The brown, red, and gold typical of the savanna and alien to the blue of an LA sunrise. The birdsong was like none I had ever heard, the smells so fresh and yet the savanna was dry.

Would it be under the African sky that I would fall in love again?

I wasn't feeling the guilt I had been feeling when I first contemplated spending time with Michael; I was filled with hope and anticipation. Hope that one day I would be able to love and feel again, and anticipation for what I already knew Michael's body could make me feel.

How could one kiss make me feel like this?

A week ago, I couldn't fathom being with anyone, but after one kiss from Michael, I was ready to surrender. Was I so fickle as to put Nolan aside so quickly after one kiss from a man I hardly knew?

Does that make him a rebound, or was I ready to have someone mend my broken heart?

Could that someone be Michael?

I went outside to the shared courtyard to enjoy my morning coffee on the sun loungers overlooking the pool. As my eyes strayed out towards the edge of the pool and beyond, I realised all that protected the guests from the animals was a mesh wire fence. While I sat contemplating my safety, and imagining a terrible scenario with a bull elephant, Michael appeared from his chalet. I couldn't help the flush that washed over me as I remembered the kiss we had shared last night.

"Good morning, Sofia." I felt little flutters in the depths of my stomach at the deep timbre of his voice.

"Morning." I smiled at him expectantly, hoping he would come closer to the lounger and perhaps even sit down next to me.

He didn't do either.

Was I wrong about last night?

"Sofia, I don't have much time, but there have been some developments with the story I am here to cover, and I need to leave immediately." He was agitated and flustered, and the urgency in his voice was hard to ignore.

"Straight away? I can be packed in ten minutes." I felt the disappointment deeply, and relief. Relief that we didn't take anything further last night, as this abrupt parting was a far cry from the attentive and charming man I spent the evening with.

"I think you should stay here, for the next two days at least. There are riots in Johannesburg, and this is where you are safest."

He had begged me to come here with him, and now he would be leaving me here, all alone. Although the more I thought about it, the more I didn't want to be near any type of riot.

"What riots? What's going on? Will you be safe? If they are anything like the riots at home, they will be dangerous." I heard the panic in my voice; I was imagining the worst, but I didn't let my mind get the better of me.

"I'll make sure to be safe, and you will be safe here too." He spoke softly, as the man from last night made a brief appearance.

This was the first time this morning he stopped and paid any attention to me, but my pride wouldn't let me scrape up tiny morsels of attention he threw my way.

"Okay, goodbye. This sounds time sensitive. Will I see you again?" I asked, trying to sound flippant.

"Of course, you will. On Monday, when you return to Johannesburg. I will send the plane back here for your return journey."

"You don't have to do that. I can find my way back." Chartering a plane for the average man is no mean feat. Although I was angry at the situation, I didn't want Micheal paying for it, literally.

"I brought you here, it is my responsibility to make sure you return safely to the Westcliff. Please let me be a gentleman." He pleaded with his eyes.

I wouldn't be petty. Were it another time, I would've argued this out, but he was agitated and needed to go. He came closer and helped me stand up.

"I was thinking about you all night, and I'm happy we were able to spend some time together, but I wish our time here could have been longer."

I didn't get a chance to respond, as he then kissed me with urgency, but not as passionately as the night before. After that, he was gone, and I was left alone in the African bush.

Inwardly, I was seething with fury. I understood that Michael's work would have him leave at a moment's notice, but as he was the one who had invited me to the reserve, I couldn't help but feel abandoned.

Is this what his commitment to work looked like?

As I floundered in my self-pity, Taryn knocked and let herself into the private courtyard. She sat down with me and had a laptop with her.

"Hi Taryn, is everything alright? Do you have any idea what has Michael rushing back to Johannesburg?"

"A lot of rioting, some looting; there are some people who have lost their lives, and some are injured. It's awful," she said, her voice taking a serious tone.

"What is it all about, though?"

"Where have you been staying since you've been here?"

"At the Four Seasons in Johannesburg."

"You probably haven't noticed, but the country is literally in the dark due to constant power cuts."

"Power cuts?"

Ahh, this is what Michael meant when he mentioned a power crisis.

"Yes, every day for up to twelve hours a day, the electricity is turned off because of a limited power supply."

"I didn't even realise that. What does everyone do?"

I had never imagined that this would even be a problem. My life was a far cry from what was happening here, and Michael was here to bring this to the world. I felt some guilt for my anger at him leaving.

"That's the issue, the few who can afford it — like the Four Seasons — have generators, everyone else is left to fumble and falter. These riots are a last resort, as everyone is disillusioned by it all."

"That's complicated. How does that even get a resolution?"

"I don't know, but it's a sad time for all our people."

She handed me her laptop as I perused article after article of what had been going on overnight, and quietly for some weeks.

Could this be the reason why Shep had discounted business in this part of the world?

At the back of mind, I was wondering what would happen with all the plans and meetings I had organised for the coming week. This situation was serious and unstable. I was worried, and concern was etched on my face until I remembered Taryn was still sitting with me.

"Are you worried about Michael? You don't have to be; this is what he does, and he knows how to stay safe," she said reassuringly.

As I contemplated the gravity of the events going on, I realised my work-related concerns were too petty to even express. I chose instead to offer a weak smile.

"We like to keep the guests as safe as possible, and against my better judgement, Phil had cameras installed outside the chalets for security. You wouldn't believe how unsafe I realised one of our guests was when I had to check one of the cameras earlier."

"What happened? Was it an animal attack, Taryn?" I was right to have been worried about that mesh wire.

"Yes, the wildest of all animals." She sighed dramatically as she accessed a camera feed on her laptop.

As she showed me, I realised this was Michael and I outside my chalet last night during that never ending kiss. I could only giggle as I looked intently on.

"I always knew Michael had the makings of a really bad friend, don't you think?"

"You got me there. I don't know what came over me, but the moment was so right."

"I'm not surprised. I can sense chemistry from many kilometres away. It's something I must have honed from living among wild animals."

Her laugh was infectious, and I soon forgot how upset I was.

"I can't believe that happened last night."

"Why not? You're both young, attractive, and available, right?"

"I've just come out of a long-term relationship."

That was all I could say to Taryn. Today was not a day to recount all that had come to define my existence over the last months.

"Still pining after the previous guy, huh?"

"Yes and no, it's complicated."

"It always is. Do you think you'll ever get back together with the other guy?"

"No, that's impossible."

"There, now you have permission to move on."

"If only it were that easy," I mused.

"Don't shut yourself away in your chalet, make sure to come and find me in the lodge, okay?"

"Sure, I will." I answered as she left.

My weekend ended all too quickly. I enjoyed every moment I spent at the reserve. Both Taryn and Themba were obliging. Every sunset I found myself at the lookout as I had done with Michael on my first night at the reserve, and every sunset was different from the last, highlighting the beauty of wild Africa.

During the day, I would be at the lodge, mingling with other guests and going out with Phil, who was the vet and owner of the reserve. Seeing the animals up close and in their natural habitat was unforgettable, and I developed a newfound respect for the gamekeepers, and for Phil. For them, I could tell it was a job they enjoyed, but for me it was therapy. It left me renewed and re-energised after my time there. I could easily have spent more time in the bush, but I had to go back to the real world to accomplish what I had travelled to Africa for.

As Philip drove me to the airport for my morning flight, I promised myself I would return to this magical corner of the world.

"Thank you, Phil. The stay was wonderful, and you were all kind to me."

"You're welcome. We hope you and Michael will return soon, together perhaps?"

"I would really like that, too. We'll see how it all works out."

"From what I hear, that seems up to you."

Why would he say that? I wondered how much Michael had shared with him, and how he would know what to share, as I wasn't sure yet what was happening between us.

"You're more informed than I am then."

The back and forth could have gone on for a while, but the plane was ready, and I had to leave. The flight was quicker than I remembered and when I arrived at the Westcliff, I felt like I had returned home. After indulging in a long bath, I got to work.

Despite the civil unrest, which had occurred over the weekend, all my meetings went on as scheduled, and more meetings were scheduled. The aviation board had several other airlines waiting in line, bidding to provide their services. They were taking their time in deciding who they would choose.

The major cleanup of the city was underway, but still the nationwide power cuts would continue. The back and forth in South Africa could take weeks, and I advised Bradley and Dad about my slow progress.

While I waited for the South Africans to decide, I would travel to Namibia and get started there. Bradley offered to come out and assist on the ground as I had five more countries which needed to be covered. I dismissed his generous offer. I was finding solace in my seclusion.

It had taken being a world away from home to finally begin to heal. I contacted the therapist with whom I had built the best rapport to help me. We arranged bi-weekly sessions to help me through what was now so different to how I had been the last time we spoke a year ago.

Chapter Eight

♥

Michael

After all we had shared at the reserve, leaving Sofia so abruptly hadn't been a part of my plan. I enjoyed her company; she was as beautiful as she was intelligent, insightful, and amusing. She had been so responsive in my arms. Even though I had promised her and myself that the trip was merely a trip for two friends, I wanted to take our relationship to the next level. The jet touched down at O.R. Tambo International Airport as the smaller airfield we had departed from was not safe to land due to the unrest. I made a quick stop at the Houghton to collect my work bag and went down to Johannesburg Central, where most of the unrest was.

There was a heavy police presence, and the crowds were slowly dispersing. However, there were many who had been injured and a lot of property destruction. I quickly got to work, documenting all I could with my camera. I spent the day following the story, from township to township. My driver, who had family and friends scattered around the country, informed me that Mpumalanga, Durban, and the Western Cape had had a lot of disturbances too.

Flying was the quickest way, and I arrived in Durban in the dark of night. It was chaos and mayhem, and the results of the looting and violence was clear to see. At regular intervals overnight and during the rest of the weekend, I edited the photos and forwarded them to the Chronicle. It was a busy time, and the situation was not only fluid but dangerous for members of the press, too. I kept in regular contact with my father, although his interest was mostly for my welfare. I worked all day and night to try to make sure I was back in Johannesburg when Sofia returned.

The frenetic pace of this story wouldn't allow me to return to Johannesburg. I desperately wanted to see Sofia; I was captivated by her and every minute I was apart from her, had me yearning to see her even more. In sixteen days, I travelled the length and breadth of the country, hearing stories, seeing the pain and suffering of economic, political, and environmental migrants. This had become more than a story about electricity, but an untold story of migration. My perceived impartiality allowed me to photograph all sides to this struggle, and when I did finally see my work in the Chronicle, I was proud that my efforts would be seen by the world too.

When I eventually returned to Johannesburg, I was worn out but happy. The story had been brought to the world, not only by me, but with the efforts of other news outlets. Though, I wasn't quite ready to leave the country yet. During the time I was travelling, I had spoken to Sofia only once, and she had been busy herself at that time. I feared the ground we had gained on our trip had somehow been lost due to the literal and figurative distance between us, as well as the communication breakdown.

When I returned to Johannesburg, she was in Windhoek with work. I was disappointed until she mentioned she would be making a stop in Walvis Bay, as a business associate had offered her their beach house to use for a while. She invited me to join her there, and I was ecstatic.

Chapter Nine

♥

Sofia

I was waiting at Walvis Bay Airport when Micheal arrived. I was happy to see him, but I didn't feel any excitement.

What if he had to leave abruptly again?

He greeted me with a hug; he wanted to linger with it but I quickly directed him to the waiting car, which took us to the house. There was distance between us again, as if a wall had been erected in the eighteen days since we last saw each other.

"Have you been busy, Sofia?" he asked as he moved closer to me, his scent enveloping me in the confines of the car.

I had longed to be close to him again, but now I had mixed feelings.

"Yes, very." I didn't elaborate as I stared out of the window, wondering if inviting him had been a good idea. When I had planned this weekend, I had imagined him with me, but because of his work schedule, I would have been content to be on my own.

"What else have you been doing while in Johannesburg?" He said, softly.

"An intense workout in the morning, work all day, and for my evenings, I found a good yoga studio close to the hotel," I answered noncommittally.

"Rinse and repeat, huh?"

"Yes, rinse and repeat." I sighed, turning my body towards the window. Seeing him again stoked the anger, which had been festering for weeks.

The drive to the Bay House was awkward, and the conversation was stiff and stilted. The natural rapport we had built was in the rear-view.

We arrived at the house, and it was breath-taking. It was built deep into the jagged cliff face, looking out onto the bay where the water was angry and choppy. We went in and it was easy enough to find the guest rooms that were made up for us. A chef was available if we needed one. We both got settled in and met on the balcony.

"This is a beautiful place. Thanks for inviting me, Sofia."

"Yes, it's wonderful. I'm glad you agreed to join me." I wasn't sure about that yet, but it was the cordial thing to say.

"I would never pass up the opportunity to see you again. I've been thinking about you."

I had been thinking about him, too. Perhaps a little too much, but anger and pride wouldn't let me own up to it. There was a prolonged silence before either of us spoke again.

"Did you get the photographs you needed?" I heard the hint of bitterness in my own voice.

"Yes, I think I satisfied the brief. I will show them to you later if you'd like. First, I need to apologise for the way I left. I took you to the reserve and leaving you like that in hindsight was impolite and in bad taste."

I had hoped to talk about how he left, but I didn't imagine he would apologise. He was sincere and the ice surrounding my heart started to thaw. A few words from him, and I would start to melt.

Is this the person I had become around him?

"That was the best place I can imagine being abandoned. Phil and Taryn were gracious hosts, but I was a little angry with you for a while," I said, truthfully.

He stepped closer to me, and all the memories of the last night we had together came flooding back.

"I realise that, and you might still be angry at me now."

Even though we were alone in this generous sized beach house, he spoke softly, and his hungry gaze sent tingles down my spine.

"Oh yes, you have a long way to go to earn my forgiveness," I said in a most flirtatious voice which took me by surprise.

"How do I do that?"

"You're a big boy; you can come up with something."

"Is that your famous imagination coming out to play?" He chuckled softly.

"I was talking about food. What did you think I was talking about?" I asked with the most confused expression I could muster.

"Definitely food." He laughed louder this time.

He took my hand and walked towards the kitchen. My hand in his felt like the most natural thing in the world, and the light stroke with his thumb on mine sent tingles down my spine.

We made our way into the kitchen, which had been stocked with enough food to feed an army.

Michael surprised me as he prepared steak and vegetables.

"Wow! Where did you learn to do that? It already smells so good. What's that you've just added?"

"Hmm, my mother taught my brothers and I everything she knows about cooking. It's only garlic granules. It's not the real deal, but it keeps your hands from smelling like garlic hours after the meal is eaten."

"Are you familiar with hand soap, Chef?" I giggled.

"Yes, I may have heard about it."

"Wait a minute, you have brothers? You only mentioned the one."

"I had two, an older brother, but he died when he was nineteen."

"Oh, that's terrible. What happened to him?" I couldn't help the pain I suddenly felt in my heart at the sober look on his face.

He put the steak on the side to rest while he spoke. "He developed Ewing's Sarcoma, bone cancer when he was sixteen, but none of the treatments worked and he died three years later." He spoke with so much emotion in his voice, as if it had happened only yesterday.

"That must have been a terrible time for your family, and your parents. Losing a child is the worst type of pain," I said, as I filled a glass of water. My mouth had suddenly become quite dry.

"It was terrible for everyone, but yes, it hit my mother really hard. She seemed to check out of life for some months. We had lost our brother and somehow our mother, too, until my grandmother got her talking to a psychiatrist."

"Yes, that would help." Checking out of life sounded very familiar. My friends and family felt that way about me; perhaps they still do. In my grief, I had never thought about anyone else. It had always been about how I was feeling about my loss.

After that heavy conversation, we went out and sat on the balcony and ate. The food was simple and yet delicious. Although it was still a little windy; the beach was beckoning, and we decided to take a walk after dinner.

"Who do you turn to help you cope with your loss? I only ask because you mentioned the pain of losing a child, and you lost two."

I had expected we would talk about this, but not this soon. His level of empathy warmed me, though, and I found it easy to talk to him.

"I have reengaged with my therapist, but for a long time, I internalised. Since being in Africa, it has become a little easier. Honestly, talking to you like this is a lot more talking than I have been able to do with friends or family. I have thrown myself into work, so I have avoided processing it all."

"You know, if you let me, I would like to be there for you whenever you want to talk about anything."

I hadn't known him long, but he was slowly breaking down my walls. I wondered how Nolan would fit into our conversations.

"I also lost my husband. That might be something you and I can't be too open about." I tried to sound as nonchalant as possible.

"Why would you think that? I am an adult and I think I can empathise with what a husband and a wife share; the bonds they have and the intimacy that comes with that," he murmured, sounding offended.

"I didn't mean to offend you at all. I know you're an adult, but I can't burden you with too much, especially about that."

"For now, let's agree to disagree. Know this, I want to know you, all of you, and that means listening and hearing whatever you have to say."

"Thank you, Michael. I'll hold you to that."

We continued the rest of the walk in silence, taking in the rugged coastline, and the rocky outcrops.

When we returned to the beach house, Michael disappeared, and when he returned he had changed into board shorts.

"I'm going for a swim," he announced suddenly, appearing back in my sight line, shirtless.

"In the bay? The water's freezing." The shock in my voice was evident. It could have been the thought of the cold water, or it could have been finally seeing him shirtless.

Underneath all his clothing, he had been hiding the perfect swimmer's body, a broad chest accentuated by a trim waist, well-built lean muscle, perfectly sculpted forearms, and the muscle definition didn't end there as it went all the way past his thighs and down to his legs. Everything I had imagined didn't come close to how he looked standing before me. In this state of semi undress, he was impressive, and he was aware of his effect on me if the grin on his face was anything to go by.

Would lugging around a bag of photography paraphernalia give him such toned hard muscle?

I wondered if he was hard beneath the board shorts. My eyes roved up and down his body while he tried to maintain eye contact with me. He cleared his throat. Again, I had been caught in my blatant perusal of him.

"Sometimes an ice cold swim is the best swimming, but no, this property has a pool on the subterranean level. You could join me if you like," he said, trying to convince me.

"I'll just get some work finished, then maybe I'll join you," I said nonchalantly, with a shrug of my shoulders. I was feeling anything but nonchalant. My heart was pounding and the invitation to swim took me by surprise.

"Okay, don't work too hard," he said in mock reproach.

I sat and did some work for a while, but I could hardly focus. I couldn't get the sight of him out of my mind and imagining him in the pool wet. I needed to see a lot more of him, and if I could get close enough to, I wanted to feel the solid planes of his body. I decided to join him.

I felt some trepidation as I changed into my white bikini. How could I have picked this one to bring on this trip? Once wet, the white fabric became translucent. The blue one piece I had packed was downright naughty, leaving nothing to the imagination. I should have tried them on before I left the store, only I had bought them to use in my own pool by myself, without an audience.

I looked great; I had never faltered in my fitness routine as it kept me balanced and clearheaded, but I wasn't sure I was ready to be so close to Michael with so little clothing. I was attracted to him and being around him made me want to get much closer to him.

I went down to the basement where he was swimming with intense ferocity; it was unbelievable. How did anyone swim like this? He was fast and powerful, moving through the water effortlessly. His arm and leg movements were well coordinated. The synchronicity was a sight, like he had been born to swim. I sat down on one of the loungers until he stopped and swam towards me.

"Are you coming in? It's heated," he said as droplets of water ran down his face.

"Yes, I think I will." I disrobed, and he gazed at me openly, not attempting to hide his admiration. I felt a momentary sense of pride until the nervous tension returned.

It had been years since I was looked at like this by a man I was attracted to and the admiration in his eyes was intense. I dived in and swam a lap away from him, to try and calm my nerves. He was soon behind me, easily catching up. Even though I was a strong swimmer, Michael was an even stronger one. He caught up and grabbed my waist.

Despite the heated pool, his hands on my skin gave me goose-bumps, and I shuddered. He pulled my soft body against his hard one. I hadn't imagined how turned on I was going to be at this moment. I wanted to wrap my body around his and have him even closer than he already was, but I was terrified.

Was this the right time? Is he the right man? Am I in my right mind? Could my judgement be askew because of how sexy he looks?

"Are you running from me?"

"No, I'm swimming away from you. There's a big difference." My flirty voice made a sudden reappearance.

"Why?"

"I love to race."

Somehow, I escaped from his strong arms, and I continued to swim. He was next to me within a millisecond; a hair's breadth away, looking down at me.

"You have got to be the sexiest woman I have ever seen. I've been wanting to have you in my arms like this since the first time we met."

"Is that all you can say, after I've just won that lap?" I giggled as I half heartedly pushed him away, not ready to acknowledge what he had just said.

"Congratulations. You won that lap because I let you win."

"What, that's..."

He didn't let me finish; he was on my lips, kissing me like only he could. I felt hotter, although it wasn't the heated pool. His strong hands were on me, rubbing me, touching me, and feeling me. I revelled in it as I moaned in assent. He was both gentle and demanding, coaxing my lips open with his tongue. He took my breath away, and he was breathing even harder than I was. I could feel his hard length straining against my stomach. Soon enough, his hands were against my neck, undoing my bikini top. In my periphery, I saw it float away. I didn't have the wherewithal to stop it floating, or to stop what was happening between us. He lifted me up and his tongue was on my nipples, licking and sucking. I threw my head back and thrust my chest towards his mouth so he could have his fill of my breasts. He kneaded them in both his hands as my legs instinctively wrapped around his waist. Then he let out a guttural moan. I ground and writhed against him, wanting to feel him, all of him, next to me, all over me, and in me. I brought his head closer as he let me slide back into the water. His lips were back on mine, and I had lost my bikini bottoms. I made a bungling attempt at tugging at his board shorts, and somehow, the moment was lost.

He stopped what he was doing and gently pushed me away. "I'm sorry, Sofia. I shouldn't have done that."

"What are you talking about?"

"I promised you I wouldn't take anything from you that you didn't want to give me."

"What makes you think I wasn't giving you what I wanted you to have?" I asked him, breathlessly.

"I don't want to pressure you," he said, as he tried to get his ragged breathing under control.

"Did I look like I was under any kind of pressure?" I asked in frustration.

Even though I was under water, I suddenly remembered I was completely naked. I looked around and saw my bikini floating away. I swam towards it to create some distance from Michael and to find something to do with my hands. After retrieving the bottoms, I swam to the lounger, got out, and wrapped a towel around me. He followed me as we towelled off in silence. My body was still pulsating from his touch, as was his from what I could see. He wouldn't look at me; I could tell he was torn. I let him have his space.

"I'll see you inside, okay?" It was a question, and he just nodded his head.

I couldn't understand his hesitation in moving forward with what was happening between us. I also couldn't understand myself; I wasn't over Nolan, far from it, but I was desperate to be as close to Michael as possible, until he decided for me that I was under pressure from him.

Was I a hopeless victim to him? Would I ever be an emotional equal or had my circumstances made me a basket case in his eyes?

I went back upstairs, showered all the chlorine off me, then got comfortable in the living room. As I sat there, I confirmed details of our excursion into the desert the next day. Even though I was hurt, and the rejection was a blow to my fragile ego, I still wanted to enjoy the time with Michael. I fell asleep waiting for him.

Chapter Ten

Sofia

The next morning, I surprisingly woke up feeling bright and sprightly. I spent an hour in the gym, which was adjacent to the pool, and then its memories. A sudden flush came over me when my mind flushed to what had happened in it not twelve hours ago.

I decided to get started on breakfast as it would be a busy day; a full English breakfast seemed like the obvious choice. After much practice, as I had been married to an Englishman, it had become second nature to me.

As I got busy, Michael came into the kitchen all dressed and ready for the day. He stood next to me, looking over my shoulder. "How did you know?"

"Know what, Michael?"

"That is my favourite type of breakfast." It couldn't be, not with the hard body hiding underneath his clothes.

"You sound like you're fawning."

"You don't miss much, do you?" he asked playfully.

He looked refreshed this morning, and well rested, like a weight was lifted off his shoulders. In fact, his outward persona mirrored how I was feeling internally. This was going to be a good day. I plated up both meals while Michael readied the coffee and juice.

"Where did you go last night?" I asked quietly.

"To the beach, with my camera," he said, as he placed the beverages on the table and pulled me close to him. I felt his length come alive against me.

"Did you get good shots?"

"Not many. I was a little preoccupied," he said, as he looked at me hungrily.

"I wouldn't have thought so. You left so quickly, I may have felt a little rejected and perhaps a little small."

"I need to apologise for how last night ended. Pushing you away is not my intention. I'm attracted to you in every way, and I'm desperate to continue what we started last night. I was worried about how you would feel after," he said, as breathed me in, lightly grazing his lips against mine.

"After?"

"Regrets, guilt. It's something you've mentioned." He spoke softly as he continued to hold me against his solid body, tasting and nibbling my lower lip. I couldn't think straight.

"That's considerate, but you need to realise I'm perfectly capable of making a decision or two," I remarked, letting him continue to tease and taste my lips.

He pulled away from me gently. "I realise that. I want everything from you. I only want you to want me too. It's easy to get caught in the moment." I did want him, too. Only I couldn't say it yet.

The intensity of the moment was becoming too much, and I stepped out of his arms.

"Shall we have breakfast before it gets cold, we have a trip into the desert today."

"The desert?" he asked, wide eyed.

"Yes, the desert. Are you worried about the sandstorms and the rattlesnakes?" I asked, in a mock concerned tone, as we both sat down and started to eat.

He chuckled softly. "I'll get my things together after breakfast, and rattlesnakes are an American thing. Here, it's all about the black mamba, the python, and the viper," he said as he counted each type of snake on his fingers, watching me intently.

"Okay, stop now. You've painted quite the picture." I might have been worried about the snake smorgasbord he had laid out, but I was determined to enjoy my trip into the desert. *With him.*

After breakfast I, too, went to my room. I had never mastered the art of travelling light and I packed several changes of clothes. I had been warned it would get dusty. I retrieved a scarf, a windbreaker, and my camera, putting them in my bag too.

Today was a new beginning; I could feel it. The embers of lust which had been fanned at breakfast still smouldered as we were driven to the airstrip. Michael kept his arm around my shoulder, stealing kisses whenever I looked out his window.

We arrived at Swakopmund Airstrip, where a helicopter was waiting for us.

"This is a treat, Sofia. I can't wait to get there. How did you come up with this?" he asked excitedly.

"I've always wanted to go into the desert and see it. Have you been out in the desert before?"

"Yes, I followed a story in the Gobi eight months ago, but not in a chopper. That would have made the assignment more comfortable. So this is your first time?"

"Yes. This is why I brought my camera. I think I will use it for the first time," I said eagerly.

"That's a great camera. Where did you get it from?"

"Oh, from a man who's not trying to get in my pants whatsoever." I laughed out loud. I was happier than I had been in a long time.

The line of conversation could have continued, but the pilot, who was also the tour guide, cleared his throat, reminding us he could hear our conversation in his headphones.

He flew us over the fascinating sun-baked desert landscape, dry and dehydrated as far as the eye could see, a bird sanctuary, and what the pilot told us was, the Kuiseb River. On this flight, I got to see Michael in his element, with a long lens camera clicking away. I might have been biased after the morning we had, but at that moment, he was the sexiest man to have ever walked in my line of sight. I couldn't look away.

Ninety minutes later, we arrived at Sandwich Harbour on the Atlantic Coast, where there was a bay and a lagoon. I saw hundreds of flamingos. I had last seen them as a child on a trip to Aruba. Aruba was how and where I had started taking photographs. I took so many photos of flamingos at Sandwich Harbour that I didn't notice Michael until he was standing next to me.

"Does it work alright?"

I could tell this was his way of acknowledging the moment; I gave him a weak smile as my eyes watered. I was both very happy and a little sad.

"Come here. I can see this was difficult for you. Little steps like this will help."

Michael held me tight and whispered in my ear. That was all I needed, and I happily accepted the comfort which his proximity offered.

We didn't stay much longer at Sandwich Harbour after that. We went back on the helicopter for the rest of our trip and landed at the Sossusvlei Lodge, a private desert reserve. I had never seen anything like it, and the look on Michael's face told me he hadn't either. The lodge was hidden deep in the Namib desert, amongst the desert topography and was so peaceful.

We were shown to our two-bedroom family suite, but something in me knew that Michael and I would be spending all night together. The suite was decorated with a mix of browns and gold; earth tones mirroring the colours of the desert. I wasn't sure what to expect, but sleek modern furniture and a fully equipped kitchenette were a pleasant surprise on land so barren, with nothing but sand to see for miles.

"Was Gobi anything like this?"

"No, far from it. I slept in a tent I shared with my interpreter."

"Looks like there won't be sharing here. You're that way, I think." I pointed to the second bedroom in the suite. "I'll get rid of all this dust before we explore," I said, as I made my way into my bathroom.

Twenty minutes later, we were sitting in the air-conditioned bar, getting a much-needed drink. The lodge didn't perpetuate any of the desert stereotypes I had imagined. A full wall of glass in the bar gave us unobstructed views of the desert expanse. The wait staff even served us a late lunch of beautiful seafood, explaining that the seafood was helicoptered in three times a week.

As we sat recounting the events of the day and enjoying an easy banter, the sun started to set. We made our way back to our suite where we sat outside, on the air-conditioned terrace, and enjoyed the vast expanse of the sand before us. Even though the private pool on our terrace was inviting, we both looked through both our cameras at the shots we had taken.

"I loved seeing the flamingos. There's something about them that brings the whimsy anywhere."

"Could be that shocking pink, within the backdrop of sparse vegetation," he said, as he critiqued one of my photographs as if it were a masterpiece.

"This camera is perfect; I love it. I think I might just never put it down again."

"I'm happy to hear you say that. You take good shots, and you have a really good eye."

"Thank you. I couldn't have done that without you," I said, moving closer to him. I inhaled deeply, wanting his scent to stay with me even after he had gone to his room.

After the day's pursuits, we were both tired but happy. I started drifting off to sleep on the lounger when Michael carried me to my bed. When he put me down, I held his hand in mine and sleepily asked him to stay. He kicked off his loafers and laid down next to me until I opened one eye and saw him watching me.

"Yes?" I inquired in a sleepy voice.

"I was just thinking how beautiful you are, both inside and out. I don't remember having this much fun with anyone in a long time."

"If you remembered, would you tell me about it?"

"Yes, just to show off."

"Michael, you're amusing," I quipped, turning on my side and facing him.

"I am here for your amusement anytime," he returned, holding my cheek in the palm of his hand, and looking deeply into my eyes trying to convey some secret message.

His voice had become husky. I pretended to miss the double entendre, but my heart pounded in my chest. There was a light fluttering in my stomach, and my lips started to dry. I quickly licked them, and this seemed to trigger something in him.

He pulled me closer and kissed me. Just like last night, with the lightest touches he played my body like a tune. I kneeled on the bed, and in an instant, I made quick work of his linen shirt, as well as his shorts. There was an urgency to what we were doing, as if we were both afraid the other would change their mind. He didn't waste any time divesting me of my clothes, either. We were both down to our underwear when he started nibbling and kissing my neck, fondling my breasts over my bra. I couldn't help the moans escaping me. He easily found the front clasp of my bra and his lips were back, nibbling and sucking my nipples, as if they had never left since the night before. I spilled out of his palms as he kneaded them. My panties were gone in an instant, and I was left completely bared to him. Laying down, my legs involuntarily parted for him in silent invitation, while he gave his gift a lustful gaze.

"You're so beautiful, and so ready for me," he said as he teased me with his fingers.

I was too far gone to come up with anything logical to say. He continued to suck and kiss down the length of my body until he reached between my legs and gently tasted me.

"You taste so sweet, just like I have been imagining," he said, as he used his fingers to hold me open to both his eyes and mouth.

He devoured me like I was his last meal, and I couldn't do anything but writhe and moan on the bed. He pushed my knees towards my shoulders and continued his tongue assault for what felt like hours. I quivered around his lips, and suddenly, I was soaking wet. He didn't waste a drop, as he cleaned me up with the gusto of a thirsty man.

"You're so good at that," I gasped, as I came down from my orgasmic high.

He slid up my body, his skin scorching, and kissed me, and I could taste myself on his lips. "Are you ready for me, Sofia?"

He knew I was. *He had made sure of it.* Before I could even answer, he entered me, and was fully sheathed in my warm channel. He was deep inside, and I could never have imagined another man could ever fill me up as he did. He rocked back and forth, flexing his hips gently at first, moaning like he had finally arrived home. This was an exercise in self-control.

Appreciative moans left him as he whispered in my ear, "I've wanted this for a while, and it was worth the wait."

"Michael, it's been a while for me. Take it slow." I could only moan as he pushed gently, inch by inch, against me.

"I don't think I can; it's never felt this good." It may have been a while, but I didn't remember it feeling this good either. I was really doing this. I loved what he was doing to me and how he was doing it. Michael was a skilled lover, and I wouldn't let my mind dwell on how much practice he had got to become a master. I had my own baggage to contend with.

He continued to rock gently, and when he felt me clench against him, he let out a low rumble, then sat me up. We were face to face, and the closeness was intense. There was no doubt I wanted this and needed him. He kissed me again and again; as he thrust deeper and deeper, hungry and demanding. I was desperate for all of his length as I canted my hips towards him. In an instant, he had me on my back again, never losing our connection. My hips sought him out, needing more. This drove him wild until he was going at an erratic pace. My body had given him permission to take it all. I knew I was there again; I exploded again with a cry, and he followed right behind me with a growl and never-ending streams of his essence inside me.

He slid up the bed and laid next to me, breathless, with a light sheen on his body. We kissed as he held me close. I felt safe in his arms. I hadn't felt this safe and secure in a long time. He must have mistaken my silence for apprehension.

"I'm sorry, but I'm clean. I can promise you that. I just got caught in the moment. I'm always careful. I'm sure we can figure out a pharmacy or a doctor as soon as we get back to Walvis Bay."

"Don't worry, I'm on the pill," I whispered.

"I haven't been with anyone in months, and I have been tested since then — wait, you're on the pill?"

"I went on it after I returned from Phil and Taryn's reserve."

"Why then?" he asked as he brought me even closer to him, wrapping my legs around him.

"I felt like we had forged a connection and I knew that I wanted this, us, to happen."

"Even though I left you there. You still felt connected?" he asked in disbelief.

"Like you, Michael, I also have a job which I am committed to, so I understood that you had to go immediately. I didn't like it, but I understood it." I couldn't help the post coital honesty.

He kissed me hungrily again, licking and nibbling, as he pulled me against him, onto him and kneading my buttocks. "Let's take a shower."

"The knees are still a little weak. I might need some help getting there," I said, as he held out his hand to me.

The four-person shower was nothing short of luxury, and the black and gold marble bench in there was where Michael sat and looked at me in wonder, shaking in anticipation as I lapped and sucked him to another roaring orgasm.

We then stood under the shower as I took in his perfection and wondered if he was real. We wrapped ourselves up in the lodge robes, and Michael called the kitchen for our dinner which we had ordered earlier before we left the bar.

"What's your week like, Sofia?"

"It's clear. Namibia has been easier to work with than South Africa. We have confirmation of routes already." I was surprised at how easily I was opening up to him, sharing myself, my body and my work.

"So, you're free all week? Would you like to extend our stay here for the week?" he asked, his eyes full of hope.

"Does that mean you prefer me to your translator in the Gobi?" I was flirting with him again. I liked myself like this. The old me was still in there but had just been lying dormant for a while. Would she ever fully awaken?

"Of course, I do. My translator wouldn't even take a shower, let alone with me."

"Do you regularly shower with everyone, Michael?" I asked as I sat astride his lap, waiting for our dinner.

"Only if they look like you, and taste like you, and smell like you." He undid my robe and let it fall off my shoulders to the floor. "How did I ever go through life without this body?" he said, as he held fistfuls of me in his hands.

I giggled. Michael was at risk of making me happy.

Another dinner and I was even happier. We didn't finish dinner, as he took me again. He took me again three more times before dawn until we both fell asleep exhausted.

When I woke up, the desert sun was high in the sky, brightening the bedroom, and I was alone. Where Michael had slept in my bed was cold. He had been up for a while, and I had wasted time sleeping when I could have been studying his body, like he had done mine. He's a quick learner, and in a short time, he knew how to make my body yearn for his. The previous night had been incredible. It was everything I had been imagining, and I couldn't wait to see him.

Even though we had been informed by the concierge about all the water saving measures in place, I opted for a shower first before I ventured to find him. He was on his computer editing some photos with a steaming mug in his hand. My eyes darted to the clock; it was only eight o'clock. I hadn't wasted any time after all.

"Good morning." He sat in the air-conditioned living room, looking out at the desert expanse. Even though it was still early in the day, we had been warned the heat could be stifling.

Before I knew it, he was up, had me in his arms, and he was kissing me. We were both breathless as we tasted each other. I couldn't get enough. His lips were gentle yet firm, his tongue probing and licking. After all the exploring we had done the night before, kissing him was still a wonder. Neither one of us wanted to stop, and when we eventually did, he spoke first.

"I am happy you trusted me enough to let last night happen. I hope you don't feel like you were coerced into something you weren't ready for," he whispered, as his eyes searched mine.

I went through to the kitchenette where the sleek coffee machine was and pressed the button for a cappuccino. I turned around and walked back into his arms as if it were the most natural thing, after one passionate night with him. For a split second, I imagined how Nolan would feel seeing me here. His anger, jealousy, and disapproval crossed my mind at me being intimate with another man. He had never been the jealous type, but this would have driven him crazy. Only, he wasn't here, or anywhere. He was gone.

How long was I meant to be loyal to him? Were there some unspoken rules to be followed?

"No, I wasn't coerced. I did consent, Detective, each and every time."

"Don't distract me with humour, Sofia. I'm serious," he said, with concern in his voice. He couldn't have been regretful about last night, was he?

"Last night was everything I have wanted for a while with you," I said truthfully.

"Your body felt so good, and I'm sure mine did too, but how do you feel about it here and here?" he asked, as he pointed at my head and my heart.

"Thank you for asking; I feel okay."

"Just okay, nothing else to tell me?" The post sex inquisition was becoming intense. *He was worried about me.*

"Since I returned from the reserve, I've been talking to my therapist nearly every day, exploring my grief, loss, and conflicted feelings about moving on, being happy, and getting intimate with you. For a long time, I had known it was all right for me to move on, but it had never become a reality, not until I met you."

"So, your therapist gave you permission to be with me?" He asked, puzzled.

"No, letting go of Nolan and coming to terms with my grief is what gave me permission, and what do you mean be with you?" I asked, confused.

"Sofia, whatever is happening between us is not casual and it's not a game to me. I'm all in. My days of playing those games are gone, and I have been waiting for you for a long time."

"How long exactly?"

"I haven't met anyone I have been able to connect with in years, Sofia. I gave up on finding that connection — until you."

"I don't think I belong on that pedestal. I'm open to what is going on between us, but can you slow down, just a little?" I was starting to feel hot; it may have been the thousand pounds of proverbial pressure coming from the man standing opposite me.

"I can go at whatever speed you want me to but tell me this, why did you look for me in Istanbul, and follow me to Africa, if you don't see exactly what is going on here?" he asked, as if he had proven a complicated mathematical theory.

"I'm here for work, and coincidentally, so are you." I tried to placate him.

"Is that what is happening here, coincidence after coincidence?" He sounded wounded.

That was the last way I wanted him to feel, because I knew he was right about everything. I wasn't ready to admit it yet, to him, or even to myself. It had only been a few weeks since we met.

The phone in the suite then rang. I answered it and stared at Michael wide-eyed, as the lodge concierge spoke to me, confirming arrangements Michael had made while I was still asleep. When I got off the phone, I couldn't help the smile on my face.

"You've paid for the rest of our week here?"

"I have. I thought we had agreed to stay longer?"

"Yes, but you don't have to spend all that money on me."

"I can afford it, I promise." He tittered.

"I'm sorry. I had made some assumptions about money based on what you had told me about yourself."

"So, you're not sleeping with me for my money, then?"

"Look who's now deflecting with humour, and we hardly slept last night."

"Is that a complaint I hear?"

"Never." He brought my playful side out to play, one I had forgotten I had.

"I was hoping to go out and meet the locals today. Get a real feel of this place, not the pomp and circumstance which is this hotel. Is that something you might want to do?"

"Oh, is there a story you want to sniff out?" I was intrigued. When and how would he have come across a story in the desert.

"No, there's no story. I find the best way to learn about any place or its people is to meet the regular people, talk to them, and learn from them."

"That makes sense. Do you think you'll go out again after today?"

"Perhaps."

"Good, I'll come with you next time. Today, I just want to relax, catch up with my assistant, and check in with my parents."

"Sure, I'll be back in a few hours."

After Michael left, I ordered breakfast and phoned Bradley.

"Hi Brad, did you receive the paperwork from Namibian Aviation?"

"Yes, all is in hand, boss; Mr Kingman is pleased. How is the desert?"

"It's extremely hot and dry, but it's beautiful. I wish you could see it."

"And the heir apparent?"

"What do you mean?"

"You said you would be in the desert with Michael Masterson? I still don't know how you've both kept that a secret."

"Yes, I did say Michael. What secret? From whom?" I asked, puzzled.

"Did you do your research on him before you left, or even something as simple as an internet search?"

I became worried. *What could I have missed?*

"I did look him up and found him on his work website. Does that count?"

He sighed heavily. "Boss, I say this because I care, but you have been out of commission for far too long. Michael doesn't work for that publication, his family owns it as well as a host of other media enterprises. He owns the news, films, and publishing... pull it out of a hat, he probably owns it, too."

"How did I miss that? Did you look him up?"

I was horrified, remembering I insinuated the hotel bill might be too expensive for him to pay.

"I didn't need to; he's a big deal. I can see how you missed all that. He's a tall drink of water; your mind must have been elsewhere."

"Okay, okay, you've made your point. So I'll be back in Johannesburg in a week, and we'll talk then?" I had to get him off the phone. I am the queen of due diligence, but how could I have been so neglectful to not thoroughly check on the man I was spending my time with.

"Yes, we will," he said, mischievously.

We ended the call, and I did what I should have done the first time I met Michael: I looked him up on the internet, properly this time.

Brad had all his facts right. What he failed to mention were the dozens of photos with different women, all the time. How could I have been so irresponsible last night? He has a type — beautiful and oozing sex appeal. This made me feel uneasy and a little queasy. I didn't want to be one of many, even if I wasn't ready to label whatever it was between us.

A few hours later, Michael returned, and try as I might, I couldn't hide my shift in mood. I sat on the terrace and stared out at the beautiful landscape. It was still and quiet, a mid-afternoon in the desert, but the sudden chill in the air around the two of us could have placed us anywhere in the arctic circle.

"May I join you?"

"Yes, of course." I was friendly, but I felt anything but.

"Really? Because I get the feeling something happened while I was out and you're not quite yourself." He slid gently onto the cushioned seat next to me.

"Nothing happened."

"So why does it feel like there is a gulf between us, and you seem upset? Is it something I said or did?"

"You are observant, but no, it's my problem," I answered in a clipped tone.

"Do you want to tell me about it?" Concern etched his handsome face.

I remained silent.

"Will you let me in? I really want to get to know you better, and I want you to know me too. The best way to do that is by talking," he said patiently as he maneuvered himself behind me and wrapped his arms around me as we sat looking out at the vast sea of copper sand.

"It's not a big deal, I don't think." I was trying to reassure myself.

"Yet, whatever it is, has you all wound up in knots. I can see and feel how tense you are," he said as he whispered in my ear, massaging my bare shoulders.

Immediately, I resented my Bardot top. I lost my train of thought as he gently nipped my ear and kissed my neck. He already knew how to distract me.

"I was on the internet while you were out, and I saw so many pictures of you with so many different women."

He let out a deep sigh. "Had you not looked me up before?"

"Yes, only when I needed to find you, and when I found you, I didn't look at anything else."

"So, what made you curious today?" he asked softly as he continued to kiss me, bringing my body closer to his.

"Not sure, just interested, I guess," I lied.

"If you want to know anything, all you have to do is ask me. I have nothing to hide from you. As for those women, that was from a time when I was sad and lonely, angry even. I thought I needed to fill the void which Vivian, the ex, had left after the whole debacle with my brother. It was a phase, and that's not who I am. I told you I was waiting for someone, and I know it's so soon, but I think you might be that someone."

"Thank you for your honesty, but why so much interest in your life?" I feigned ignorance as I completely ignored the last part of his speech.

"Oh, something tells me after your internet study session you already know why. I'm sorry I omitted some other things too. I figured we would talk about that as time went on."

"What else have you lied to me about?" The vulnerability in my own voice was hard to miss.

"I haven't lied; I didn't get into everything about me, and in a way, I thought I was doing it for you, until you were comfortable with me." He was reassuring, and I was falling for every word.

"If I had trillions in the bank, I wouldn't go around telling people either."

He laughed. "A trillion, huh? You're not far off. Although, we need to talk about internet searches and using websites with authority, but not straight away. What we need to do now is get to know each other some more so you can stop looking me up."

"How do you propose we do that?" I asked him breathlessly, already distracted, imagining all the ways we would.

"I have some ideas, but I would need your help. Come inside with me."

He led me back inside our desert love nest, where talking was over as he took me to even higher heights than the night before.

Chapter Eleven

Sofia

Our magical week in the desert passed by in a haze of intimacy, food, wine, and a lot of getting to know each other. Michael proved to be knowledgeable, witty, and insatiable. We explored the desert in a 4x4, ATVs, and again in the helicopter. I even enjoyed a couples' massage, which he sat out after five minutes. He later told me there was too much manhandling from a stranger. Even though he hated receiving massages, I found out giving them was another hidden talent he had.

He was right about visiting and getting to know the locals. They were a world away from the luxury of our hotel — this I already knew — but the desert, I realised looking at it through the eyes of the locals, was a harsh environment. I wondered how many places I had visited but had never really opened my eyes to what was around me. On the last day of our trip, before we returned to Walvis Bay, I bravely asked him what I suspected we both had been thinking.

"How are we going to make this work? We live in different cities, and I travel all over the world with my job."

"I've been thinking the same thing too, and I'm not sure. Can we promise to always talk and be available for each other though, because I see you in my future."

"You always say the right things." How could I have become so attached, so quickly? I still had a lot to work through, and he might be the reason I needed to try harder.

"I'm not just saying things. I mean every word. I've enjoyed every minute we've spent together here, and I want more of that."

"Where are you going from here?"

"Back to Seattle. I've been away from HQ for too long, and my father needs me."

"Of course, you're his number two, after all."

My heart was breaking a little as I contemplated even one day without him. Could I drop everything in Africa and go back home to cultivate whatever this is between us? I could, but I didn't start what I couldn't finish, and I assured my father that I was the person for the Africa trip even as he tried to dissuade me. I hadn't considered what was going on with Michael as a possibility, not even to myself.

Our trip back to Walvis Bay was bittersweet, so was our coupling the next morning before we parted ways. I was falling for him, but I was terrified of losing him like I had lost before when I had dared to love.

When I returned to Johannesburg, I continued with work, and I began to get out and explore the country. On my first weekend after returning from the desert, I travelled to the magnificent mountain kingdom of Lesotho, an entire country within another country. I had been to both the Vatican and to San Marino, both being countries within other countries, but this time, it felt like I had been transposed to another world.

I stayed for three nights in an authentic, cosy stone and thatch Rondavel. I had only ever seen those in books, and the novelty of it was as magical as it had looked. By day, the Drakensberg escarpment provided a wonderful backdrop for the photographs I took, and with each click, I celebrated the happy but short lives of my sons. By night, I tended to my hike weary legs and feet by soaking in the glorious roll tin tub, which they had somehow managed to squeeze into the Rondavel. This was not the most luxurious hotel stay I had ever had, but it was by far the most meaningful. I enjoyed authentic African food, which I wouldn't begin to know where to get in any restaurant once I returned home to LA.

The mountain kingdom allowed me to enjoy outdoor pursuits like trail running, horse riding, and kayaking, which I hadn't allowed myself to enjoy since becoming a mother and a wife. I didn't begrudge Nolan and the boys, but I was only able to do all this because they were no longer there to share my time. The fresh, crisp mountain air proved to be more valuable than all the therapy I had, and it helped with perspective. Even coming to the obvious realisation that it was all right to be happy; to live, to breathe, and to smile again, and to not feel uneasy about my happiness. My three boys had loved me, and they would want me to be happy.

The next time I could get away from work, I ventured out to Durban, where I enjoyed the beach. I ate too much, indulged in too many cocktails, and treated myself to a well-deserved shopping trip. This was a trip for both Michael and I, as he would likely be the beneficiary for all the lacy and frilly things I had splurged on. I overspent, and I loved it. I hadn't spent much on myself, as I had never tried to enjoy anything since I lost my boys. I finally learned to stand up paddleboard. *Why hadn't I before? – I had lived in LA all my life.* Swimming with sharks was unforgettable, although I didn't think I would try that again. I was able to take in the sights and take some photographs too. I was finally starting to feel alive again.

It had been a month since our trip into the desert, and I was looking forward to a video call with Michael. Our time difference made talking on the phone difficult for both of us, and our phone calls had become a practiced choreography. While I was in my thoughts, my phone rang. I answered it straight away.

"You can't have been waiting for this call, were you?"

"I was. I've been looking forward to it all day," I said, as I looked at him with a wide grin.

"I've missed you, Sofia.," he said, gazing at me unflinchingly.

"I missed you too. Do you think you can get away for a few days?" I asked, sounding hopelessly needy.

When did this happen?

"I would love to do that, but it could be a little tricky. I'll let you know," he said, distracted, as if someone had interrupted him.

"Do you need to go? We'll talk later."

"I'm sorry, but yes, I need to. I'll let you know if I can come to you." The conversation became impersonal; I suspected he had company.

"Okay, I'll see you, maybe?" My smile grew wider.

"Yes, you will. Very soon." He looked straight into the camera, and although he was half a world away, and distracted, those few seconds belonged to me.

When I woke up the next morning, I had a message from him telling me he would be visiting for a little over a week. I was ecstatic, and

I knew exactly what I wanted to do while he was here. I had been thinking about taking a road trip down the Garden Route. While I had been enjoying and taking pleasure in my solitary travels, I wanted to go on this trip with Michael. In tandem with Brad, I was able to rearrange work to allow for the trip.

Three days later, I was making my way to Michael's jet, which had landed only moments before at Grand Central Airport close to the Westcliff. As I arrived at the jet, the door opened. He came down the airstair, and I met him at the bottom; my heart pounding and my palms sweaty. Time stood still as he kissed me like he had been waiting a lifetime to do so. He didn't stop, and I couldn't stop. I had been imagining this kiss for weeks.

He pulled away gently and mouthed over the loud idling plane, "I missed you so much."

I could only reach for him and kiss him repeatedly. Eventually, we stopped, and he helped me up the airstair. We sat next to each other and readied ourselves for take-off.

"I missed you too," I said, as my breathing returned to normal.

Chapter Twelve

Michael

I couldn't believe how happy I was to see Sofia, and she kissed exactly like I remembered, with wild abandon. She was in my arms again, and I didn't know how I was ever going to let her go again. The past month had been excruciating without her. Work had kept me busy, but life had become mundane and commonplace without her.

We made small talk until my pilot announced it was safe to remove our seatbelts, but we both knew how we wanted and needed to get reacquainted. After we had been in the air for a few minutes, I took Sofia's hand and led her towards the stateroom.

"Can I show you around the plane?" I asked, hoping my voice wouldn't betray the lust brimming beneath each breath I took.

"Seen one, seen 'em all," she said, as she laughed, letting me lead the way.

I led her straight to the stateroom, then turned around to look at her.

"This is where I sleep," I said, hoarsely.

"Do you need to sleep now?" she asked as she stepped closer to me.

"That would be time wasted." I pulled her flush against me, and she felt how much I had missed her.

My intentions were clear, and I didn't need to say anymore; she wanted the same thing I needed since we last had each other in Walvis Bay. I had taken my time and learned her body in the desert, and it didn't take her long to come undone again and again. How I had lived a month without her was beyond me, but now, I knew I needed to have her for a lifetime.

We arrived at George Airport in three hours, and we had used our three-hour flight time wisely.

Upon landing at George Airport, a sturdy SUV was awaiting us at the tarmac. It had been years since I had indulged in a road trip, but I knew I wanted to take this one and spend all my time with her.

"I'll drive first, while you relax. You've worked hard, and you need the rest," she said playfully as she took the keys from me.

"Okay, but I'll have you know I can work harder if you need me to."

She laughed. After all our bags were loaded into the car, Sofia drove us to a game reserve, where we arrived in the late afternoon.

"Since you couldn't stay with me at the last game reserve, here we are," she said excitedly.

"Phil is not going to like this, Sofia," I said to her, shaking my head and bringing her body against mine. I wanted her in my arms all the time.

"He'll never know, as long as you don't tell him."

The authenticity of the Rondavel had impressed me. She had stayed in one when she was in Lesotho, so when she told me about this game reserve along our route, I was looking forward to experiencing it with her. This reserve had new and ultra-modern huts. They even had panoramic windows on one entire side to allow for viewing any of the passing animals. These huts were even more special as they were built along a watering hole, so we could watch the animals when they came to drink. Much like Phil's reserve, this one also had a restaurant to rival any I had ever been to. After freshening up and getting settled in our hut, we went to have dinner.

"So do you know how long you can actually stay for this time?" she asked, looking at me expectantly.

"About ten days before my assistant has a grand mal," I said, gazing at her, as if seeing her for the very first time. She looked younger, more playful, and, if it were possible, more beautiful than I remembered.

"That's good news. I've really been looking forward to seeing you again. What is it? You're staring?"

"I can't believe you; everything. I'm just thinking about the first time we had dinner together. I couldn't get you to speak or tell me what was on your mind, but today, you're so different. I like it a lot."

"It's this place; it's healing, and I've been able to get out of my own head."

"I'm glad you're happier, and I'm happy being here has helped you."

"Perhaps, but it's more than just being here, which is making me happier." She had suddenly become coy.

"Really? What else is helping?" I asked her, catching her hand in mine.

"Having you in my life."

"Sofia, you make me happy, too. I've been looking forward to seeing you again since the day we parted ways a month ago. If it wasn't for work, I would have been back here much sooner."

We finished eating and decided to return to our hut as it had the best vantage point of the watering hole.

The road trip was everything I had imagined it would be. We made several stops, and with each mile we travelled, I realised how compatible we were. We both loved the outdoors; we tried everything dangerous; we enjoyed white water rafting, bungee jumping, and diving. We even enjoyed a scenic hot air balloon ride, even though it was slower than we both would have liked.

Sofia was unencumbered and uninhibited, more sensual than I would have ever known. She let me have her at the secluded Kaaimans Waterfall, and whenever we couldn't wait. The spacious Range Rover proved to be a good road trip choice, as it provided enough room for me to show her how much I couldn't get enough of her. I had met my equal in every way and never in my wildest fantasy would I have thought I would fall for a woman in the wilds of the African bush. On the eighth day of our road trip, we arrived in Cape Town. Although we were both exhausted, we rode the cable car over the Table Mountains. The view from the summit at Table Mountain was still a wonder, and the perfect culmination to our road trip.

"I don't want to leave," I said truthfully.

"I wish you didn't have to. I've had so much fun with you," she said as we walked down the track, away from the cableway.

"Next time, you could come to me instead, and I'll show you my city."

"I would love that. I can't wait." She had a new lease of life. Her demeanour had changed since we first met.

Was I too cocky to try and take all the credit for that?

As we neared the Range Rover, I had to hold her in my arms and feel her. I was already dreading the goodbye.

She belonged next to me, whether she knew it or not. I didn't want to leave, but I couldn't stay any longer than I already had. We arrived at the airstrip where my pilot was waiting to fly us both back. We had each other one more time before the distance separated us again. The stop in Johannesburg was brief, just long enough for Sofia to disembark, and the final goodbye was as agonising as they had all become.

Sofia

After returning to Johannesburg for a few more weeks, Kingman Air was finally granted the licences we needed. All was finalised, and we had agreed to favourable terms. This was my best work for my father. Though, I wanted to leave and be closer to Michael. My mind flashed back to my impassioned pleas to my father to let me come to Africa and grow Kingman. I couldn't let him down and I didn't want to lose credibility. I was more than the boss's daughter. I was a professional and I would stay the course.

Brad found an apartment for me to stay in one of the Northern Suburbs in Harare. After spending a week there working, I had become terribly lonely. The twins' birthday coming up was a difficult milestone. Somehow, I had regressed and retreated into my cocoon of sadness.

How could this be? Was there a purpose to all this suffering? Would the despair ever come to an end?

My therapist was still so invaluable, and I spoke to her a lot of the time.

It had been five weeks since I last saw Michael. We tried to speak as often as possible, but the time difference was still a perpetual enemy. The day before the twins' birthday, Michael surprised me in Harare. I cried a lot because I was happy to see him, but also because I had someone to comfort me. I was too spent to be useful, and Michael packed a bag for me. I didn't know where we were going, but I was just glad to be with him. I got on his plane in a daze, and an hour later, we landed somewhere.

We were in Bumi Hills, I later found out, but I didn't notice the beauty and the splendour. In my slump, the wild African beauty had suddenly become commonplace. The pain of not having my children with me was amplified on their birthday. Michael tried everything he could to help me, but I couldn't stop crying for hours on end.

When my father telephoned me, I was able to compose myself long enough to speak to him. He begged me to come home immediately, but I assured him I was with a friend, which he begrudgingly accepted.

After three days in Bumi Hills, I woke up to a beautiful sunset and wildlife meandering down to the watering hole. This had been the first time I was lucid since Michael arrived. He joined me on our private viewing terrace and held me.

"Are you feeling better?" He asked softly.

I nodded my head gingerly, and the kindness in his eyes made me want to start crying again.

"Why don't you take a bath, and I'll order us some dinner?" he said in the caring voice I was becoming accustomed to hearing.

"Why? Do I smell?" I asked him in jest.

"Yes, just a little," he answered with a wide grin.

I knew right then that I was in love with all that he was. I might have been mourning my children, but I was in my right mind. I wanted him in my life, for as long as I could have him. I went and freshened up, and by the time I returned, the table was filled with all the items on the menu.

"I'm sorry, but I'm not really hungry," I said regretfully, sitting down next to him.

"You need to eat. You haven't eaten anything in three days," he said, tucking my hair behind my ear.

"Three days, huh? What have you been doing while I was not eating?"

It's unbelievable that I have been this way for three days, and he was with me the whole time. The kindness in his eyes made me want to melt into him.

"I was worried sick about you, and in between that, I managed to get some work done."

"I don't know how I lost control. I don't even know where that flood of emotions came from. I thought I was doing well, and I'd been feeling better. I hadn't felt this way in a long time." I offered up that explanation. I might have been apologetic too.

"I spoke to your therapist, and she told me it was all very normal. She wants to speak to you when you're ready."

"You spoke to her? How?" I asked in alarm. I wondered what else they had talked about, as lately he had become the subject of our sessions.

"I had to go through your phone. I'm sorry," he answered remorsefully.

"Under the circumstances, that was the right thing to do."

"I also saw the picture of your sons on your screensaver. You had a beautiful family. I'm so sorry you lost them."

"Thank you for looking after me."

"What do you think about most when you think about them? We don't have to talk about it if you'd rather not." He spoke tenderly, as if I was glass ready to break if he spoke any louder.

"I would love to tell you about them. Where do I begin? They both loved Spider-Man and that Sunflower song that comes with it."

"Yes, I think I've heard it," he said, hand on his chin nodding his head.

"Whenever I can, I fill my penthouse with sunflowers, and that makes me feel close to them. For a while, they wore their spidey suits for days on end."

He chuckled softly. "They did? Laundry day must have been a fight, how would you convince to get them out of them?"

"You have no idea, but cookie bribery worked, and they loved to play tricks on everyone, pretending to be each other. They were identical, and when I was tired, *I* couldn't even tell them apart sometimes." I exhaled, already starting to feel lighter.

"They would've had fun with that." He smiled.

"Yes, they did. They had lots of plane figurines, loved all stories about brothers, especially about Orville and Wilbur Wright. They went flying with their father often. Mine too, when my mother wasn't spoiling them rotten." As I continued to speak, the tears I had been fighting hard to hold back started spilling.

"I didn't mean to upset you," he said, his eyes watering too.

"I'm not upset; I don't talk about them often, and this conversation with you is cathartic," I said as I dabbed my eyes with a Kleenex. They had become a constant in my palm over the last three days.

"I'm not a twin, but I have a brother. When things were still good between us, before life happened, he was the person I wanted to be with most in the world. Wherever your boys are, they are together.

With their dad looking out for them, and that should give you comfort."

"It's the only thing that does, and now you do too," I said, trying to smile through my tears.

"I'm happy to hear that. You're important to me, too." He kissed me lightly on my forehead, a far cry from the kisses we had become used to.

I started on the spread in front of me. As I ate, I realised just how hungry I was. I didn't eat everything, but I ate a lot.

I started to feel much better, and I was even able to laugh a little. I caught him up on what had been going on with my work in Harare.

"I feel like there's an undercurrent of corruption, you know, and I have had so many people wanting to discuss 'a small fee' to proceed with things."

"You've never had that problem anywhere else?" He asked, both in surprise and disbelief.

"No, I don't think so," I said, trying to remember.

"This may come as a shock to you, but there is corruption and cronyism everywhere. Where we're from, it may be subtle and more nuanced. You've just had pure luck that you haven't had any problems until now. What do you want to do about it?"

"I want to take a step back and let them come to me instead."

"If they don't?"

"I'm ready to go home. They are the last country in this region. I've done well otherwise."

"Will your father be okay with that?"

"Yes he will, he's pleased with what I've managed to do here. How has HQ been?"

He sighed, and it was only then that I noticed the resignation on his face. "My father hasn't been in good health, and he needs me more at work."

"What's wrong with him?" I asked, worried about both Michael and his father.

"Dizzy spells and blackouts, but his specialists can't pinpoint exactly what the problem is. I suspect he's stressed and overworked."

"How do you feel about this? I know you love the flexibility of leaving at a moment's notice for the photography."

"I knew the day would come when I had to give it up and be permanently based at HQ. I just never imagined it would be this soon." His words were laced with resignation.

"At least, now I know where to find you when I need you," I teased.

That joke fell flat. Michael tensed; he was quite unhappy about giving up the work he loved so much.

The days in Bumi Hills weren't the idyll the desert had been, nor the sensuality that had punctuated our road trip. He was tense, and I was still so sad. We went out sometimes, but mostly found comfort in each other's arms. The lovemaking was both so tender, and sometimes filled with anger, which Michael would apologise for afterwards. Secretly, I was happy for the show of emotion from him; the passion was intensified. The last two days were spent in bed, as neither of us had the heart to let go of the other.

"When you're done here, I want you to think about moving in together, Sofia. I need you to be close to me," he said as he made love to me.

"Already thinking about it. I need you, too, every day, all the time."

This elicited a delicious moan from him, as my body arched upwards involuntarily towards him. Without any warning, he drove deeper into me, taking my breath away. His legendary self-control shattered as he took everything I willingly gave him, thrust after thrust. He was as deep as he could be, my body was protesting, but I needed more. I anchored my heels on his calf and against his hip as he gave me all he had. Our bodies spoke a language of their own, as he conquered mine over and over.

The next day, we went back to Harare, and Michael returned to HQ. I loved Africa, and all it had done for me, but my heart wasn't into being here anymore. I should have told Michael I was in love with him, but I was too overwhelmed by my own feelings.

Did loving Michael mean I didn't love Nolan anymore? Is this what letting go feels like?

It was bittersweet, and it made me feel free. As if Nolan himself was freeing me from him.

Chapter Fourteen

Sofia

It was midday when I entered my rental after returning from Bumi Hills. Although I had been sad, it had been a sweet reunion and the last few hours, that Michael and I had spent making love over and over, kept replaying on my mind. Concentrating on anything would be nearly impossible until I saw him again. My phone's shrill ring interrupted my reverie, and it was Alex.

"Hello there, stranger. I thought you had forgotten all about me." I said, lightheartedly, still in my love drunk daze.

"Sofia, I have something really complicated and sensitive to discuss with you in person," he said tersely. He was making me nervous, and this was all reminiscent of the phone call I had received from my father in Istanbul.

"I'm in Harare. I don't know when we can meet. Can we talk about this now, over the phone? You're making me nervous."

"No, we can't. I'm in Cairo, so I can be there in six hours."

Alex had never sounded like this before, and I was suddenly on edge. For the six hours that Alex was on his way, all I could do was sit still and wait. Michael called from his jet, and that was a welcome distraction. I didn't tell him about Alex, as there was nothing to tell, but I wondered if I could lift his spirits as much as he had lifted mine. I didn't need to wait long; at six o'clock, Alex called me and told me he had landed and was on his way to the apartment. Within twenty minutes, he had arrived at my door.

"Hi Alex."

When I saw him, I had a very uneasy feeling about what he needed to say, but I waited for him to tell me. Alex was fidgety and wouldn't look at me. The wait for him to speak was much worse than waiting for him to arrive from Cairo. This was unlike him, and the news he had to deliver couldn't be good.

"It was your mother," he said without preamble.

"It was my mother, who what?" I was suddenly on guard and spat the question at him.

He took out a large envelope with printouts and photographs. "After you asked me to investigate what happened to your family, I used every resource and cashed in on all the favours I was owed. I'm sorry it took me so long to get back to you, but I had to be sure about everything I found out. This is going to be upsetting, but all I can do is just say it, Sof."

"Go ahead and just say it; the suspense is killing me." Even though my knees felt weak, I couldn't sit down as I stood transfixed on the opposite end of the dining room table in the apartment. I felt an unfamiliar constriction in my chest.

"This company here belonged to your maternal grandfather. There had been no transactions for twenty-four years, but a month before your husband and kids died, there was a transfer from it for a million bucks to this group here."

Alex was direct, but he made sure he explained in a way I understood.

"This organisation has mercenaries in South America. Normally used by Drug Lords and Cartels as a vehicle for exacting revenge, sending messages, kidnappings, and the like."

I took a deep breath. "Alex, listen to yourself for just one second. Cartels, drug lords. Is this a movie? I still don't understand how any of this has to do with my mother."

"When your grandfather died, all his holdings and assets went to your mother, an obscene amount of money. Your mother is in control of this company, and this transaction is the only outgoing transaction from this account in twenty-four years."

"My mother uses a legitimate wealth management firm to manage her inheritance and my grandfather's estate. This doesn't ring true. What else have you got?" I asked dismissively.

"We, my employer, has a man in this group, and he has told me, face to face, that on the day your husband's plane was downed, his colleague went and parked exactly one mile from San Marcos Airstrip and directed a miniature drone missile into the 'British Man's plane' as they had been paid to do."

I could only laugh at the absurdity of it all.

"I know you're a professional, and good at what you do, but you're mistaken. My mother can't even begin to know how to do all this. She lunches and goes shopping. You've been misled and your intelligence is wrong." I spoke to him in a patronising tone. I would have screamed otherwise. I couldn't believe that Alex, who I had imagined to be a friend, flew out to accuse my mother of the worst thing anyone could do.

"I had hoped that was the case, because you and I have been friends since we were kids and I know your mother too, but I have triple checked my information and I trust all my sources. I wouldn't have travelled all this way to bring you a pack of lies."

"I don't understand. Both you and your lies. Have I upset you in some way? Is this some kind of joke? Because it's not funny."

"I'm sorry. I wish I had never found this out either. What are you going to do?" He sounded concerned, and I could see the pity in his eyes.

"I don't know. With this tall tale you're spinning, is my father involved too?" I couldn't help the sarcastic tone. This had to be the most harebrained thing I had ever heard.

"I did think about that for a while, but there's nothing from my information which suggests that he is. Common sense tells me he wouldn't down his own plane."

"But does common sense tell you that my mother is involved? This is ridiculous!" I shrieked, all composure now lost.

"The Intelligence, Sofia." He pleaded with me.

"The Intelligence is hardly intelligent, is it? All these months, I thought you were helping me, and you brought me some modern day fable? Spinning tales about how a grandmother killed her own grandchildren? Did you even think?" I was now furious, screaming like a banshee.

"You're angry," he said, defeated.

"What gave it away? I can't believe this is how you would treat fifteen years of friendship."

"Don't you think your anger is a little misguided?"

"Are you still talking?" I screamed at him.

"I know you're in shock, and I understand. I followed the evidence like I would do with anything else in my work."

"Have you never been wrong?"

"I have, but this is all in black and white."

"Yes, and a little too convenient."

"I'm sorry this is hard to swallow. I would never do anything to hurt you. I was only trying to give you the answers you were looking for."

"It's just that your findings are ridiculous, for want of a better word. I didn't mean to take out my anger on you. I'm sorry," I said, as I finally calmed my screaming thoughts.

"That's why it's called shooting the messenger. I would be hurt, too. What can I do now?"

"Help me pack, Alex. I'm done here. You're a good friend." I was now speaking softly, the gravity of Alex's accusations finally sinking in.

"You're so strong. How are you not in tears?"

"I've cried all my tears. I just want answers. I have a jet; do you need to get back to Cairo?"

"Yes, please, that would be helpful." He spoke with the dejection I felt.

"I'm just going to sit down. I feel like I'm going to pass out," I said, as I started to feel hot.

"Here, lay down and lift your feet," he said as he put two cushions underneath them. He went into the kitchen and brought me a glass of water.

Alex packed silently and haphazardly, while I closed my eyes just for a moment to will this information out of existence. I was never one to leave without finishing an assignment, but this was the mother of all extenuating circumstances. I was relieved I had my jet and a pilot and while I tried to calm down, I called my pilot and told him to ready the plane. Travelling this way would buy me time to gather my thoughts before I went to see my parents. I had to think about how I would approach my mother and ask her the most difficult question of my life, and perhaps hers, too.

The flight felt long, and I was ill. My heart was breaking over and over as I tried to make sense of all the information Alex had brought to me. It all seemed ridiculous. When, how, and why would my mother conceive and execute something so bold and audacious? She was the original socialite, with a lot of time on her hands, but not for this.

The bizarre fact was the reams of documents to prove all of Alex's theories, and the closer I got to my mother, the more worried I became that this could be true.

Would she and could she even do this?

Even though we were slowly making our way back to each other, could this be the reason why she had never been my comforter?

Had she been racked with guilt that she couldn't be there when I needed her, or was she so cold and calculating that my emotions didn't matter?

She was hardly a wilting flower, but she was not a murderer. At least this was how I comforted myself on the plane ride to Boeing Field Airport in Seattle.

I decided to go to the only person who was far removed from the whole situation. I left some of my luggage on my plane, but what I took with me I left with the security officers in the reception area at HQ. This was an old landmark building, which had undergone a sympathetic refurbishment, bringing it straight into the twenty-first century. It oozed class and elegance. I was awestruck as I took it all in and, with great difficulty, slipped past security to the Forty fifth floor, where it proved even harder to see Michael without an appointment. He had a pit bull at his door in the form of his executive assistant who insisted an appointment was needed to see him. No explanations would grant me access, as she insisted she knew everyone of any significance to Michael.

I sat down in the double height majestic lobby of the Forty fifth floor and called him.

"Sofia, this is a pleasant surprise. Why aren't you sleeping?"

"It would be difficult to sleep outside your office door, Michael." I sighed, exasperated by the ordeal of getting to Seattle and not seeing him straight away.

"You're here!"

In an instant, he came bounding to where I was, and he gave me the most exuberant greeting. He picked me up, as if I weighed nothing, and kissed me as if we were the only two people in the world. The pit bull was apologetic, but I was exhausted and past caring. It had only been less than a day, but I was happy to see him, forgetting for a moment the reason I was there. I had never seen him in his place of work, and he looked the part of an executive. He was clean shaven, his blue suit that was clearly made just for him, didn't do much to conceal his hard physique. Immediately, I realised why women constantly worshiped at his feet.

"We need to talk. Can you take the rest of the day?" I spoke with an urgency I didn't recognise.

The concern was immediately stamped on his face. "Yes, let me get a few things from my office, and I'll take you home."

"Of course. My luggage is downstairs."

"You came straight here? Is everything okay?" he asked, the alarm registered on his handsome features.

"No, nothing will ever be right again." My breathing remained steady; my heartbeat was anything but.

"We'll go straight home. My driver will bring your luggage."

His long strides ate up the distance as I followed him into his office, where he had spectacular views of the city. He was more important than he had made himself out to be if this office was anything to go by. It was large, and like a cliche, in the corner with a two hundred and seventy degree view of the Seattle cityscape. A concealed paneled door leading to what I realised was a bathroom and a full size closet with rows of suits. After giving instructions to his assistant, he collected some paperwork and his laptop, hurriedly putting them in his bag, then led me down to the garage. When we got to the underground garage, I didn't know what I was expecting, but it was not a sporty red car I had never seen before.

"Which one of the super cars is this one?"

"It's a Ferrari Spider." He grinned like a little boy, proud of his shiny toy.

"Not sure I've seen it before. Is this the one that will bring my luggage?" I said, making a half-hearted attempt at humour.

He chuckled. "We can barely fit your handbag and my work bag in here."

He maneuvered the Spider with ease and the skill of a practised driver, driving carefully through the city streets. It was a soft, smooth drive, and it took my mind off my troubles in the twenty minutes it took to get to his home.

We arrived at a beautiful large house with a classy light Danish brick facade that would be right at home in New York or London. He led me straight into a beautiful gourmet kitchen, past a massive island surrounded by a fleet of upscale appliances. We both sat down on a deep grey plush wraparound banquette, highlighted by dramatic lake views framed by a wall of floor-to-ceiling windows.

"I am happy to see you, but why are you here? What happened?"

"I don't know where to start from, but I have some information that points to my mother as being the one responsible for the deaths of my family." I had been composed for hours, but I started gasping, my chin quivered, and an errant tear rolled down my cheek.

"What kind of information? Is it a trustworthy source?" He couldn't hide the look of shock and disbelief on his face as pulled in closer to me and used his thumb to wipe away the lone tear.

"I trust the source with my life, Michael. This is an old high school friend who works for an intelligence organisation. I don't know which, but this is what he has brought to me." I took the bulky envelope I had been holding onto since I left Harare and I handed it to him.

He thoroughly and silently went through each sheet of paper while I slowly died.

"This is compelling information, but it doesn't ring true," he said as a matter-of-fact, pushing the offensive material away from both of us to a far corner of the table.

"What makes you doubt it?" I was hopeful. I didn't want this to be true.

"First, it points to your mother. Nature dictates that she's your number one protector, and this goes against that. Second, it's too tidy. The signposts are obvious and there's too much information — clear for anyone who can read to see. I've had to sift through a lot of investigative work over the years and it's never as straightforward as what you have here. If anyone wanted to do something so heinous, they would cover their tracks as if their life depended on it."

"I hear you, but why go through all this trouble?" All this had already crossed my mind, but I was weary.

"First thing that springs to my mind is that someone wants this to look like your mother's doing. Can I check its authenticity?"

"I trust you, but I don't want any of this in the newspapers."

"It won't be. I have an investigator I trust who can verify a few more things."

"Verify all you like, but I trust Alex."

"Alex? Do I need to be worried about him?" he growled, in a low tone bordering on insecure.

Why would he be so insecure? I had never given him a reason to be.

Suddenly, my energy was back. "Will you get a grip? I have this life-changing information, and you're worried about who Alex is?" The outburst even took me by surprise.

He sighed, regret on his face. "You're right. I'm sorry, I don't know what came over me. I've never been the possessive, jealous type, at least I didn't think so, not until now, when I thought what we are nurturing might be under threat."

"Nothing's under threat. By now, you should know it's you I love," I said, as my eyes watered and my voice cracked.

He didn't miss a beat. "What did you say?"

"I'm hopelessly in love with you," I whispered as I held my breath. I had said it, what I had been feeling since I was lucid in Bumi Hills.

He smiled, a full genuine smile. Leaning forward, he put his forehead against mine and spoke gently.

"I love you too. There's no need to cry. I'm not the worst person to love," he said, as he kissed the tears off my cheeks.

"Don't tease, these are happy tears," I whispered.

He continued speaking softly, "I love you, and I've wanted to tell you for a while, but it never seemed to be the right time, and I was worried I would push you away. I seem to have a knack for putting pressure on you."

"For a while, I wasn't ready to hear it, but now I'm right there with you."

"I'm not a patient man, and it may not seem like it, but I would have waited for however long it took to hear you tell me that you love me," he said as he kissed me over and over.

"Do you want to call your investigator, then you can show me around?" I asked, catching my breath.

"I'll call him, but this is what I prefer," he said as he gave me one last lingering kiss.

After calling his investigator, Michael showed me around his home, and I couldn't understand how he could ever leave to go around the world. I've always found modern homes to be cold and austere, but this one was decorated in warm tones and down-to-earth furniture. It had a softness to it, a feminine touch, and I couldn't help but wonder who had decorated it. The double modular sofas, although custom, were unmistakably Boca Do Lobo. They fit the grand scale of the living room. A more intimate sitting arrangement was arranged closer to the dining room, with a half moon sofa and a fur throw. Directly in front of it was a picture frame television.

While he was showing me around, his investigator arrived. Michael explained the situation to him, and the sensitivity of the matter at hand. He seemed very professional and left after promising he would be as discreet as possible.

As soon as he left, much to my exasperation, the doorbell rang again. *How could one man be so popular?*

All I needed was some quiet to gather my thoughts. Michael was surprised, too, as he would have been at work. He went and answered the bell, and I heard a female voice coming through into the kitchen, talking animatedly to Michael. As soon as she saw me, she stopped walking and turned around to look at Michael.

"Son, you didn't tell me you had company."

"You didn't give me a chance to."

"Can I say hello?"

"It would be rude not to, and don't be too much, she wasn't expecting to meet you today." Micheal chuckled.

"I'll be on my best behaviour."

"Promise?" I'm not sure if I was meant to hear their conversation, but I was thoroughly entertained.

"Hello, I'm Christine Masterson, Michael's mother." As she came closer, I saw a regal beauty with a dazzling smile and flawless skin. She could easily pass as Michael's sister.

"Mum, this is Sofia Kingman, my girlfriend." Even though I was tired, and the eighteen hour sleepless flight had taken its toll on me, I had to be gracious.

Christine beamed from ear to ear. "Michael, why would you keep her a secret, especially from your mother? It's so lovely to meet you," she said, extending her hand adorned with a perfect dusk coloured manicure.

"You too, Mrs Masterson." She was bubbly and warm, Michael couldn't have gone any other way.

"Call me Chris. Is this why you skipped our lunch date? I would skip lunch with my mother too for you, Sofia; you're stunning." She spoke as she looked at both Michael and me.

"Was that today? Sorry it slipped my mind," Michael chimed in, now standing next to me.

"I'm sorry. It's my fault he missed your lunch date. I ambushed him at work. I've just arrived back from Africa, and I just had to see him."

"Africa, wow. We need to have lunch, so you can tell me all about that. What's your phone number?"

I smiled inwardly, a social butterfly just like my own mother, who, at this moment, I was trying not to think about. I gave Christine my number and Michael was amused as he looked on quietly.

"Okay, kids. I'll be off now. I'll see you soon, Sofia."

"Mum, what am I — chopped liver?"

"Yes, I'll see you too, Michael; you're still my favourite, both you and Miles," she said as she smiled sweetly at him.

Michael was a male version of his mother, both in looks and personality. Michael walked her to the door, and I couldn't have been more pleased with how that went.

"I think my mother loves you more than she loves me," he said as he walked back into the living room.

"Are you jealous of that, too?" I asked him playfully.

"Not in the least bit. She's figured out how important you are to me."

"We've only met for five minutes. She can't be clairvoyant." I giggled.

"That's true, but in the four years I have owned this place, I've never bought any woman here. It's my sanctuary."

"You haven't?" I fell in love with him even more.

"No, I haven't met anyone I imagined sharing it with, but now I finally have," he said as his brown eyes gazed unblinkingly into mine.

"I would share this view with you any day. You have Lake Washington literally in your backyard, and what's that mountain range?"

"Those are the Cascades, and to your left is downtown Seattle, and right there is the Space Needle." He showed me his vista as he wrapped his hands around me and brought my back closer to his chest.

As he held me close, he made me forget why I was there; I was in awe. "Wow, it is a sanctuary. You're so close to everything, yet still far enough for it to be peaceful. I love it." We stared out at the view for a while until we found ourselves upstairs.

After Michael had shown me his bedroom, and we had reconnected in the only way we knew how, I finally had a chance to take a bath. The bathroom was yet another masterpiece, with a walk-in shower, a deep soaking tub, and an unexpected boudoir area adding to its luxurious feel. Despite being surrounded by this grandeur, the gravity of what was happening was finally hitting me. Whether my mother had done this or not, whatever it all meant, was serious. Who and why would anyone want to do this to my family, then make it seem as though it was my mother behind it all?

With all the thoughts running through my mind, I remembered Michael had told me he was in love with me. When I arrived at HQ and saw him, he had seemed unattainable, but he was all mine and wasn't afraid to show it. This thought alone made me smile. I thought I was alone until I heard him speak to me.

"Sofia, I am here for you. You did the right thing coming to me first; you can trust me."

"I do trust you. Why are you standing so far away? Are you afraid of getting wet?" I asked seductively. I didn't need to ask him twice as he stripped out of the low slung shorts he now wore.

"I'm not afraid of getting wet," he said as he winked, sliding behind me. He took the sponge from me and started gently washing my back. "I love every little thing about your body. The way you feel, how it responds to even the lightest touch, and I even love those little sounds you make when you don't know you're making them."

"You love everything? You've got to have a favourite part."

"I don't play favourites. If, however, I had to choose..." he said as he cupped both my slippery breasts, tugging and twisting. To prove his point, an involuntary moan left me.

"Hmm, I think you do play favourites." When I whispered to him, he let go of my left breast, moved me closer to him, and reached around, pushing a finger deep inside my core.

"Maybe I do," he whispered as he continued to give me so much pleasure. When he added another finger, I heard myself whimper.

"Don't stop."

He listened and didn't stop. Just when I was close to the edge, both fingers slipped out and left me empty. He started the slow tease again, this time rubbing me slowly and torturing me, while his length grew against my back. Writhing against his fingers, I held on to his biceps with both hands as he continued his merciless assault on my sensitive bundle of nerves. He had long since found the spot which drove me crazy, and he stroked it until I exploded. I was panting as I came down, weak and malleable against his chest, needing a much deeper connection with him.

"We're getting out of the bath. I need you," he said with ragged breaths as I witnessed a ferocious intensity I had yet to see from him. We scrambled out of the bath. We should have rinsed off the bubbles, but we were both mindless with need. Carelessly, I threw a big fluffy towel on the boudoir chaise, then backed onto it as I wrapped my legs around him. He slid his arousal deep inside me. He thrust hard and then harder, as our wet bodies played a symphony echoing in the white marble tomb. My whimpers and moans filled the luxurious bathroom, as he unleashed a beast, I had never guessed resided in the most urbane sophisticate I had ever known. He took what he needed from me and came with a ground shaking roar.

"I don't think I could ever live without you," he said to me as he came down and peppered my neck with kisses.

"You don't have to; I'm here now." I was finally ready to be honest with him.

"I love you, Sofia."

"I love you too. How have you taken over my heart and soul and have become my world?"

"Everything about today has made me happy; you coming to HQ and knowing what I've suspected for a while to be true, that you are in love with me, like I am in love with you."

This time when I kissed him, I never wanted to let him go. "Looks like I might be staying a while."

"I want you to stay with me, and I want this to be your home, too. I may have been drunk on you, but I meant what I said in Bumi Hills. I need you by my side. I know you have a lot going on right now, but one day I will make you my wife, if you will have me."

"As proposals go, that might need some work." I made light of the seriousness of his declarations.

How could we have come so far in a few short months?

"You're right; it does. Get dressed, or don't, and come to the kitchen. I'll make us some dinner."

I rinsed off in the shower and dressed in a light front zip-through sleeveless dress. Although the autumn chill was starting to set in, Michael's house was warm and comfortable. I got my laptop out and sent Brad an email. I told him I had left Africa, but begged him to keep it a secret, especially from my father. The subterfuge was not my style, but these were extenuating circumstances.

Once I was finished, my laptop was running out of power. Tucking it underneath my arm, I went into what I remembered from the house tour to be Michael's office. As I pushed through the door, I realised this wasn't his office, but a fanciful bright pink princess bedroom with twin beds. A girls' bedroom with toys and books to one side, and a pretty ensuite bathroom too. I smiled as I looked around, and briefly remembered the dishevelled man I met in Istanbul and how far removed he was from the man I knew now. I made my way downstairs, where I eventually found his home office.

After dinner, we sat in the living room, with its oversized crescent shaped comfortable couch, as if it were made for lovers. I looked outside; the city lights danced and twinkled on the surface of Lake Washington and couldn't imagine being anywhere else.

"My place seems so cold compared to yours."

"This place is only warm because you're here with me."

He pulled my back closer to his chest and wound his hands around me, softly kneading my breasts and kissing my neck as he unzipped my dress. Even though we were alone, he whispered in my ear with his signature husky voice.

"I'm not sure why you bothered to get dressed when you knew clothes would just get in our way."

"We needed to eat, and I don't eat in the nude."

"When I eat, I prefer to eat you in the nude."

"That's clever, but no one's eating anything. We've just had dinner. You never told me you're going through a princess phase." I smiled and waited expectantly.

"I'm happy you're exploring. That's Maxie and Laila's room — my nieces for when they visit," he said as he licked and nibbled my ear.

"Do they stay over often?" Resentment snarled through me as thoughts of their mother made an unexpected appearance.

"Once a month, sometimes twice. They are both good girls."

"I don't doubt that at all."

"Yet you sound doubtful. Their mother rarely comes here. This whole setup was my mum's idea to try and mend the rift between my brother and I." he said as he sat us both upright to face each other.

"Do you see her?" When and how had I become proprietary, *over him*?

"Yes, at family events, so will you. She's a nonissue to me. Although, I know the situation is new to you. Try not to worry about it."

"Easier said than done. Do you get along with the girls?"

"I do. They love it here. I taught them both to swim," he said proudly.

"Wow, at their age, that takes patience. I think you'll make a great Dad one day."

A boyish grin appeared on his face, and he looked at me closely. "I hope so. I'm in no rush as long as I've got you, but I would really love to practise making one, perhaps right now." His hands were already back on the zipper of my dress.

Was Michael talking about starting a family? He had already talked about marriage.

Was I ready to be a mother again?

I knew I was ready to be with Michael in every way because he made me feel everything again.

Could I ever be a mother again? Would I even remember how it's done?

How could I love any other child as much as I loved my boys?

Chapter Fifteen

♥

Sofia

The next morning, I woke up later than my usual to an empty bed. After we had made love late into the night, and I was drifting off into a dreamless sleep, Micheal whispered to me that he would need to go into work, but he wouldn't be long.

I was home alone. My soul felt weary, and my heart was heavy. Being alone with my thoughts and the situation with my mother was weighing me down.

After an hour, I couldn't stay in bed much longer. Just as I was getting up, Michael arrived back home.

"Good morning, I thought you would still be asleep," he said as he kissed me tenderly.

"I can't sleep anymore," I said as tears filled my eyes.

"Want to go for a swim? Always makes me feel better. It might work for you, too."

"Not today. I'm feeling a little disenchanted and I think I might drown." I managed a weak smile.

"You wouldn't. I'm here to save you from any kind of drowning," he said as he pulled me in closer and held me.

I breathed him in, and a calm settled over me. "I love that scent; it's so you. I would recognise it anywhere."

"It was made for me by a perfumer in Covent Garden in London."

"Right. Is that when you get interviewed, and they drill down on all your subtleties?"

"Yes, that's it, and they make the scent based on your answers and personality."

"The perfumer got it so right. It's strong without being overpowering with real depth; it's refined and so sexy."

"Are we still talking about my cologne?" he asked with a cocky smile.

"Your head just gets bigger and bigger." I laughed.

"You walked right into that one. Come downstairs, wear something warm." I couldn't resist his pleading eyes.

"I'll freshen up first." I felt a little lighter as I walked downstairs fifteen minutes later. He was on his phone as he pointed to a freshly made, steaming mug of cappuccino and blueberry muffins. I took my mug and went outside.

The grounds were beautiful and well-manicured. A lavish covered patio offered a dining and living space, with a fully equipped outdoor kitchen, and lake views as far as the eye could see. A herb garden was adjacent to the backdoor of the kitchen and delicious smells filled it. In addition to an indoor pool, Michael also had one outdoors, taking centre stage. I walked down to the very edge of the two-acre lot and found a bench where I sat for a while and looked out onto the lake. There was a mild chill in the air, the sun was trying to break out from behind the clouds and the Cascades in full view; it looked like a watercolour painting.

Michael eventually came out to find me and held his hand out to me. "Come with me."

We made our way to the Spider, which Michael eased out of the city. He looked young and free as he expertly manoeuvred the car around the bends. An hour later, we arrived at what he told me was his favourite city beach. As we strolled along the shoreline, with the small waves lapping at our feet, I let out a sigh and he looked at me.

"I only want you to be happy. When I first met you in Istanbul, I could see how unhappy you were and now that I know you and understand the depths of your unhappiness, I see how strong you are."

"Today, I don't feel strong." I sighed, despondent.

"You might not feel it, but living through what you've lived through, and still going through, takes a certain kind of strength that I can't begin to imagine. Don't be too hard on yourself. Please," he said as he pulled my hand to his lips.

"You're my hero. You love me even with all my issues." I was feeling a little too sorry for myself.

"You don't have issues. Something tragic happened to you; it could happen to anyone. I love you. After all that had happened in my love life, I had given up all hope of ever finding you."

I smiled at him, a really wide smile. Every word that came from him made me fall in love even more. He seemed to always say all the right things; he made me feel needed.

"I need to go and see my parents. I'll leave on Monday."

"Why so soon?" he asked, surprised.

"I don't want to keep putting it off. I've been thinking about this and you're right. There's no way my mother could have done this, but we still need to talk about it, and I need to understand why she has been off ever since this happened."

"She's off because she lost her grandsons, not because she had anything to do with their deaths," he explained patiently.

"I really want to hear that from her."

"You're right. You do need to talk, but I'll come with you." He was concerned, and I was still so fragile. I was already broken, but I had to face this alone.

"I think I should do this on my own; I'm ready to hear what she has to say."

"I don't like that plan one bit, but I respect that. I will be waiting for you at home when you're ready to come back."

Home — I'm in love with him. The last home I had with a man was with Nolan, and it was everything to us.

Was Michael's home now mine too?

"Yes, I'll be back. I also need to pack up my place."

"I can send people to do that, or if you prefer, I can at least come and help you."

"I'm pedantic about packing, but I would love some help with it."

He smiled an indulgent smile, stopped walking, and pulled me closer. "You have made me so happy, and I love that you are moving in with me. I will spend the rest of my days making you happy."

"You already make me happy. I just hope I will have less bad days."

"I'll be here for you, even when you have the bad days." He spoke as he gazed deeply into my eyes, and when I looked in his eyes, I arrived home.

We stood on the shoreline and kissed until the sun began to sink over the horizon.

When we drove back to the house, Michael and I were desperate to have each other again. We didn't make it upstairs as our need overwhelmed us. After hunger forced us into the kitchen, we found the fridge restocked and some meals prepared. The house was pristine; someone had been busy while we were out.

"You have a fairy godmother?" I gushed in mock astonishment.

"My housekeeper, Marianne, comes twice weekly when I'm in the country. I'll have to introduce you two. You don't mind having a housekeeper, do you?"

"Not at all. I couldn't keep this huge place clean, even if I tried."

After eating a delicious lasagne and polishing off a bottle of wine, we tried watching a movie in the home theatre, but our need for each other was too great, and Michael took me again in the theatre, all the while my trip to LA played on my mind.

Chapter Sixteen

Sofia

As the Bombardier neared the runway at Van Nuys Airport, I was struggling with how I would approach my father. I had rehearsed it over the last two hours, but every way I had come up with made me sweat more and more. I had emptied my breakfast down the toilet three times, and I couldn't calm my racing heart.

After contending with lunchtime traffic on the highway, I arrived at Kingman Air a little after lunch. Penny showed me into my father's office while he finished a call. I maintained my composure, although on the inside I was anything but.

"Sofia, what a wonderful surprise. When did you arrive?" He came round from his desk and gave me a warm embrace.

"I got in four days ago, Daddy," I said as my voice broke. I willed the tears to stay at bay. The only secret I had ever kept from my father was when I first started dating his employee — Nolan, and that lasted three whole days. It broke me that I had kept my arrival from him.

"You took a while to come and see your old man. Your mother will be so happy to see you."

"You're not old, just refined." I tried charm; I felt anything but charming.

"Come, let's sit and tell me the highlights. I'm impressed with what you did in Africa. This has got to be your *magnum opus*." He was beaming with pride, oblivious to my anguish.

"About my mother; I need you to be completely honest with me," I said as I took out the brown envelope from my bag. "Have you heard anything at all from your investigator about Nolan's plane?" My voice shook.

"Nothing of substance. I'm sorry. Sweetheart, don't upset yourself now..." I cut him off. I couldn't continue without saying what I had come for.

"Dad, my investigator brought me this treasure trove of information, and I need you to make sense of it before I start to tell you what it all means."

"You have an investigator? Since when?" he asked in surprise, finally starting to take notice of my demeanour.

"They were my family. I couldn't sit around and wait. I needed to know."

Dad was silent for five minutes as he sifted through the paperwork. I was shaking like a leaf. Speaking to my mother would have me in an even worse state.

"Sofia, the plane was downed by mercenaries?" he said aghast.

"That's not the worst of it all. They were paid with funds transferred from this company here, the company which is controlled by Mum!" I showed him as my hand shook, and my eyes watered.

"Are you accusing my wife of doing this?" he roared.

"It's all in black and white, Daddy." I had become a little girl again, but I needed to stay the course. I had never cowered before my father; I wouldn't start now.

"Think, Sofia! That's what you do best! She's your mother and the love of my life!" His tone was caustic as he stood up and stood over me.

At this point, I was hysterical.

"This is all I've been thinking about for the last four days!" I cried, looking up at him.

"No, this can't be. Your mother would never do this. This must be some kind of mistake. You should know that." His face paled as he bellowed at me.

"Believe what you will. This information has been verified by yet another different source, and the paper trail leads back to Mum."

"A different source? How many investigators do you have working on this?" Alarm registered on his face. Everything about this seemed to be a revelation to him.

"Let me speak to your mother. I will get to the bottom of this; she would never do anything like this. She loved the boys too. They were her everything."

"I don't doubt she loved them, but did she know they would be on that plane with Nolan?"

"Why would she want Nolan dead? You sound like you don't know your mother at all. Is this why you haven't been to see me since you returned from Africa?" He had become a raging bull.

"Yes, it is. I was afraid you might somehow be involved, too." I couldn't look him in the eye as I voiced my fears.

"In murder? Who do you think I am?" he growled incredulously.

"I didn't know what to think, or to do. My heart is breaking over this," I said as tears trickled down my face.

"It must be, but how could your first instinct lead you to believe this? Where have you been?" he asked, as he took out his handkerchief and handed it to me.

"That's another thing I wanted to tell you. I was in Seattle with the man I mentioned when we last spoke a week ago."

He smiled tenderly; his eyes suddenly glazed over. "Is he good to you, Sofia? Does he understand what you've been through?"

"Dad, I'm in love with him, and I am moving to Seattle to be with him."

"This is all so sudden. How long have you known him?" His protective side rearing its head, despite my accusations.

"We met in Istanbul five months ago."

"I see. Will you continue to work for Kingman Air?"

"I want to cut back on travelling because I want to see how things go with Michael. That's his name."

"So, what does Michael do for a living?" This was fast becoming a fact-finding mission for my father, and he sounded suspicious.

"He is the interim CEO at Worldwide Media."

"David Masterson is the CEO. What happened to him?" he asked, warily.

"Michael's father is not well, so he's had to step up."

"Is Masterson the one who brought you this information about your mother? What is he trying to get at?"

I didn't want my father's image of Micheal tainted before they had even met. "No, an old high school friend working for one of the intelligence organisations did. Michael is not trying to get at anything. In fact, he's doubtful about the information, too."

"This is a complex matter. Do you want to come to the house tonight so we can speak to your mother together?"

"I really wish we could go now. I need to talk to her and understand. Is she at home today?"

"Yes, she is at home, getting over a cold."

We left immediately. Ross Kingman, as a pilot himself, was always cool under pressure, but this new development had him unnerved. He didn't speak much on the way. When we arrived, we both went upstairs to find my mother where she was finishing up getting dressed.

"Sofia, this is a treat. How are you?" She beamed with the most genuine smile.

How could I not trust her implicitly? My heart stilled.

She came towards me with arms outstretched, and when I flinched, she held me even closer. She had finally become my comforter.

"Sofia, what's happened?" she asked, concern and worry written all over her face, all the while she held me at arm's length looking deeply in my eyes.

"I need you to be completely honest with me." My voice shook as I looked at the delicate and elegant woman before me.

"Sofia, this is all unusual. What is going on with you? Did something happen to you in Africa?" she asked as she tried to lead me to the loveseat in her bedroom.

I resisted and faced her. My father hovered at the doorway.

"Not exactly. I have some information, which was brought to me by someone I trust, and it implicates one of your companies as having paid mercenaries to blow Nolan's plane out of the sky."

"What, that's ridiculous..." Instantly, she began hyperventilating, and then fell to the floor with a resounding thud.

My father was at her side in an instant while I called for an ambulance. The histrionics were not in my mother's nature, and I suspected something wasn't right.

I looked over at her as she was starting to turn an unhealthy purple hue. "Start CPR, Dad; she's not breathing!" I yelled. Instant regret hit me as I looked at my mother on the floor, unresponsive.

How could I have done this to her?

Tears streamed down my face as Dad, and I took turns performing CPR while we waited for what felt like aeons for the paramedics to arrive. I was angry at the situation, and at my mother, too. I needed answers, and she needed to be alive to provide them. The paramedics arrived and loaded her into an ambulance and sped towards the hospital. My father rode with her, and I followed closely behind, driven by Thomas.

When we arrived at Cedars, she was barely breathing, and had to be sustained by oxygen. It didn't take long for my father to be recognised, and we were quickly ushered into a private waiting room while the doctors and nurses worked to preserve her life. I was torn; it seemed she was behind the worst thing to have ever happened to me, but she was still my mother and I loved her. I said a silent prayer, willing for her to be returned to us. My father was in pain, and I had caused it. We looked at each other.

"I'm sorry, Dad. This is not what I wanted. All I needed were answers."

"I am not angry at you, Sofia. You didn't do this."

Unconvinced, this was of little comfort to my conflicted heart.

After an hour of waiting and hoping, a doctor who introduced himself as a cardiologist came in and explained my mother had suffered a heart attack and was stable. My father and I continued to sit in silence. Raw anger emanating from his body.

Defeated, my father eventually spoke. "Sofia, go home and rest a while. I'll wait here for your mother."

"No, I'll stay here with you." Every word I spoke had become a chore. I didn't even know how to talk to him.

Dad and I managed to eat some sandwiches, which Thomas brought. I fell asleep in the waiting room, and hours later, I woke up with a start, my head against Michael's shoulder.

"What, how are you here?" I immediately sat up. Relief at seeing him washed through me until I remembered why I was in hospital.

"After you left, I had to find out how you are, and when you were not answering your phone, I was worried about you, so I flew out here."

"How did you know I was here?" My eyes flooded.

"Your dad found out from his assistant that I was trying to find you, and he told me where you were," he said as he kissed me softly.

"Where is he?" A few errant tears now ran down my face.

"He has just gone in to see your mother, but only one visitor at a time," he said, handing me tissues.

"Thank you for being here. I was so afraid I may have killed her."

"No, you can't think that. She's alive, and you needed to talk; remember?" He spoke gently.

My dad returned to the waiting room, tears in his eyes. "She's waiting to see you. She's now talking and breathing on her own," he said as he held my hand briefly.

"I'm so relieved to hear that, Dad."

As soon as I walked into my mother's room, the dam broke, and all the tears I had been holding in came in torrents. She was clearly upset, too, but trying hard to be strong.

"Sofia, thank you for being here. I was afraid you wouldn't be after what you told me you had learned." She had aged ten years in the hours since I had first seen her.

"Mum let's not talk about that now. I want you to concentrate on getting better. You've been through something very serious."

"No! You need to listen to me. I am hurting that you have had to live with this information even for one minute. Why didn't you come to me straight away?" This was the mother I knew, but where had she been for so long?

Her voice was hoarse, and with the little effort she had used to speak to me, she became tired. How could I have believed my mother could be capable of this? Both my father and Michael had seen through all that evidence the minute they laid eyes on it. Why had I been so quick to believe it? I had never despised myself more than I did then.

"Under the circumstances, it was difficult to do that."

"We need to get to the bottom of this, and I've asked your father to get the authorities involved. If I really have to say it, I had nothing to do with any of it."

"The evidence against you is so strong. Once the authorities get hold of it, you will go to prison."

"We need help to find out what happened to that plane, and also finding out how your grandfather's companies became entangled in all this. You think I despised Nolan? I resented him for a while — you were so young, and I worried about you. When I realised how happy he made you, I loved him like a mother would love their own son." She winced as she spoke.

Mum was getting tired and was starting to become breathless, so I put the oxygen mask closer to her face and she took some deep breaths.

"Thank you for telling me that. It means everything to me. Don't think about this for now; get better, then we can deal with it. I don't want to lose anyone else."

"You're strong. I can be strong for you, too. I missed you on the boys' birthday. Were you okay?"

"No, it was difficult, but I wasn't alone."

"I'm happy to hear that. Perhaps you can tell me about him in the morning; you have a love glow about you."

"I do, because I'm in love." My smile broke through, and I felt lighter.

"That makes me happy," she said as she smiled weakly.

"Rest up. I'll see you in the morning." I returned to the waiting room, where Michael and Dad were talking quietly. They both stood up when I entered the room.

"She's tired, but she's trying to be strong. She told me what you talked about. Please don't call the authorities yet until she's better."

Downcast, he held my hand as we spoke. "I'll hold off for now, but by law, I am required to report this, otherwise all our planes will be grounded."

"I understand, but if it is indeed some kind of set-up, we need to keep this information really close, because whoever set her up has to be someone really close to her, to us, and to Kingman Air."

"You are keeping a level head. We'll keep this quiet. Go home. I'll stay the night here and look after her. Take Thomas with you."

"It was good to meet you, sir," Micheal said as we made to leave.

"The pleasure is all mine, son. Thank you for everything." He was impressed with Michael; not once had I ever heard him call Nolan "son". I filed that information away for later.

Michael and I walked out of the hospital and into my father's waiting car. Thomas drove us to my penthouse. As we walked out into the cool air, Michael took my hand in his.

"Are you okay? Today has been intense."

"Intense is right. I have more questions than answers now. Did your investigator find anything new?"

"Whoever did this covered their tracks well. He hasn't been able to find anything contradicting the information you already have."

"I wonder why and who could and would do something like this."

"Are there any business associates of your dad's that you may suspect, or even any of his competitors?"

I was thoughtful for a while, but nothing came to me. "I would really have to think about that. I'm not sure."

"I have to ask, your late husband, could he have been targeted for any reason at all?"

"He was a fighter pilot for the Royal Air Force before he came to work for Kingman, but nothing else stands out."

"Okay," he answered softly, looking a touch intimidated.

"Do you want to eat before we go up? I haven't been here in months, and I don't have anything in my apartment."

"Sure, what's good around here?"

It was nearly midnight when we walked into a late-night bistro close to my penthouse. I wasn't hungry, but I knew I had to eat. After our meal and sharing a serve of honeycomb ice cream, we walked to my building.

"Welcome home." I kept it tidy, and a cleaning service provided the touch ups, but the California coastal decor with its warm white walls, designer furniture, and all the beautiful art I had on the walls didn't make it a home like Michael's was.

"I love this place; it's so calming. Have you always lived here?"

I could read between the lines straight away.

"No, I moved in after putting up my house for sale. You're the only one..." The last words were a mere whisper.

"I didn't mean to make you uncomfortable," he said as he held me close for the first time since he had arrived in LA.

"I'm glad you came to find me today. Aren't they missing you at HQ?" I had to change the subject.

"No, they are not. Dad had a good weekend, and he plans on going to work all week."

"That's great news. I'm glad he's feeling better."

"For now. I'm still responsible," he said, seriously.

"What does that mean?"

"It means I'll be busy, but I will always make time for you, for us, and for the family we will eventually have." Michael's warp speed was dizzying. He was planning a family, where I was still learning to let go of my old one.

"That's quite the speech. Where's this coming from?" I asked lightly.

"Your dad asked me if I would 'allow' you to work for Kingman Air after moving in with me. I would never stop you from working or doing what you want, but if you're in any doubt about me and my resources, you don't ever need to work if you don't want to."

"Okay, Mr Moneybags. Thank you for clarifying that. For now, I will keep working for Kingman, travelling; maybe not so much. Eventually, I might stop. We'll see."

He came closer to me, close enough to whisper in my ear. "Why would you eventually stop?"

I whispered back, "To spend all that money you've just told me about, of course." I didn't have it in me to get into the family conversation now. "Let me show you around, moneybags."

"I'll never live that one down, will I?" he said as he followed close behind.

"No, you won't. I'm not with you for your money. Take a look around you; I've got my own." I didn't realise how defensive I sounded until I looked up into his eyes.

"I meant no offense. It's something you never have to worry about," he said as he tried to placate me.

"It's been a tough day. Let's not argue about money. I'll show you my bedroom instead, and perhaps we can have a different kind of fight."

"I like that idea." He chuckled, pulling my body flush against his.

Chapter Seventeen

♥

Michael

Sofia's arrival at HQ had been one of my life's highlights. I had made up my mind in the Namib desert that she was the one I had been waiting for. I had bought the ring when I returned from there, but I was still nervous and worried it might be too soon. I had with absolute certainty felt Vivian was the woman for me, but I had been wrong, and I had promised her the world and given her a ring, too. My instincts had failed me before, and I didn't want to be wrong again.

I worked from her home office, which, despite her long absence, had a scent that was distinctively hers. She had photographs of her children and *him* in there, and they were all very happy. When I found myself staring at her previous life, I decided it was time to go out.

I arrived at the hospital, hoping to see Sofia, but she wasn't there, neither was her father, so I decided to see Mrs Kingman and introduce myself. Everything about Sofia's situation was a minefield. It had taken some doing but our investigator had managed to find out some information about the company which had supposedly paid for the plane incident. It did seem to be a set- up, - but it was difficult to prove.

"Good afternoon, Mrs Kingman," I said softly as I entered her room so as not to startle her.

She looked up in interest and beckoned me to come closer. I couldn't get over how alike Sofia and her mother looked.

"Hello, you brought flowers, so you can't be one of my doctors." Even though she spoke in a hushed tone, she even sounded like Sofia.

"No, I'm not one of your doctors. I'm Michael, a friend of Sofia's."

"Sofia has plenty of friends, but none of them have deigned to visit me. Why don't you tell me exactly who you are," she said with a mischievous smile.

I was speechless and could only smile while she looked at me expectantly.

"Cat got your tongue?"

I could see where Sofia got her smarts and wit. I had only been in her presence for five minutes, and I already loved her.

"Come in, sit down, and tell me how you know Sofia." She patted the space next to her on her bed.

I got the feeling she already knew about me, but I was enjoying this game. At that moment, Sofia arrived at her mother's door.

"Michael, you're here to see Mum, with flowers; those are beautiful," she said in surprise.

"Yes, Sofia. I'm here to see Mum." I smiled at Mrs Kingman, sitting down where she had invited me to.

"You were about to tell me who you are, Michael."

Sofia looked at me with keen interest and wide eyes. This was not a problem as I knew exactly who I was.

"Mrs Kingman, I am the man who's desperately in love with Sofia."

"If I hadn't already done so yesterday, I believe I might have swooned. Please call me Bianca."

"It's lovely to meet you, Bianca."

"The pleasure is all mine. I'm sorry we are meeting while they try to mend my broken heart."

"Don't apologise. You just might be the loveliest broken-hearted patient in here."

"I see why my daughter has fallen for you. You say all the right things. Are you a writer?"

She was just as charming as she looked. How was it possible that Sofia was quick to believe she could be capable of the unthinkable?

"No, nothing as interesting as that. I help my father run a media company."

"That sounds busy. What do you like to do when you're not busy with that?"

"Photography is my passion."

"Really? Sofia loves photography too; always has since she was just out of nappies."

"Mum, I was four. I had been out of nappies for a while," she said as she poured some water in a glass for Bianca.

"Okay, my mistake." She tried speaking through a coughing fit.

"Mum, let me help you lay back down so you can have some rest. You've had too much fun for one day." I watched as Sofia took charge, and it was a revelation.

Could I have been stifling her all along, imagining that somehow, I had to be in control because of her fragility?

"Now you're making me out to be a four-year-old. Soon you'll want to feed me." She smiled sweetly at Sofia.

Sofia kissed her on the cheek. "I probably will, rest up before I make you say, 'ahh'."

"I hope to see you again soon, Bianca."

"Thanks for coming to see me, Michael," she said as she blew me a kiss. Evil incarnate didn't behave like this.

We left her and walked towards the bank of elevators.

"Thanks for coming to see my mum. The irony is even though she's in a hospital bed, I haven't seen her so alive and so happy in such a long time. I think you charmed her."

"I did? Did I also charm you too?" I spoke in her ear as the elevator arrived.

"Yes, every day."

I couldn't help smiling. "Sofia, I'm sorry I need to return to HQ."

"When do you need to go?" she asked as her face fell.

"Early in the morning, so I can be in the office during business hours."

"I know you have to go, but I'll miss you."

"I will be thinking about you. I'll make sure to be back on Friday night."

"I know, because you're desperately in love with me," she deadpanned.

"I meant that too, Sofia. I wasn't just saying it to make Bianca smile. I meant every word I said."

"I love you too, Michael."

"With all of you?"

"What do you mean? Of course, with all of me."

"Do I have your whole heart?"

"What are you talking about?" Suddenly, she was on guard.

"Are you over him?" The question was out before I could stop it. It had been on my mind, while I sat in her office, surrounded by him.

The elevator doors opened to the ground floor, and as we left the elevators and walked out of the hospital, she quickly let go of my hand.

"Why would you ask me that now?" she spat, face flushed, turning an angry red.

"I need to know that you're all mine, and I'm not sharing you with a phantom," I said calmly.

"How very dare you," she hissed, the rancour clear in her tone. "What reason have I given you to make you doubt how I feel about you?"

"You love me, that's for certain, but do you still love him, too?"

Blowing out a breath, she fought for composure. "There's no need to go to Seattle in the morning. Leave now, so I can be with my phantom in peace." Sarcasm and anger seeped through her.

"You don't mean that." I kept calm, but she was furious.

"I do. Grab your things and leave my apartment."

She walked away in the opposite direction.

With all the hysterics, she hadn't denied that she was still in love with him. My instincts had kept me safe in a lot of volatile situations. I was right about this. I wasn't angry, just resigned to the fact that I might always be second best to the hero pilot. I wasn't ready to be second best again.

I went back to the penthouse and collected my bag, and as irony would have it, called my own pilot and didn't look back.

Chapter Eighteen

♥

Sofia

My time in Africa had been bittersweet. I had finally found myself. I had let go of the pain and moved on from the hurt and sorrow. Within a minute, Michael had minimised all my emotional achievements, and I was livid. Nolan had left me too soon, before we had fully lived our lives, when we were happy and so in love.

I was now focused on building a life with Michael. Michael, who was self-absorbed, and seemingly indulged, couldn't see how much I was giving up for him. The memories in this city with my children, much needed proximity to my parents, my friends, and my job. He didn't consider all this when he accused me of stringing him along while I pined for Nolan. The doubts from Michael were a setback, and they were hurtful. I needed space from him while he worked on himself.

I had never noticed how large my apartment was until he left, and I was alone. I had been so sure about how angry I was with him, but now that I was here, and could smell the lingering scent of his custom cologne, I missed him terribly. Finding his T-shirt in the bathroom made me happy, and in my sorry state, I wore it. I made my way into my office, and his scent was strongest there. This was where he had been working, the only place in my apartment where I had photographs of Nolan and the boys on all four walls.

Had the photographs sent him into a tailspin? Was that why he doubted my feelings for him?

I became even more angry at him. I returned to this apartment for the first time in five months, two days ago. He needed to work on himself more than he knew.

The next day, I went to my parents' home and waited for Mum to arrive back from the hospital. When she did, we sat down to eat together.

"Where's Michael? I loved meeting him yesterday. You know a man who can talk about his feelings like that is a keeper."

"He had to go back to work." I made sure my voice didn't betray my inner turmoil.

"Your father mentioned you're thinking of moving in with him?"

"Yes, that had been the plan, but I am not so sure anymore. He thinks I am still pining for Nolan."

"Are you?"

"I think about him sometimes, but not as often as I used to. Instead of dreaming about Nolan, it's Michael in my dreams, and when I want to be held and touched and kissed, it's Michael I long for." I explained this to my mother, even though I was telling myself all this.

"That's beautiful, darling, but does Michael know any of this?" she asked as she took my hand in hers in silent comfort.

"He must, I'm sure he does." We have shared so much, how could he not know?

"Have you told him, like you have told me?" She pressed in that motherly way she had always had about her. For a long time, it had disappeared, but now it was in full effect.

"No, when he confronted me yesterday about my feelings for Nolan, I became hysterical and told him to leave. I was angry about his myopic outlook and lack of empathy for what I was sacrificing by moving to Seattle to be with him."

"Perhaps it's best to spell it out for him so he is absolutely certain of where he stands with you. He wasn't shy about voicing where you stand with him. Terms of endearment and open communication might just be his love language."

Where was this Mum all along? I could have coped better if she had given me even a fraction of this over the last two years.

"What's Dad's love language?" I asked, worried about confronting her with what was really on my mind. Where she had been when I had needed her.

"Money, and perhaps Penny." She chuckled softly, which gave way to a cough. She sipped some water gingerly.

"I love the James Bond reference, but I don't believe there's anything going on there. I've worked with both of them for a long time."

"A woman knows, darling. Have you met Michael's family?"

Knows what? Were my father and Penny in a relationship?

"His mother briefly. She has an effervescent personality, and she is very easy to like," I said wistfully.

"I'm sorry, Sofia."

"About his mother?" I asked gently.

"No, not about her. I'm sorry that I haven't been the mother you've always known. When we lost the boys, my world imploded, and I was of no use to my daughter who was going through the worst of it. I left you flailing in the wind, and when I started to feel better, I left you all alone in your nightmare, and I am so sorry."

"Why did you?"

"I didn't know how to help you. When my fog had finally cleared, and I was starting to feel better, I thought, like me, all you needed was time. I shouldn't have left you alone in the depths of despair. I should have been there for you." She swallowed down a sob.

"Don't cry, please, it means so much to hear you say that. I'm sorry I ever doubted the love you have for our family. I don't know what would possess me to think that you would do what I accused you of." We had both become a blubbering mess.

"It's very convincing evidence you have, and you don't ever have to apologise. We all want to know the truth of what happened," she replied after she composed herself.

This was more talking than Mum and I had done in a long time. We had lost so much of our relationship, but this conversation was what we both needed.

"Do you need to rest, Mum?"

"Yes, I think I will. Thank you for visiting, and for having faith in me." A tear rolled down her cheek, but she smiled through it.

"I love you, Mum."

I kissed her on the cheek, walked her to her bedroom suite, and left her in her bed.

Chapter Nineteen

Michael

It had been two weeks since I left Sofia. We hadn't had any contact since our argument outside the hospital, and I needed to apologise. I was missing her, but I wasn't sure how my presence would be received. I had been angry at her response, but with the benefit of time and distance, I realised I might have overreacted. I had been wrong and needed to get back to what we were.

At lunch time, I left for Boeing Field, hoping to arrive just as Sofia was finishing work. When I arrived at Kingman Air, I was greeted by Brad, who seemed a little too excited to see me.

"Sofia's not in, in fact, she has been working from her home office for the last fortnight," he said in a sing-song voice as he scrambled from his chair and stood a little too close to me.

"Thank you," I said, trying to restore my personal space.

"Would you like me to tell her you are on your way to see her?"

"I'd rather you didn't, if that's okay?"

"No problem."

I arrived at Sofia's apartment and her doorman told me she was out. I had left my key on her console in a fit of rage to prove to her that

I wasn't returning. I waited for her in the lobby. Just after dusk, she arrived with a Phase One camera bag strapped across her body and what looked like her dinner.

Was she out taking photos? She needed that, like I needed her. She looked refreshed and happy until she saw me. Then a scowl covered her beautiful face.

"Michael, have you heard anything else about my mother?"

"No, I came to see you."

"Whatever for?" Her spine stiffened as she spoke bluntly.

"May I come up? I need to speak to you."

"Do you think you can bear to be in my space, *with my things*!" she shrieked.

"Sofia, I'm not here to fight with you. I need to speak to you. Can I come up with you, please?"

She didn't seem as affected by me as I was by her. She was radiant, happy, and still as breath-taking as the first time I met her. I followed her into the elevator, and we rode up in silence. Her scent was heady, and it took all my willpower to remain in my corner of the elevator and not pull her into my arms. I had missed her, and standing next to her reminded me I needed her with me.

We arrived upstairs, and I followed her into her inviting kitchen.

"Would you like some water, or wine, or whatever?" she asked me, seemingly disinterested.

"I just want you," I said softly as I walked towards her.

She scoffed. "I'll get changed. You can wait for me right here," she said as she put some distance between us.

Being in her presence felt like I had come home; I had to do everything in my power to get back to where we were. She returned, having changed into a very baggy beige sweater and some frumpy bottoms. I suspected to hide her body from me. No amount of clothing could ever let me forget how her body looked, and how it felt. Her attempt at keeping me at arm's length was amusing. I schooled my facial expressions, as I didn't want to provoke her in any way. She broke me out of my blatant perusal of her.

"Have you eaten? I have more than enough."

"I would love to eat. What are we having?"

"It doesn't matter; you'll eat what you're given."

She didn't look at me as she gave a biting response and shot down my attempt at a conversation.

She busied herself in the kitchen, then placed the plates on the island. She sat next to me, and with a tight smile, motioned for me to eat.

How had we departed so far from what we had been two weeks ago?

After a couple of forkfuls of the delicious carbonara, I decided to say what needed to be said. "Sofia, the last time we spoke, I was cruel. I shouldn't have said all those things to you."

"Yes you were cruel," she agreed.

"I'm sorry."

"You hurt me, and you set me back emotionally. That accusation was baseless, and I didn't understand what I had done to deserve what you said." Hopelessness layered her voice.

How could I have made her feel this way, when all I wanted was to make her happy?

"I was affected by all the photos you had in your office. I had spent all day looking at your happy family, and I started second guessing your feelings for me."

"You didn't have to. I was here to pack up my apartment and move in with you." Sad brown eyes looked at me.

"Will you still move in with me?"

"I don't know. I am still so angry with you."

"What can I do to make you feel better about us?"

"Only you know how to fix this. I was blissfully happy until you spoiled everything for me," she said, as she picked up her fork, ending the conversation.

She was angry, and I didn't know what to do. I'd always won every negotiation I've ever had. I hadn't anticipated this being the one I would lose. How could I show her how much I needed her? She loved gifts, but she hated any overt display of wealth.

We sat in silence for a while until she told me she was going to sleep.

"Can I join you?"

"No, you can't," she spat.

"Can I hold you, at least? I miss you."

"No, you don't. It's been two weeks with no phone call, text, email, smoke signal, or carrier pigeon. The only thing I see is a photo of you at a fancy party with some woman on your arm. Do you expect me to just fall back into your arms like one of your fawning women?"

"Fawning women! Where's this coming from? That was an annual charity gala sponsored by my company. The woman in the photo was an attendee who I was photographed with. Don't make that out to be what it's not."

"When I came to HQ, your assistant wouldn't let me see you. Do you know what she said to me?"

"No, I don't, but what does that have to do with this?"

"She told me if she let every pretty girl into your office who insisted that you would want to see them, you would never get any work done. So yes, those fawning women."

"I'm sorry she said that to you, but that is her job."

"Exactly, to keep the fawning women away. I'm going to bed! Alone!" she yelled after starting a brand new argument from left field.

I knew it was going to be difficult with Sofia, but I didn't realise it would be this bad. She was infuriated and unreasonable and it was my fault, but I needed to win her back.

I could have used any of her three guest rooms, but in her sour mood, she could easily have left her penthouse, and I wouldn't have been the wiser. So, I stretched out on the sofa and fell asleep.

It was an uncomfortable night and when I stirred the next morning, Sofia was getting ready to sneak out for a run. I opened one eye and saw her filling up her water bottle.

"If you wait for me, I can be ready in five."

"Sure, don't take too long," she said obligingly.

This was friendly. Was I forgiven?

Sofia wasn't much of a runner, but she was fit; however, I was fitter. She tired sooner than I did, but she wouldn't give in. We ran around her local park in silence until she tripped on an exposed tree root, rolling her ankle, and landing on the ground. Her ankle immediately ballooned to an orange sized lump. She couldn't bear weight on that foot, and the only thing to do was to carry her. In her pride, she was reluctant to get onto my back, but after attempting to hobble a few steps, and realising how painful it was, she eventually agreed to. This was the closest I had gotten to her in a long time. The sociopath residing deep inside me was secretly pleased that, in that moment, she needed me.

When we got back to her apartment, I helped her into the shower, as she was muddy and sweaty.

"I can manage a shower." She sighed.

I left her, took my own shower, and quickly returned to her.

"Sofia, are you ready to come out?"

She had become quite subdued, and the fight seemed to have left her.

"Yes, I am."

"Are you in a lot of pain?"

"No. Mostly humiliated about tripping while out running with you, but sad and upset about us."

"Don't feel humiliated about that. I'm sure we'll see each other at our worst, and if this is your worst, I think I love it. We can be fixed, I'm sure of it, but first, I need to get you out of here, get you dry, and dressed," I said, as I lifted her chin so she could look at me.

"Okay," she said and finally smiled at me.

"Okay? I love that word from your lips. Can you say it again?"

She laughed, and that was progress. I got her to bed, where she insisted on wearing pyjamas. The short silk pyjama set clung dangerously to her curves and it had me wondering why she would insist on wearing any at all. I wanted back in her life, and particularly back in her bed.

I elevated her foot on some pillows, placed an ice pack on it, and gave her some pain medication. Despite all the events that morning, it was still only seven o'clock, and Sofia napped while I made us breakfast.

"I've brought you something to eat." I woke her up, and she sat up and we both started to eat.

"Thank you. I like that you've brought this little tub of yoghurt; that's invalid food," she said as she licked the lid.

"Will you let me have a taste?" I asked, inching closer to her.

"A taste of what?" she whispered, gazing at my lips.

My eyes widened as I took her in. She licked her lips instead and looked me over.

"A taste of anything you would like me to try."

"Okay, I'll let you have some yoghurt," she said as she scooped some out of the tub and held out the spoon towards me. As I leaned in closer, she brought the spoon back towards her.

"That's not fair."

"You might need to come closer," she teased playfully. I loved it when she was like this.

That was all I could take. I inched closer to her lips until she moved closer to me. She gave me the softest strawberry flavoured kiss, and that was all the invitation I needed. I showed her how hungry I was, for her kisses, her touch, and for all of her.

"I missed every part of you. I need to see you, properly this time," I said, as I hooked my fingers into the thin straps of her pyjama top and pulled on it. The shorts were next to go, and she was left bared to me.

Her breathing quickened as she tried to undress me without moving her foot but failed. I was out of my clothes when I heard her moan as her brown eyes took me in. We didn't take our time like we always did. As soon as we were both undressed, I pushed against her right to the hilt, and I was home. She was slick for me, like she always was. I was as gentle as I could be, but that wasn't enough for her. She begged me for all I had to give, and I obliged, thrusting harder and going deeper. With my finger rubbing feverishly against her soft bundle of nerves, we both reached an intense climax within minutes. As we lay there panting and trying to catch our breaths, she spoke first.

"I missed you too, and while we were apart, I found myself clinging to the hope that you were missing me, too."

Once my breathing returned to normal, I said, "I was, with everything I am. Let's not spend that much time apart again."

"I can't go anywhere. My mother was placed under house arrest."

"She was? When?" I asked, surprised at this new development.

"Five days ago. She could've been in jail, but because of her heart, her lawyers were able to move mountains and have her at home. She's charged with some serious offences."

"How do we do this? Us?"

"It sounds like we are back at the beginning." She sighed.

"I have a jet, and we're now two hours apart. It's not the same."

"So do I, but it's the time spent hopping on and off planes to be together, which is time wasted. I don't want to waste time anymore." She burst into tears.

"Shh, what's brought this on, Sofia? We'll be together, in fact, we are together," I said, as I held her naked body close to mine.

"The time we spent apart, me stewing in anger, and you doing whatever was difficult, and I know from first-hand experience that life is short, and time is fleeting."

"Hey, don't get upset. First, I wasn't doing whatever. I was working all hours, and you were all I could think about. Second, I appreciate time and how fleeting it is. We have both loved and lost, and we can't spend our lives fearing the worst. We need to figure out what will work for both of us."

"I'm not being unreasonable, am I?"

"No, you're not. Your feelings are not unfounded. How often have you been able to see Bianca?"

"Daily at the moment. This situation is not favouring her psyche, and a very small superficial part of her is also worried about how this will impact her socially, and she's worried about my father's airline; it's his life's work."

"In that case, if you'll have me, I can stay here for a while, but I may need to go to HQ at a moment's notice."

"Can you really stay? Here? With Me?" she asked, beaming with excitement."

"Yes, I can."

"That's just perfect. I love that idea. I will finally have a live-in Chef-Masseuse."

"Is that all I'm good for?"

"Hmm, mostly."

Sofia was showing me exactly how happy she was with my decision when I held her smaller hands in mine and looked at her.

"Before you get other ideas, let's get one thing straight."

"This sounds serious. Am I in trouble?"

"You're the only woman I have in my life, and the only one I want."

"And your fan club?"

"Static and white noise."

That seemed to put her mind at ease, as she returned to showing me how pleased she was that I would be staying in LA with her.

Chapter Twenty

♥

Sofia

I was thrilled with Michael's decision to make my apartment his base for now. During his absence and getting some perspective, I had redecorated my office in a contemporary African theme. Taryn had shipped some pieces of furniture, vases, urns, and some soft furnishings from the store at the lodge out to my home after I had left the game reserve. I used some Fortuny lamps too. I first saw them on a work trip and fell in love, then bought some when I saw them at the Four Seasons in Kuwait. They fit right in with the African theme. I had selected and framed some photographs I took on my solo trips in Africa. On my desk, I still had one of the last photographs of the twins taken by Nolan on their third birthday; a week before the crash. I wanted Michael in my life, but he needed to respect that I had led a very fulfilled life before we met. Removing Nolan from the walls in my office wasn't a difficult decision, as he would always be in my heart but I needed Michael to feel comfortable when he was in my home.

A week after he had moved in, he finally ventured into my office. He was shocked by the transformation.

"You didn't redecorate on my account, did you? You're really good at it," he said, awe-struck.

"My time in Africa was important to me, I had to bring a little bit of it back here with me. I just hadn't had the opportunity to do this the last time you were here."

He kissed me with fervour. "It's beautiful; you have a good eye. These photos are so authentic. I especially love this one," he said, pointing to the twins' photo on my desk.

"I love that one too. It was on their third birthday."

"I love you, Sofia. I appreciate what you did here. I'm the one who was in the wrong. I let my insecurities get in the way."

"You've apologised already, Michael. I know your apology is sincere." He was apologetic, but that didn't take away from the fact that he still had insecurities around my feelings for Nolan. Would that ever change?

"If you're feeling up to it, I would like us to go away for a few days. Can you get away from work?"

"I'm sure I can clear some things. When would you like to leave?"

"Tonight, if you can."

"Tonight! Where are we going so I know what to pack?" I asked, rubbing my hands together excitedly.

"That's a surprise. I'll do the packing."

"You will pack for me? This is a full service trip, but I can always find out where we are going, you know?" This was special, and I loved surprises. I wouldn't spoil it by worrying about wardrobe choices.

"That will just spoil the surprise."

"Michael, anywhere I'm with you is magical, even if you decide to take me to an underground bunker."

"Is that on your bucket list?" he said as he pretended to think.

"If it were, I know I would love it with you. In that case, I'll go into the office now and quickly visit Mum. Do you want to come with me?"

"I saw both Bianca and Ross yesterday," he said as he nervously cleared his throat.

Surprised by this, I asked him, "You went to see my parents without me? Why?"

"To have lunch, and you were in a meeting."

He was being evasive, but why?

I let it go, as I was now so excited about taking a trip with him.

I arrived back home after work and seeing my mother finding bags packed and waiting at the elevator door. I was agog with excitement. I wondered where we were going and how long we would be there for, but most of all, I was looking forward to going away on a trip with him. Even though we were under the same roof, our jobs kept us apart, as they were both busy.

I started for the bedroom when he stopped me and begged to leave.

"I just need to grab some things from my medicine cabinet; I won't be long."

"I've packed those too, Sofia," he told me knowingly.

"You've definitely thought of everything."

"I considered leaving them because you don't need them. You're the one for me and you will have our children."

This was something Michael had said before, but he was so intense at that moment, and I wanted to know why. I chose not to spoil the moment and kissed him instead. We left the penthouse, and I drove my Panamera to the hangar where Michael's jet was kept while he was in town, and in no time, we were flying away to parts unknown.

It was a long flight filled with a lot of failed attempts at persuasion on my part to find out what our destination was, but no matter the tactic, Michael remained steadfast and wouldn't tell me. When we started the descent, surrounded by azure seas, white sands, and a calming serenity, I realised we were somewhere in French Polynesia. I had been everywhere but there.

"Where are we? Tahiti or Bora Bora? This is the best surprise; you did well," I said as I hugged him and gave him a ravenous kiss.

"You're good. We're in Bora Bora, and I'm glad you approve." Suddenly, he had lost his vim.

I glanced at him, and he appeared ill, pale, almost a light shade of green. I felt his forehead, and he was cool, but clammy.

"Are you okay? You don't look well at all," I asked as I looked at him closely.

"It must have been the long flight. I just need a bit of rest."

He seemed lethargic. He was fit, swimming at least an hour every day and he put in time in the gym. A simple flight wouldn't have him in this condition.

As we sat on the ferry to the resort, I wondered what had him so fragile and tense. He wouldn't say much, only nodding his head when he thought it was appropriate. We checked in and were led to The Royal Estate. I was astounded by its beauty, a mansion-sized modern villa right by the beach, so private and magnificent. I was speechless and impressed as I took it all in. The butler and some maids brought in our luggage and unpacked it for us in the palatial grand master suite. While I was talking to the chef, and discussing our preferences, a doctor came out to see Michael; they spoke alone for a while, then he left. I went in to see Michael, who was still looking worse for wear.

"He says it's dehydration. He left me some electrolytes and ordered me to drink plenty of liquids," he said, still looking green and avoiding eye contact.

"Hmm, really? We need to get a second opinion because you look like death warmed up, and I don't like this green colour." I was worried. How could he have become so ill, so quickly?

"Do I look that terrible? That won't be necessary. I'll drink lots and maybe after a good night's rest I'll feel better." He tried to convince me. But if he was still this way in the morning, we would be flying back to LA.

"Right, but I'm running you a bath."

He begrudgingly got into a bath, and while he was in there, he drank a litre of his electrolytes. We ate a light meal where he remained quiet and straight afterwards went to sleep as it was night-time.

I woke up just before sunrise to a cold bed. I sat up in bed and instinctively looked around the room for his camera, and I found it gone. I was pleased; glad he was well enough to go out and take photographs of the sunrise. I knew he would take photos of me once I joined him, so I made myself presentable, wearing the blue swimsuit, which had quickly become his favourite, and found a coverall to keep warm in the early morning. He was right about packing for me. In my closet, he had easily found everything that suited where we were.

I opened the double doors to the beach, and I was greeted by clean, fresh air. I made my way to the private and secluded beach and saw Michael sitting on a boulder, looking out at the ocean as the sun tried to push through the darkness. I loved the tranquillity at this time of the morning. Around him were at least twenty flame lit torches, a blanket, and a sea of red rose petals blanketing the private beach.

"What's all this, Michael? Do you feel better?" Why would he wake up so early to set up some photography set? He was really unwell, and I was worried about him all over again.

"I'm glad you woke up. I couldn't wait anymore." He inhaled deeply. I had never seen him act this strange.

He led me onto the blanket and fell onto one knee. "Sofia, ever since we met, I knew you were special, and the more time I spend with you, the more I realise I can never live this life without you by my side. I brought you here to ask you, convince you, and even beg you to be my wife," he said as he held his breath.

"Michael, I don't know what to say. Everything is so beautiful and perfect." I could never have imagined this. Somehow, my breathing remained steady, but I was now shaking and surprised. I couldn't speak. This was really happening.

"Say yes, Sofia, please."

My eyes opened wider as I took in what I later found out was a four carat cushion cut diamond ring.

"Yes, I will marry you, Michael."

As he exhaled, I said a silent final goodbye to Nolan.

I was on my knees, too, as we kissed and hugged, and I cried happy tears.

"You have made me so happy, Sofia. I was worried you would say no."

"Why would you even doubt that? Is that why you were ill? Oh no, you could have killed yourself."

"I was really worried, and I'd been carrying the ring around for months, never finding the right moment." He sounded relieved, and he looked like a huge weight lifted from his shoulders.

"Months? Since when?" This was a surprise. He had been thinking about marriage for months.

"Since we left the desert, I knew you were the woman I would spend the rest of my days with." He confessed with a sweet smile on his handsome face. I would be waking up to that face for the rest of my life.

"Well, this proposal was simply perfect; I loved it, and I love you. I can't wait to be your wife."

We kissed on the secluded Polynesian beach and made love over and over until the sun was high up.

As we showered off all the sand, in the beautiful outdoor shower, I couldn't stop looking at my ring.

"This ring is beautiful. I love it, and it's the perfect size. How did you do that?"

"After it had been made for you, it took a while for me to access your jewellery drawer. When I eventually did, I had it resized to fit one of your other rings, at the penthouse. When your parents gave me permission, I couldn't wait any longer."

"You asked my parents' permission? On your mystery lunch? So, they know?" she asked, as each piece of the puzzle fell into place for her.

"Yes, I did; it's respectful. I'm sure they would love to hear the news from you, but yes, they already know."

I kissed him again and again. He was thoughtful to involve them. They had worried about me for a long time, concerned I would never allow myself to be happy again.

"Now we just need to tell your family, Michael, and my friends, and yours, too. I want to shout from the rooftops that I'm happy. You make me happy." I was giddy. I was excited, and I couldn't contain it.

"I am too, but do you think we could just enjoy each other for a little while, while we are here? There's so much we can do, and I want to do it all with you."

Enjoy each other, we did. We made love late into the night and early mornings; we made good use of our personal chef. I already knew Michael loved to sail, surf, and snorkel. He was at home in the water and was so free without the worries of a billion-dollar company, if only for a little while. Even on a secluded island he still found a way to engage with the locals and take photographs. He was energetic and full of life and vitality, telling anyone who would listen that I had agreed to be his wife. I also found out his favourite subject to photograph was me, and when I looked back at his photographs, a lot of the time I was unaware he had been taking pictures of me.

"Michael, some of these photographs are too private to have on this camera. What if you lose it and it falls into the wrong hands? I would be so embarrassed." Michael was skilled, and his photographs made me look sexy and beautiful. *Was this how he saw me?*

"You're the most ravishing woman, and you're mine. No one will ever see them, but I'll remove them from the camera when we get home. Will that make you feel better?"

"Yes, it will."

Our time in Bora Bora ended too quickly, but this time there was no bittersweet parting or long goodbyes. We were leaving the island together to return home as a man and woman who had made a promise to marry. We would be returning to Seattle, as he needed to go into HQ after his absence. Brad was keeping everything under control and my father had been delegating less work to me.

When we arrived in Seattle, I realised how much I had missed it, and how much it felt like home. Michael went into HQ daily and I worked in his home office.

Chapter Twenty One

♥

Michael

It was only four in the morning, but I had to wake Sofia up and be the one to tell her the news before she found out from anybody else. My father had always warned me that this was a real possibility and there would be very little to be done to protect Sofia or anyone else in her orbit from the media firestorm which would ensue. A nondescript online publication had broken the story about the plane crash and Bianca's possible involvement in it. The story came with the sensationalism and all the ugliness that involved wealthy family sagas, so-called family secrets, and anything to make it palatable to the gossip hungry masses. Given the fact that Bianca had inherited billions of dollars from her own father, it made the story even more salacious. This was going to dredge up so much Sofia had worked through, but she needed to know.

I made her a cappuccino, hoping it would help soften the blow, and took it back to bed.

"Sofia, will you wake up, please?"

"Hmm, you're insatiable. I'll be up soon," she said sleepily.

"Sofia, I need to talk to you. It's important. Here, drink this," I said, with urgency.

She turned around and faced me, and in that moment, she was wide awake as she took in my facial expression.

"Has something happened?" Fear was written all over her face. I should have been more sensitive.

"The plane crash conspiracy theories are now a news story online, and they have named Bianca, among other things."

"Show me." She held out her shaking hand as tears filled her eyes.

She took my tablet and shook, reading it word for word. Brow creasing as she took it all in. "I need to talk to my mother. Her lawyers assured her this case was sealed." She broke out into a sweat. Her voice shook as she struggled to breathe.

"You need to breathe, Sofia; you're hyperventilating," I said as I breathed deeply with her.

"This is all my fault. I should never have involved Alex, and now both my parents' reputations are ruined. Ahh, dear god!" she cried out.

"This is not your fault. It's the fault of whoever is actually behind this, and that is the story. The actual who and why, which no one has been able to figure out yet."

"That's the bigger picture, I know, but both my parents will be eaten alive, cast out by their friends, and I am sure Kingman Air will lose all integrity and all the business my father has spent years cultivating. I also need to contact Nolan's family. They knew some of what was happening, but not every detail."

"I'm here to help, in any way I can, but remember the media hysteria will pass. This is how these companies make their money. Try to not let anything in the news upset you because this has the potential to get messy," I said, trying to preempt what could happen.

The first forty-eight hours after the story broke online were the most gruesome. Bianca maintained a dignified silence, even in the midst of the worst journalism I had ever witnessed. My relationship with Sofia and our impending marriage became gossip fodder, as my past relationships and some non-relationships were dissected and analysed. Old, really old photographs taken of me with women were dredged up from the confines of past history, and Sofia was embarrassed and humiliated as I was called all manner of unsavoury names. Our news outlets reported, in a different tone, to the rest of the media corporations. We maintained neutrality and didn't speculate nor provide any commentary that wasn't fact.

Nolan's sister was a different story. She agreed to a television interview and ripped Sofia to shreds. She discussed everything from her relentless work ethic, which she claimed had not spilled into motherhood. She described Sofia as having abandoned her children at home to jet all over the world at her father's behest, to how she had quickly moved on to a wealthy man to finance her love for the finer things. Sofia was devastated; I was livid. This had to end.

We were both at home, as the media frenzy was too much to venture out. Sofia was subdued and hurt, but we did everything we could to stay upbeat. On the eighth day after the story broke, Alex Mcvie contacted Sofia. He wanted to talk, but she wasn't interested in talking to him. She mistakenly blamed Alex's involvement in what had resulted. I told him I would speak to him and invited him to HQ, which he refused; he didn't want to be seen anywhere near this story, as he needed to maintain his privacy for his work, which was a legitimate reason. Instead, we met at a disused factory downtown.

"Hi Alex, I'm Michael." I sized him up, trying to see anything that he and Sofia could possibly have in common. He wore a wedding band, but that didn't tell me much about his character. I couldn't read him. Maybe this benign persona was his best asset as whatever type of spy he was.

"Michael, I am so sorry for what's happening to Sofia, her family, and yours; it's terrible." He sounded sincere, but platitudes come easily to some.

"Thanks, Alex. I need to get back to her. What have you got?"

"This just becomes more complex. The communications with the mercenaries came from an IP address at Kingman Air, specifically from the offices of Ross Kingman."

"In your line of work, do mercenaries communicate via email so openly? And why would Ross orchestrate the downing of his own plane? Even if he had no regard for human life, that's his business, which he built himself."

"I have to admit, this has been very strange right from the beginning. So a friend and I kept digging until we looked closely at the bank transfer. It was made from this IP address, belonging to Penelope Warner."

I drew a blank as I didn't know Penelope Warner. "Do you know who that is?"

"Yes, it's Ross Kingman's Personal Assistant." My stomach dropped, and my mind raced as the pieces of this inconceivable puzzle started to come together. She was someone close with intimate knowledge of the family and the airline.

"What, Penny! Alex, last time it was Bianca. This time, it's Penny. What is her motive?" I tried to reason.

"I can only provide you with evidence. I don't know. Perhaps you can ask Sofia." He spoke gently.

"No, I'm not asking Sofia anything. She is in no condition to deal with this convoluted mess. I can't take this back to her; I'll look into it myself."

"How? You are too visible and too close to remain objective."

"Leave that to me; I'll find a way," I said, striding past him.

I left Alex; I had to go back to Sofia. I had left her with Marianne, but I couldn't be gone for too long. I made a call and even told him to use my plane. This was time sensitive, and it had to end.

When I got back home, Sofia was slumped at the banquette with a bowl of soup in front of her; Marianne could get anyone to eat. She had stopped short of spoon-feeding me after Vivian had called off our engagement.

"Hi."

"Michael, I need to see my mother today. I don't know if her heart can take all this. I need to be with her," she said with tears in her eyes.

"I can't look after you when you're not here with me," I protested.

"My mum needs me, and I need to know she's okay. My father, too."

"Ok, what time do you want to leave?" I didn't want her to go anywhere. Her vulnerability made me want her as close to me as possible.

"Whenever I can get there. I have my plane waiting now. Brad organised it."

"I see, I'm not happy about this. I'll drive you to Boeing Field."

"I don't want to leave either, but I need to." She quickly glanced away, although I had already seen the tears brimming at her eyelids. This needed to stop. I needed her free from this.

Chapter Twenty Two

♥

Sofia

Leaving Michael was difficult, but I needed to breathe, so did he. The whole situation was suffocating us both, and I needed to think. Brad was waiting for me when I landed, and this was all very discreet until I arrived at my apartment besieged by reporters. Brad continued on to my parents' home, which was much worse. They were ensconced by the large walls and gates, so once inside the walls, it was peaceful. I arrived to find my parents sitting together mindlessly watching television.

"Sofia, you're here. Oh, my baby. I'm sorry for what you're going through again."

I couldn't help it, and I broke down crying. This whole situation had turned me into an emotional mess.

"I'm okay, Mum. I was more worried about you."

"I'm fine. Everybody who needs to, knows the truth. I'm just angry about all the viciousness on the television. I can't believe Nina could be so deceitful, even after you and I spoke to her only a month ago and explained everything."

"Bianca, let Sofia sit down. How are you?" Dad said, getting up and giving me a warm hug. Then, he sat me down next to Mum.

"I was missing you and Mum, and I just had to see you."

"Thank you for coming, and congratulations on the engagement. When you and Michael are feeling up to it, we need to celebrate."

"Thanks, Dad. I was happy, for a while, until this happened."

"It will blow over. Will you excuse me for a minute? I have a call I need to take," he said, as he left the room.

I moved closer to Mum and laid my head on her shoulder.

"How are you really?"

"It's all hurtful, Mum. Everything; my love for my children being questioned. Hearing that I am with Michael for his money; you are accused of something you didn't do, even small things like parading all of Michael's past conquests on the television. I've never been so humiliated in my life."

"Where there is a story, they really dig in. Your father and I had hoped to keep everything quiet, but they found it."

"I hope you haven't lost friends over this, Mum."

"It's at times like these when you know who your real friends are, and there are not as many as I would have liked, but I know our family will come out stronger at the end of this."

"I hope so too, but that's awful to hear about your friends. Although, I did know some of your friends were a little spineless."

Mum laughed a deep and genuine laugh, one I hadn't heard in a long time. "You're absolutely right."

"What was so funny? What have I missed?" Dad said, as he came back into the living room.

"The obvious, Ross. My spineless friends."

"Oh, those, you've had them for years." We all laughed.

"Dad, how is work?"

"Bookings are low, but we haven't lost any routes for the time being. We are just not landing anywhere in Guatemala. You needn't worry about this."

"Have I been dismissed from my job?"

"Of course not. You have a lot on your plate, and work shouldn't be one of them."

"Thank you, but I love Kingman too."

"Shall we have dinner? Martha left something for us in the oven."

"I'm not hungry."

"You will come and watch us eat, anyway. You came all this way to be with us," Mum said as she stood up and held out her hand to me.

The three of us walked together into the kitchen.

Spending time with my parents was therapeutic. They were calm and took everything in stride. That was until three days later, when Michael arrived with his private investigator. I knew this was big. Michael was cordial, but business-like, trying to keep some distance from what the investigator was about to tell us.

"I am sorry, Ross and Bianca, for the information which has been brought to light. This will at best exonerate you, Bianca, but it's difficult information."

This was huge, new information which would help my mother. I wish Michael would have told me first to put me out of my misery.

"Shall I get my lawyers to come over?"

"Yes, Bianca, that's a good idea."

The lawyers didn't take long to arrive, and as soon as they sat down, the investigator started to speak and was very matter-of-fact.

"The information I have points to Penelope Warner as the one who has transferred funds to the organisation. Mr Masterson wanted as much information as possible before bringing this to you."

"What! Penny? Why would she do that, and how does she have that kind of access, Dad?"

Was *this what Mum meant about Penny? Was she really involved with my father?* The thought made me sick to my stomach.

The investigator didn't let the interruption deter him from his delivery. "Mr Kingman, this is a birth certificate I have found. Even though it says father is unknown, there is a paternity test which was conducted at this lab fifteen years ago, confirming you as a paternal match for this child, Penelope Warner's son."

I looked at Mum. She didn't bat an eyelid, as if she already knew. I wasn't entirely surprised Dad had fathered a child with Penny, as Mum had alluded to some type of indiscretion when I saw her after her heart attack.

"I don't know anything about this!" Dad barked.

"Dad, let's all try to keep calm so he can finish. Michael already said this will be difficult. We can discuss this when we have all the information. Continue, please." I was determined to hear what Penny had to do with the plane crash.

"Penny Walker has been receiving a yearly sum of half a million from this account. It's another subsidiary belonging to Mrs Kingman's late father."

Realisation dawned on my father's face, then both he and my mother looked at each other, and I could see the understanding in their eyes. I was the only one who now didn't know what was going on. Michael took my hand in his, and that was comforting.

"I have some gaps in my information, and I apologise, but on this date and in this location here, which I suspect might be in her office, Penny was able to access banking details for this company, which she used to transfer the funds. Penny's brother lives in Colombia, where this group is most active, and his wife is a distant relation of the leader who is referred to as The General. It is my understanding that he may have been the middleman responsible for organising the attack, while Penny financed it using the funds from Mrs Kingman's company bank account."

After he finished speaking and producing reams and reams of paperwork, which he handed to Mum's lawyers, Michael stood up and walked him out.

"Mum, Dad, do you know what that was? Do I have a brother? Did his mother orchestrate my children's deaths? What is going on here?" I was in a daze, and my mouth was suddenly dry.

"Sofia, will you let a husband talk to his wife in private? I will tell you everything after I have spoken to your mother." After all this, he expected me to leave so he could do damage control with his wife. I was livid.

"There's no need to excuse her from this conversation. She's a big girl, and this affects her, more so than it does us."

My father nodded silently and solemnly.

"Sofia, sixteen years ago when your grandfather died, and you were away at Thacher, I left your father and that was the biggest mistake of my life. I was grief stricken and miserable. The grief was unbearable, and I felt your father was to blame for how I felt." My mouth was ajar, and I was in disbelief.

"When she left, Penny was there for me in every way."

My mother then picked up from where my father left off. "When I returned, three months later, your father and I reconciled, as if nothing had ever happened. He forgave me for all I had done, and I did the same. What I didn't know was that Penny had fallen in love with your father and she was pregnant with his child."

"You knew about this child? What did you do, Bianca?" My father growled.

He really didn't know about Penny's son.

"If you remember, she asked you for some time away from work to go and look after her sick mother. I gave her some money. I told her never to tell you about the baby, and that I would look after him for as long as it was needed."

"You had no right, Bianca!" he thundered.

"I had every right! You are my husband, and I did it for our family!" she defended.

"So, why did you allow her to come back and work for me? She obviously didn't need the money."

"That was the worst mistake, Ross. I shouldn't have let that happen."

"Mum, Dad, not to minimise this nuclear bomb, but I still need to know how any of this is connected to the downing of Nolan's plane."

"Penny asked for more money, and for a while, I gave in until she demanded two million monthly, which I refused. Then she told me I would be sorry. I assumed this had something to do with your father, as it's no secret she is besotted with him. I never imagined she was homicidal, or this unhinged."

"Why didn't you tell me? We could have worked this out. No amount of money is worth what our family has been through." My father's shoulders sagged as he sat with his head in his hands in anguish.

I couldn't help myself as I wept silently on the floor. Michael returned to the room. He silently picked me up, took me to my room, and sat me on my bed.

"Thank you for everything. Do you think you could take me home? I don't want to be here anymore."

"I can do that. Do you need to pack anything?"

"No, I have everything I need," I said as I looked into his eyes, with tears glazing mine.

As we were leaving, we ran into my father coming to find me.

"Sofia, no words can make this right, but I need you to know that I'm so sorry about everything."

Despite being very eloquent, I was unusually silent and at a loss for words.

"Michael, thank you for looking out for my family. I'm in your debt."

"It's my family too, but right now, I'm taking Sofia home. I'll be in touch."

I gave my dad a hug and a kiss. "I love you, Dad."

"I love you, Sofia."

Chapter Twenty Three

Sofia

On the plane, I sat on Michael's lap all the way home. He whispered sweetly to me, and I was grateful for his care and attention. The car ride from Boeing Field was no different. I felt like I was the most important person in Michael's world. He was fully present, but I knew he had been neglectful of his work while he dedicated his time to help me.

After arriving back home and avoiding the few photographers lingering at the gates, I took a bath and felt some relief. The heat of the bath cleansed me, while the lavender scent filling the bathroom was soothing to my weeping soul. I was relieved I now had answers; however, I deeply felt the agony of knowing my family had died in vain and in a senseless act of misplaced retribution. Nolan had no idea that flight would be his last, and the twins were blissfully unaware of the horror they were to meet on that tarmac. This was all perpetrated by my only brother's mother. The woman I had worked alongside for years, and had trusted, she had betrayed me and our family in the worst way.

The secrets my parents had kept from me, and each other, informed how I was going to proceed in my own relationship with Michael. The halo I had always imagined above my father's head was suddenly not so bright. I felt anger during the moments my parents had been going back and forth about Penny. By the time I had left their home, I had already forgiven them. I didn't want the burden of carrying any anger or resentment towards either of them. I was enraged whenever I thought about Penny, and I didn't know what to do with those emotions.

After I had been in the bath for an hour, Michael came to find me.

"Are you feeling any better?"

"I feel clean, not sure about better. I think I will re-engage with my therapist. We had wrapped things up in Africa, but I need her help."

"Anything that helps you, I'm all for it. Are you feeling like company tomorrow? My mother wants to see you and Dad has been looking forward to meeting you."

"I want to see them, but I'm so humiliated with everything that's been said about me in the press. It's all been so exhausting, and I feel depleted. I've met Chris, and I know she knows me, but I don't think I can face your father, not yet anyway."

"Have a little faith. My dad has worked in the media all his life. If you should know something, he doesn't even watch, listen to, or read the news."

"He doesn't? The irony." I chuckled. I had to meet him sooner rather than later; I decided sooner was better than waiting.

"He's my hero, and the reason I'm me," he said resolutely.

"That's very convincing. How can I say no? But what shall we feed them?"

"Marianne will help with that, and don't worry, everything will be fine."

When we went to bed that night, there was burning and screaming in my dreams until Michael woke me up to tell me it was a bad dream, but I knew it wasn't just a dream. Everything in my dream had happened, and the burning flames, the heat, and the smell were as real in that dream as they had been on the day it had happened.

The next morning, after Michael left for work, I reconnected with my therapist and set up regular appointments. The events of the last fortnight had brought all the memories back with a vengeance. I felt as if I was right back at the beginning. I was a simmering pot of tension. My psyche had been macerated all over again. The only thing that seemed right in my world was Michael.

Even though I wasn't feeling like having company over, at six o'clock, David and Chris Masterson arrived to visit. Chris was her usual warm and charming self. David was quietly observant and very amusing.

"It's so lovely to meet you, Sofia. Congratulations on the engagement. We are happy for you both."

"Thank you. It's wonderful to meet you too, Mr Masterson."

"It's David; Mr Masterson makes me feel old."

"You're not old, David. Now, stop fishing for compliments. Sofia, you look beautiful as always."

I chuckled. "Thank you, Chris. It's lovely to see you again."

"So, have you been keeping busy? Show me your office, Sofia."

Chris wanted to get me alone, and I was pleased about that.

I took her downstairs to the wellness floor, where I had chosen a room looking out at the garden as my office. Once we got there, I turned around and smiled a weak smile. Tears glazed my eyes again, and I fought hard not to cry.

"Come here. Are you okay?"

As she hugged me, I felt genuine warmth, and I couldn't help but start sobbing.

"The media was so cruel to you last week. I was worried sick about you." She gave me another warm hug, which was most welcome.

"I was embarrassed and humiliated every time I turned on the television. I just had to stop watching."

"I'm so sorry, darling. What was the worst part?"

"All parts in equal measure. If I had to choose, it would be my sister-in-law's interview. Everything they said about my mother and that segment about Michael and his so-called 'harem'."

"Yes, all that was brutal, but you need to continue to hold your head up high and don't ever let them make you feel small."

"Easier said than done, but I'll try."

"You've already been through the worst thing that can happen, and you made it through. This is just a bump in the road. Don't worry about your parents; they will pull through. Is Michael looking after you well?"

"Yes, he's been wonderful."

"I'm happy to hear that."

We heard footsteps coming towards the office. "Dinner's ready. Are you ready to join us?"

"Of course, my darling son," Chris said as she gave him a warm smile. "Michael, hold on to Sofia. She's wonderful and I love her."

"I plan on it. I love her too," he said as he took my hand, and we all went upstairs to join David.

The rest of the week was calm; Penny's arrest and my mother's release from house arrest were simultaneous. It all made me ill. My brain was foggy, and I was constantly tired. My appetite was non-existent, no matter the delicacies Marianne offered. My only release was when

Michael came home from work, we would make love well into the early hours of the morning. I had never needed a man as much as I found myself craving his touch.

Chapter Twenty Four

♥

Michael

Sofia still wasn't herself after the whole media onslaught. She had been looking pale. Marianne and I both made sure she ate, but she only picked. I was worried about her as I needed to leave for New York on an overnight trip. I asked her to come with me, but she wasn't feeling up to it. Marianne had been coming in daily, so Sofia would at least eat something while I was away. I hadn't had much need to travel lately because I was now primarily based at HQ, but my father couldn't go on this trip and asked me to.

I left Sofia at home. I checked into the hotel and spent the rest of the day in endless meetings. As I sat through another mind numbing presentation, it became apparent that all this could have been done in Seattle and I willed the time to move quicker. I was missing Sofia and I wanted her in every way.

I even tried to call her before I turned in for the night, but she didn't answer, which was troubling. The next day, I found myself impatient and hurrying everything and everyone's presentations along. Excusing myself to make phone calls to her. I couldn't take it any longer and by midmorning, I had cancelled the rest of the day. As soon as a car was ready, I left the hotel for Teterboro Airport. My pilot made good time, and I arrived at Boeing Field within two hours.

An eerie silence greeted me when I arrived home. The blinds were drawn, and the house seemed empty. I looked for Sofia everywhere.

Could she have left? Had everything proved too much, and she decided she couldn't be with me anymore?

When I had left home things between us had been good. *What had changed her mind?*

I went upstairs to check if she had taken her things with her. This was where I found her in bed, fast asleep. I breathed a sigh of relief, and my body started to uncoil from the hours of built-up tension.

I woke her up gently. "Sofia, wake up, I'm home."

"Hmm, good morning."

"Good morning? It's just after one o'clock in the afternoon. Have you slept the day away?" I put my wrist against her forehead, and she didn't seem to be running a fever.

"One in the afternoon! How? Why didn't you call me?" she asked as she tried to sit up, but quickly closed her eyes.

"I did. Last night a few times, and again today. How long have you been asleep?"

"I'm not sure. I talked to Brad at four yesterday, and I felt so tired, I just went to sleep. Now my head's spinning." She rested back against the pillow.

"You've been asleep for nearly twenty-two hours straight! That's not right. Are you okay?" I was worried; this was unlike her. Even when she was going through everything with the media, she never slept into oblivion; she must be ill.

"I'm exhausted."

"Just exhausted?" I brushed her hair from her face and caressed her cheek. "I'll make you something to eat."

"That sounds good. I'll follow you down after I get dressed," she said as she laid her head on my palm.

"Ok, that's a good plan. Are you sure you can stand with your head spinning?"

"I think I can. I'll be down as soon as I'm dressed," she said, blowing me a kiss.

I made us an omelette and remembered that Marianne often visits her mother in her care facility on Fridays, which is why she wouldn't have come to the house today. When Sofia didn't come downstairs after half an hour, I went upstairs to investigate. I found her in the shower, asleep. I woke her up again, helped her get dressed, and finally she was able to stay awake and eat.

While she was eating, I called my doctor and told him I was on my way in with Sofia. She was adamant that all she needed was sleep, but I promised her she could sleep in the car.

I drove her car, one of my many gifts to her, as it was more spacious. We arrived at the clinic where Sofia answered a million questions; the usual rigmarole. Blood work was done, and the nurse took Sofia's urine away.

We waited for a while until the doctor called us back into his office. "Sofia, how long have you been feeling this way?"

"Weeks now, but a lot of things have been going on, so I'm not sure when exactly this all started."

"I see, well we are still waiting for your blood test results, but I have one test we have a result for, and I'm pleased to tell you you're pregnant."

"What? Really? How?" She immediately sat up and looked at me, with a million questions on her face. I smiled at her and took her hand in mine.

He gave her an indulgent smile. "I'm sure you know how, but did you miss any of your pills, or were you physically ill in the last few weeks? That may explain it if you have been absolutely careful with them."

"Well, no, I haven't been ill," she answered, trying to remember.

"I'll find out if our obstetrician, Dr Smyth, is still here, so you can get a few more answers before you leave."

He stepped out of the room.

"Oh my God, Michael, is this ok?" she asked animatedly, as she suddenly got a burst of energy.

"Of course, it's ok. This is the best news ever. Come here." I hugged and kissed her. She had made me a happy man.

She was still in disbelief when the doctor returned. I was stunned too. I was ready, and I wanted this for us.

Was Sofia ready, or would the grief take a hold of her again? I wondered.

"You're in luck. Our obstetrician is still here. She can check on you and make sure the baby is growing well. You can choose your own obstetrician later, if that's what you want."

We left the doctor's office and went into an exam room, where Sofia changed into a tissue paper gown. As she laid down on the exam table, the obstetrician arrived. She explained that if it was too early and we couldn't see clearly, she would need to do an internal scan with an ominous-looking instrument. Then the scan began. Dr Smyth didn't say much to begin with as she worked. After a while, she turned a knob, and the room was filled with the sounds of a heartbeat. Sofia cracked, and tears streamed down her face. This was bitter-sweet for her, yet the best day of my life.

"Now, by my measurements, this looks like you're fourteen weeks along. You've done very well."

"Fourteen weeks? That's three and a half months. Oh no, I've drunk wine, and I have been flying, and exercising. Just doing everything I shouldn't have," she said as her words trailed off. She was in a daze.

What could be so wrong with flying and exercise? What else shouldn't she have been doing? I needed to read the books.

"Yes, it's three and a half months, but you didn't know. I will prescribe you some vitamins, and that exercise, keep it up, but in moderation."

We were both trying to remember how and when this happened. Dr Smyth finished all her checks. She told us the baby was a little small for her expectations at fourteen weeks, and we should make an appointment to see her again in the next week if we wanted to proceed with her as our obstetrician.

We left the doctor's office and went home. We both laid down on Sophia's favourite couch, the soft crescent shaped one. She was just as tired as before, but this time, she was much happier. She was back in my arms where she belonged, and she was growing our baby inside her.

"Sofia, how are you feeling about all this?" I kissed her softly, reverently.

"I'm so happy; it's a miracle."

"Do you have any idea when and how this happened?" I put my hand where I suspected the baby was. I had an overwhelming need to protect them both.

She smiled sadly. "Yes, I do. In Bumi Hills."

The irony of it wasn't lost on me. While she had been grieving her children, we had managed to make another. I also remembered she cried and slept for three days straight and had not eaten or drank much, not even taken her pill.

"You have made me the happiest man. I've always known that this is what I want for us. Do you want to go out and celebrate?"

"I don't think I could. I'm too tired. I could sleep until next week."

"Not to worry. We'll stay in and celebrate. Is that ok with a baby in there?"

"Of course, it's ok. You would almost certainly perish from need otherwise." She giggled.

"You're probably right."

I picked her up and carried her upstairs, where we celebrated again and again, before she fell asleep. Her need for me wasn't diminished, only stopping, as she couldn't keep her eyes anymore.

The weekend spent with Sofia was quiet. After breakfast in bed on Sunday, Sofia announced the next weekend's plan.

"I want to avoid flying at the moment, but I need to see Mum and Dad to tell them about the baby. I'll invite them to come out next weekend."

"That's perfect. Would they want to stay in the guesthouse?"

"They would love it. Perhaps we could get both sets of parents together and tell them the happy news then." All I had ever wanted was to see Sofia happy, and now she was.

"I love that idea and sometime this week, we could have my brother and the girls over, just for a few hours, after they finish up at kindergarten so you can meet them. What do you think?" I asked expectantly. The girls were important to me, and I had wanted Sofia to meet them for a while.

"Of course, I would love to meet them. How about his wife?" she asked with her eyebrows raised in question.

"Things are a little complicated between them. She's left him and the girls. She won't be making an appearance."

"Oh, do you know what the issue is?" she gasped, genuinely shocked.

"No, Miles was too upset to get into it with me."

"That's a shame. The girls must be missing her."

"Yes. Now that we know who's coming when, I need to tell you something."

"What's that?" She smiled expectantly.

"I love you, and I love our baby."

I lowered my lips towards her, coaxing her lips, and she kissed me back with a kiss so hungry it set my body alight. Our kisses turned desperate and even though she had been exhausted, Sofia became more insatiable than ever, and I was the beneficiary. She straddled me and when we connected, she wouldn't stop, even when I begged her to slow down.

I don't know how I had missed that she was pregnant with the now glaringly obvious changes to her body. Her breasts had become fuller; more than a handful; her nipples were so much darker and beckoned to me with every bounce. She had always been ready, slippery, and soft for me. I had been immersing myself inch by inch into what felt like wet moist velvet, and try as I might, I couldn't help but release all I had deep in her, much too soon. That didn't seem to matter to her, as she would wake me up what felt like only minutes later, begging me to please her again.

I worked from my home office for the rest of the week, as I couldn't bear to leave her at home alone.

Chapter Twenty Five

♥

Sofia

I was having a baby. I wanted to chide myself for being so irresponsible in Bumi Hills, but this was happy news and a pleasant surprise. Michael was just as overjoyed; this baby was already so loved. I couldn't wait to tell my parents, who had been pleased about the invitation to come and visit us for the weekend. Michael had the guesthouse redecorated with tones and furniture mimicking the main residence, and his designer had also done some sketches for the nursery. We discussed a bespoke crib which we commissioned, and I asked Michael for some baby friendly wildlife photographs.

My parents arrived at Boeing Field on Friday. When they arrived, they went to the guesthouse and freshened up for dinner. They returned to the main residence just as Michael's parents were arriving. Introductions were made and everyone fell into easy conversation. This baby already had a loving family.

"Michael, this is a lovely home you have," Mum said.

We sat around the dinner table, tucked into dessert after dinner prepared by Chris' chef. I enjoyed dinner, but adrenaline was coursing through me. All I wanted to do was share the happy news with everyone.

"Thank you, Bianca, but you know I have a roommate now, so it's her home too."

They all laughed.

"Speaking of which, the reason Michael and I asked you over is because we have some news to share with you."

They all quietened down and looked at us expectantly. My parents and David wore blank expressions, but Chris smiled at Michael knowingly.

Did she already know? I wondered.

"Sofia and I are having a baby." He declared proudly, with a glimmer of tears in his eyes as he looked at me and held out his hand for mine.

Instantly tears filled my mother's eyes, and my father was just as overcome with emotion. For a split second, I wondered how much longer my previous life would continue to overshadow my current one.

"These are happy tears. I never imagined I would be a grandfather again. Congratulations to you both," my father said as he came round the table to kiss me.

My mother was too overcome with emotion to speak.

Chris spoke up. "Bianca, why don't I show you the lake so we can both get some air? This is too much excitement for two grandmothers waiting." She said in a conspiratorial tone.

My mother stood quietly, and I made to stand up to follow when Michael shook his head surreptitiously. It was best Chris was with her, as I would have started crying too.

David was quick to fill the silence. "So, when will the baby be here, Sofia?"

"We are fifteen weeks along, so another twenty-five weeks," I told him, still excited about the news despite the awkwardness with my parents.

My father silently observed me and Michael, beaming. At one point, he looked away from the table and wiped an errant tear from his cheek.

"That will fly by. I have never understood why it's all measured in weeks and not months."

"It's just to confuse the hapless men, Dad," Michael answered with a shrug of his shoulders as he continued to hold my hand under the table.

After some more baby small talk, I went to find my mother and Chris. Chris had worked her magic on my mother, and they were now giggling like schoolgirls.

My mother stood up to hug me. "Sofia, I am so happy. I'm sorry I was so overcome and lost my composure. I hope I didn't embarrass you."

"No, I'm not embarrassed. We are all family."

"That's exactly what Chris said." The three of us sat in the atrium as we talked about all things babies. It had been so long since I had been this happy, save for when we got engaged. I sat and basked in it.

The next morning, Mum and I went shopping. Dad decided to tag along, but only lasted fifteen minutes before he found a hotel lounge to wait in. After two hours of intense retail therapy, both Mum and I were tired. Moreso Mum, as she still suffered the occasional shortness of breath. Some purchases would be delivered to the house, and some we were able to lumber with great difficulty. After collecting Dad from the Lotte Hotel Lounge, we returned home, where we attended an impromptu dinner party arranged by Chris and David.

The weekend flew by quickly and my parents left. Michael and I spent a lot of time together, he had his camera on him all the time, and we were both very happy. He spent too much on baby clothes, and even more on me. At the end of the week, Michael told me he had to return to Istanbul. He assured me he would be back home within three days, and I couldn't wait.

Chapter Twenty Six

♥

Michael

Leaving Sofia was one of the most difficult decisions I ever had to make. Although she was happy and looking forward to our baby, she was not as strong as she usually was. Her appetite was non-existent, and her weekly blood work showed she was severely anaemic. After consulting with Dr Smyth, who had become Sofia's obstetrician, we both decided that flying together to Istanbul wasn't a risk either of us wanted to take. She pleaded with me to find a different way to have this meeting, but I needed to be there to wrap up the assignment about the prison conditions, which I had been on when I had first met her.

Marianne was to come in daily and attend to her housekeeping duties. Much to Sofia's amusement, my mother's chef prepared a week's worth of meals, with the understanding of returning a week later to do the same if he was needed. I wouldn't be gone for more than three days; however, it was comforting.

On the day of my departure, we lingered in the kitchen. I didn't want to say goodbye. I walked her back to bed and didn't leave for another two hours, laying in bed with her. She didn't seem to want me to leave either, as she held onto me even as she slept. I left Sofia asleep in our bed with a note reminding her that I would be back home in seventy-two hours.

Travelling to Istanbul was simple. As this was work, I took the company jet and arrived there in record time. After checking into the hotel, I called Kaan Zehra; the prison warden. If I could spend a few hours in Istanbul and return home straight away, it would be an even better outcome. I called Sofia, and she was awake and sounding energetic.

"Did you arrive safely?"

"Yes, the journey was bearable, but I miss you already."

"Well, I have news!" she said, and as if it were possible, I imagined I could hear her smile through the phone.

"What news? I've been gone only eighteen hours, and you're already up to no good," I said lightheartedly.

"Today has been the best day. I've felt the baby move!" The excitement in her voice was difficult to miss.

"What! You have? I should have been there with you. I can't believe I missed that."

"Yes, you should have been. I was so happy. Hurry home and you'll feel the baby, and other things too. I miss you so much."

"Don't be naughty; you know I want to feel you all the time. I can't wait to get back to you."

"You're the naughty one. What time's your meeting?"

"In twenty minutes, so I need to leave my suite now."

"Okay, don't be late. I love you."

"I love you too."

After that call, Kaan called me, and we decided to meet at a restaurant I knew well. It was frequented by tourists and close to where I was staying. I took my work bag with me and made my way there. I hadn't been waiting long when I saw him arrive. He sat down, retrieved the camera I had left with him, and he ordered three shots of Macallan.

Chapter Twenty Seven

Sofia

It had been a good day. I was about to sit down to my meal when the intrusive gate bell sounded on my phone. David's black Rolls Royce was at the gate. He didn't visit often, and this was unexpected.

Why would he be here when he knew that Michael was overseas?

His driver spoke into the intercom, and I let them in. I was waiting at the front door for David when I noticed Chris was also with him. They both didn't look right, and a feeling of foreboding and doom washed over me. My mind raced to the worst place. I couldn't believe this could be happening to me again. I sat down on the front step; my knees were suddenly weak, and my legs couldn't carry my weight. My mouth was dry, and my heart felt as though it would leap out of my chest.

As they ascended the few steps to the entryway, I could see the look of a mother in anguish. They both got to the door at the same time and assisted me to stand up and move into the house.

"Please, just say it. Tell me what has happened. Please." I heard my voice break.

Chris looked at me as tears streamed down her face. She had been crying. Her eyes were bloodshot, her lips quivering, and the pulse in her neck was visible and so fast. She couldn't bring herself to speak.

"Sofia, will you look at me, please?" I pulled my eyes from Chris to look at David, who was just as worse for wear as Chris was. "There's been an incident at a restaurant where Michael was, and he's not awake."

Why won't David say what he means? I'm not a child.

"What do you mean, not awake? Is he asleep or is he dead? What kind of incident?"

"He's unconscious with a head injury. We're not sure yet what has happened, but there seems to have been some kind of explosion."

"Oh my God, this can't be happening. Oh no, no, no, no, noooo. We need to get to him straight away." There was a tightness in my chest, and the bile rose right to the back of my throat. I swallowed the bitterness down, then the tears started to run down my face. I felt dizzy and saw the shining lights in my vision. David held me up as he spoke softly to me.

"We have the jet at Boeing Field. You need to be ready to leave in ten minutes. Do you think you can do that?"

I couldn't speak, but I nodded my head. I didn't feel like I owned my body.

How could this be happening again, in one lifetime, my own.

I went upstairs and threw clothes haphazardly in a bag. I remembered all my medication and threw that in the bag, too. I had the presence of mind to pack a bag for Michael, although I wasn't sure if he was in any condition to be wearing any clothes, or if he even needed them. Within ten minutes, I finished packing. I put the bags in the internal elevator, and I took the stairs. David and his driver loaded them into the car while I got in and sat next to Chris, who I had never realised could be so hushed. We rode mutely as I quietly sobbed.

"You need to call your parents. Let them hear this from you," David said to me from the front seat.

I took my phone out, but my tears wouldn't let me see to make the call and my hands were slippery and trembling. Chris took the phone from me and pressed the call button.

My father answered on the first ring, as if he had been waiting for this dreadful phone call.

"Dad, are you with Mum?"

"Yes. We are out at dinner, is everything alright. You don't sound so good?"

"It's Michael. He was caught up in some kind of accident, but I'm not sure if he will be okay, or what else is going on. I don't know anything, and I'm so scared."

"We will be there soon. We will leave now," he said with urgency.

"He's not here with me. He's not in the country. I shouldn't have let him leave."

At that moment, all the pent-up emotions took over, and I was overcome. David took my phone from me and hurriedly explained to my father what he knew so far. In the background, for the second time in her life, my mother sounded hysterical. She had to calm down.

"I don't want her to have another heart attack," I whispered to Chris.

She held me quietly and let me cry. David hung up after promising to keep my parents informed.

We arrived at Boeing Field, and I suddenly remembered what Dr Smyth had told me about flying. She had assured me that ordinarily at seventeen weeks' gestation, one would be okay to fly, but her concerns were my iron levels, and how I had been prone to fainting.

Chris took my hand. "We have a doctor on the plane. His name is Francis, and he's a friend of David's. On the flight, he will be able to keep an eye on you."

"That's good. What is his specialty?"

"He is a trauma surgeon," she replied quietly.

"Oh no, is Michael in a really bad way?" I cried out. I couldn't take the not knowing, and my body slumped in the seat of the G700.

"We don't know. We wanted to be prepared for any eventualities, so he's here to help with anything."

"You said he had a head injury. Wouldn't a neurosurgeon be the best?"

"None of David's friends are that clever," she said, offering a weak smile through her own tears.

We shared that light moment, and I knew it could be the last smile we would share for a while.

The flight to Istanbul was a difficult and long one. I wanted to comfort Chris, but I had no words. I suspected I knew how she felt as a mother. I willed the jet to speed up, so I could get to his bedside and hold him close. I felt helpless, but I was hopeful. Unconsciousness was better than death.

As I wallowed in my self-pity, I heard a commotion at the front of the plane where David was sitting, and my heart and head filled with dread. I couldn't make out the words, but I had to get closer to hear why David was so enraged.

"Miles, buy those news outlets if you must. I don't want any videos or photographs of Michael circulating anywhere. He has a child on the way, and my grandchild will not see pictures of their father in that way."

This took me straight back to the week from hell, where mine and my family's lives were paraded on television for the world's entertainment. I couldn't help breaking down in tears again.

"What sort of pictures, David? Who would do that?" I asked, wheezing and sobbing. How could I still have so many tears in this lifetime?

"Journalists without scruples, but I'll keep them from seeing the light of day."

"But how?"

"Money. I don't want you upsetting yourself with this part. I'll handle it, so will Miles. He's the best at what he does."

I'd only met Miles in the last week; he was a broken man after his wife left him. How could he be strong enough to deal with what David was talking about?

I went back next to Chris and sat down. She appeared calm, but the anguish on her face was still so visible. I held her hand the rest of the flight. Its purpose was twofold; it comforted her, and it also grounded me.

After the jet landed, we were driven to the American Hospital in Istanbul, where it was mayhem. There had been a lot of presentations to the Emergency Department, and many others all over the city. Due to what we were learning might have been a suicide bomber in the restaurant. Francis suddenly looked at home in the Emergency Department, where he asked to see Michael immediately. Michael had been transferred upstairs to the Intensive Care Unit. I grew more nervous as we rode in the elevator, nearing the ICU.

Once we arrived in the ICU, it was only marginally less chaotic than the Emergency Department. They had stationed a patient liaison officer to meet, greet, and vet visitors. Due to the high-profile nature of the incident, it was important to protect the privacy and dignity of the patients; we were told. Chris and David were immediately allowed to see Michael. While Francis's credentials were checked, I was shown to a private waiting room. This waiting took me back to when my mother had the heart attack only weeks before.

Was this really happening? Would this run of bad luck ever end?

While I was sitting there, Francis came to find me with a bowl of soup and some bread.

"Sofia, this is the best I can do under the circumstances, but you need to eat. I'm not sure how long we will be here for, and it's important to look after yourself and the baby."

I didn't have much of an appetite, but Francis was right. I thanked him and took the tray, but I wouldn't be able to stomach any food, not until I saw Michael.

"What's going on?"

"Chris and David are in with Michael now, and they've paged his treating doctor so I can speak to him directly."

"When can I see him?" I asked nervously, wringing my hands.

"They have a strict privacy policy here at the moment, but I will speak to his doctor when he arrives to give us an update on Michael's condition and let him know it's important that you have access to him."

"Thank you."

"No need to thank me; Michael is like a son to me. I have known his parents since before he was even born. Both my wife and I are so happy that he now has you. He explained to us he had finally found the one he had been waiting for. My wife thought it sounded like poetry."

"He does seem to have a flair for the dramatic."

Francis was being kind, but I didn't have it in me to hold a conversation. I was fearful and uneasy about Michael's condition, and the more I sat in the waiting room, the more anxious I became.

As we were speaking, Michael's doctor arrived, followed by Chris and David. He introduced himself, as did the rest of us.

"Please forgive me if I come across as abrupt. I am going to speak directly. Mr Masterson was in a restaurant where we believe the bomb went off. I don't have much information about what exactly happened during that incident, but from the injuries he sustained, we can only surmise. As he didn't sustain any burns, it would seem he was launched into the air and out of a window. He has a severe head injury, which is why we have him in an induced coma. He has extreme swelling to the brain and what we are attempting to do by inducing the coma is buy time to allow for the swelling in his brain to reduce naturally.

In addition to the head injury, he has a fractured left clavicle, fractured ribs on the left, as well as the lacerations which you may have noticed. These we assume are from the window where he was launched out of. He's been examined by a plastic surgeon who has confirmed all lacerations are superficial and don't need any surgical intervention. An orthopaedic surgeon has also assessed him, and no surgical intervention is indicated. All his other tests and exams are of little consequence. Does he have any medical conditions to speak of?"

"No, he doesn't have any medical history. Doctor, when are you expecting to bring him out of the coma?" Chris asked in a less than confident tone.

"As soon as we are satisfied, the swelling on his brain has abated," he answered patiently.

"Do you know if there will be any residual effects from the brain injury after he wakes up?" David asked, his lips quivering.

"We can only tell once he is awake, and he is talking and communicating with us. It's difficult to say with certainty while he's still in this condition. I need to leave you, as you can imagine, I have many loved ones to speak to. I can talk again tomorrow after he has had twenty-four hours. Doctor, may we speak?" he said to Francis.

Francis followed him out of the waiting room, and I was left with Chris and David.

"How is he?" I asked as soon as his doctor had left.

"He's unconscious. He didn't respond to us, but he looked peaceful and comfortable. I don't think he knew we were with him by his bedside," Chris said softly, her voice shaking.

"So, he was breathing okay, and not in any pain?" I asked, a lone tear running down my cheek.

This time, David answered as tactfully as he possibly could. "He has a machine doing the breathing for him."

I broke down; I was upset that I hadn't seen him yet. I was tired from the long flight, and angry at the whole situation. I was finally happy again; I had been lucky enough to find true love for the second time, in one lifetime. We were getting married and would soon have a baby, but all this hung on a precarious tightrope.

Francis returned to the waiting room. "Sofia, you can see him, but with either Chris or David present. It's the policy in this hospital. I'm sorry."

"That's okay. I would like to see him now, please."

"David, I can't possibly go back in there, not now. Please take Sofia." Chris sobbed softly.

What horrors laid in Michael's room?

As David and I walked into Michael's room, I wasn't sure what to expect, but I knew it wouldn't be good. I walked into the room; my internal heat overwhelmed me, and I thought I would combust. The nausea was not far behind. Michael was unrecognisable. His face was swollen to twice its usual size, his eyes merely slits.

"David, are we sure this is Michael?" My shoulders slumped. My voice was weak, and so was I.

"It is. Look at his right wrist; that's a burn mark from a campfire in Africa when he was twelve."

I took his lifeless hand in mine and looked at his wrist. It was just as David had said, but I still didn't recognise him. He had cuts, lacerations, and the bruising had started to show all over his face, arms, and torso. I wasn't sure about the rest of his body, as he was covered with a sheet. I went closer and noticed some shards of glass still embedded in his lacerations. I ran my hands across his skin and felt the glass.

"He has glass in the lacerations. Will you call for a nurse? I need to help him. This must be uncomfortable." The nurses might be swamped with all that's happening, but he shouldn't be left in this state.

David walked out silently, and for the first time, I was alone with him.

"I'm here now and the baby and I need you to wake up. Please, Michael. We need you to wake up." I sat by his bedside and held his hand. He looked nothing like my handsome Michael, but he was in there.

David returned with the nurse.

"Did you call for me?" she asked gently.

"Yes, I did. I'm Sofia, Michael's fiancée. Thank you so much for looking after him. You're probably busy and haven't had a chance to do it yet, but he has bits of glass underneath his skin all over his body." My voice shook as I tried hard not to cry.

"He does?" she asked, wide eyed, taking his arm from underneath the sheet and running her hand across it. "I'm sorry we overlooked that. I'll remove them straight away."

"There's no need to apologise. You must be busy. I know my way around tweezers. If you give me a pair, I can do it for him now," I said, smiling weakly.

"I'll get you some now. I'm Isra, his nurse for today."

"Thank you Isra."

She returned with the tweezers, and I sat by Michael's bedside, removing them as carefully as I could. David sniffled at the far end of the room; after a while, he got up and left us.

I had heard somewhere that people in a coma could hear, so I proceeded to tell Michael about the flight, and some of the goings on he would have been interested in. After I had removed all the glass from his upper body, I checked both his legs, and he had a few shards which I removed. I ran both my hands across his skin until I was satisfied all the shards were gone. I sat with him for a little while longer, then I told him I was tired and had to leave him so we could both rest, but I promised to return to see him the next day.

I left his room and walked to the waiting room, where I found Chris waiting for me.

"Chris, why didn't you join me?"

"You needed time with Michael. I don't understand why you can't be alone with him, anyway. The whole reason you're in this predicament is because you had far too much alone time with him," she said as she pointed to my stomach. My laugh was half hearted.

"Did you remove all the glass? Michael is so lucky to have you" she said as she grabbed hold of my forearm.

"I think I got it all. It would be infuriating if he could feel it but couldn't move to do it himself. Can we go to his hotel room and get his things before anyone else gets to them?"

"That's a good idea. Do you know where he was staying?"

"Yes, where we first met; at the Raffles."

"You met here, in Istanbul?" Chris was surprised. Neither Michael nor I had mentioned it to her.

"Yes, but I wasn't in the right mind frame, and so rebuffed his advances." I smiled wistfully.

"You did? I would love to hear about that. I don't think he had ever heard the word 'no' until he met you." She chuckled as we made our way towards the elevator.

"I'll tell you all about it on our way to the hotel. If the hospital strict security measures are anything to go by, they won't let me in without you."

Chris and I took a car to the Raffles. The city was in chaos after the catastrophic bombing, but we eventually arrived. After showing her identification, Chris didn't have much trouble getting access to Michael's suite. It held his scent, even though he hadn't stayed there long. His bag remained unpacked, only his computer was charging at the desk; I suspect ready to upload his photographs. I packed that away and checked the rest of the rooms; although it was obvious he hadn't planned on staying long.

We were driven to the property where we would be staying while we waited for Michael to wake up. Francis and David were already there.

"How is he?" Francis asked, pushing back his hair, worry etched on his face.

"Unrecognisable, and I felt so hopeless and helpless seeing him that way. Do you think he's getting the best care there, Francis?"

"I believe he is. His doctor seems quite competent, and the hospital he is in is internationally renowned."

"When do you think we could get him back to Seattle?"

"Practically speaking, on a Medi plane, he could go home at any time. I don't recommend that, as he is receiving a very high standard of care here. Today, we met his intensivist. Tomorrow, we meet the neurosurgeon, and he'll be able to tell us more. If you or Michael's parents are doubtful about the plan, then we can start the process of repatriation."

"It really helps that you're here. You really help to put everything into perspective."

"That's okay. I'm here to help. Before you get something to eat, I just need to check and make sure you're ok. Would you let me do that? Today has been quite heavy for everyone, but especially for you."

"I feel alright, perhaps tomorrow?" I didn't want to be examined by Francis. He was a friend of David's and that alone was awkward. Michael was the patient, not me.

"That's okay."

"Sofia, let's eat something, shall we?" Chris encouraged as she stood up to go towards the kitchen.

We found some prepared meals in the warming drawers in the kitchen. I was grateful someone had organised a comfortable place to stay with chef-prepared meals in the midst of a terrible disaster. It was difficult to eat as I sat and imagined what must have happened to Michael for him to be injured the way he was. I didn't want to let my imagination run wild, but I thought the worst as I tried to stomach the food in front of me. It didn't taste like much.

Chris and I ate quietly for a while until she eventually spoke. "Are you thinking about getting Michael back home?"

"Not straight away, and definitely not without discussing it with you and David first. I think his recovery would be best in a familiar place, but Francis makes sense about not moving him while he's still so fragile."

"When I saw Michael, I couldn't bring myself to touch him, let alone move him. He seems so delicate at the moment. How have you thought so far into the future already?" Chris asked with a faraway look in her eyes.

"I'm comfortable with medical repatriation. I had to learn a lot about it as I developed that division from inception at Kingman. We have a fleet of Medi planes, and when we need to, we can get Michael home safely."

"I'm in awe of you all the time. I see why Michael fell in love with you. Let's get through tomorrow, and hear what the neurosurgeon's opinion is, then we will make up our minds about moving him." She was reassuring, and just for a second, my confidence in him getting better soared until my mind veered back to how he looked in his hospital bed.

"I agree. I'm tired now, and I think I will try and get some sleep."

"Good night. You know where I will be if you need anything," she said as we embraced. That went a long way.

"Thank you, Chris."

Chapter Twenty Eight

♥

Sofia

When I went up to my room, I unpacked and organised what little I had brought with me. I was tired but I couldn't sleep. I was worried and restless. Every time I closed my eyes, I kept seeing Michael so unrecognisable in his hospital bed. I was relieved he was alive, but only barely. I wanted him back, completely and absolutely. Hope was an empty vessel for the weak and desperate and, in that moment, I was both. I held on tightly to the hope that Michael would soon wake up, and also wake me up from yet another nightmare. Michael was his own man, yet still I was angry at myself for having allowed him to come here. I should have made him realise how ill I was, and how I needed him at home.

I managed to fall asleep for a few hours. The moment I woke up, I got myself ready to visit him. I couldn't wait for Chris or David; I had to be with him. I called Mum first and gave her the cliffs notes. I didn't get into too much detail as I worried about her heart. Then I sent Chris a message so she would know I had left already when she eventually woke up.

After packing some snacks, I called for a car and made my way to the hospital. It was only five o'clock in the morning, so the nursing staff were surprised to see me. By removing those glass shards from Michael last night, I had unwittingly ingratiated myself with the nursing staff. They bent the rules and let me see him without a fuss. I was led to Michael's room by his night nurse, and I sat next to him, holding his hand.

"Good morning. You're usually awake by five o'clock, but this time, I beat you to it. Did you sleep well? Are you dreaming? I think I only slept for ten minutes, and I dreamt of Bora Bora." I laid my head on his bed and spoke to him.

As I was talking, I drifted off to sleep despite the constant beep from his machine and the whooshing from the ventilator.

Isra, his nurse from last night, entered his room at seven o'clock and was genuinely pleased to see me. She wanted to freshen Michael up, and she asked if I wanted to help. I told her to give me whatever was needed to do that, and I would do it myself. Seeing him lifeless and unresponsive made me want to cry, but I kept the tears at bay and was strong for the both of us.

After Isra had been gone for twenty minutes, she returned with another nurse, and they helped each other to change his bedding, reposition him, and complete their nurse checks, as well as other nursing tasks, like emptying his urine bag while I waited outside his door. When they called me back in, I asked his nurse what could be done to bring the visible swelling down, and she offered me cool moist cloths to use on him.

At nine o'clock, Chris and David arrived, and both their faces lit up when they saw Michael.

"He looks different today; his face is less swollen." Chris smiled.

I was pleased when I heard that. I told myself the cool cloths were working; though, I could never be sure, especially since the swelling was mostly internal. I excused myself so they could spend some time with him. I went to the hospital café and ordered breakfast. Our baby hadn't moved again since the last time I had told Michael about it, but in my preoccupied state, I let it go.

I opened Michael's computer to catch up on the news. I found Michael's handsome face on every international news channel. In some reports, they had used our engagement photo, which the news outlets must have obtained from any one of our friends. We were happy and in love, and once more I prayed our love story wouldn't be cut short.

Sixty-nine people had died from the bomb blast, and one hundred and ten people were injured. Michael was the highest profile individual in that group, so he had become the story. Something which he would never have wanted. He would have wanted the fatalities, and the other victims' stories, to be heard by the world. I closed out the news feeds after I had started to see articles calling me the black widow.

Was this who I had become, and how the world perceived me?

If I had learned anything from Michael, it was to ignore the media's white noise, and that was what I decided to do. Instead, I found a folder with some of our photographs together and became lost in those for a while.

I bought all the muffins left in the cafeteria for the nurses in the ICU. They were working hard, and it was the least I could do. I returned to Michael's room just as his intensivist and neurosurgeon were arriving. They didn't bring much news. There had been no improvement overnight with Michael. The elevated intracranial pressure was unchanged, and it was a matter of waiting and patience.

They said they would return and reassess his condition in twelve hours, and if he hadn't improved, they would perform a ventriculostomy. A procedure that allowed the medical team to monitor the pressure as well as to help drain any excess fluid on his brain by inserting a tube into his skull. Meanwhile, they would also lower his body temperature as this neurosurgeon, in his practice as a doctor, had seen hypothermia helping to reduce swelling and speed up healing of the brain.

Francis then asked if surgery was an option to help relieve the pressure, if it wasn't decreasing any faster. They left Michael's room and had their discussions elsewhere. We were all subdued after that update. Chris and David suggested lunch, which I declined, opting to stay with Michael. When they left, I spoke to Michael, updating him on the current affairs — which I made sure didn't include him.

I also launched into our trip to Phil and Taryn's game reserve, and what I had been doing after he had left me there. By mid-afternoon, I was tired. I said my goodbyes to Michael and promised him to come back at night-time.

I returned to our base, ate a good meal, and fell asleep for a good six hours. I woke up to my phone ringing, and it was my father. He just arrived in Istanbul. We would meet at the hospital. As I was approaching the entrance, I saw my father's unmistakable tall frame. We embraced, and only then did I realise how much his presence meant to me. I felt renewed, and my spirits lifted; my father was my strength and had always been; how had I never not noticed this before?

"How are you?" he asked as he embraced me.

"I have no words, but I'm fine, I guess," I answered with a single shoulder shrug. "Everything is upsetting and overwhelming, and when I left earlier, there had been no improvement in his condition." I spoke softly, so he wouldn't catch the dejection in my voice.

"I'm sorry this is happening. Let's go inside and hear if anything has changed since you were last here." He took my hand and walked with me into the hospital.

We made our way to the ICU, where a weary Chris and David were in the waiting room. When my father arrived, they both got up and embraced him. Dad offered some words of comfort to both of them, and that set Chris off; she started crying again. Dad held her and let her cry in his arms.

"What's happening? Where's Francis?" I asked.

David was composed enough to give me an update. "The neurosurgeon consulted with his colleagues. He came back an hour ago and decided to proceed with the ventriculostomy. If there are no changes tomorrow morning when he returns, he will perform the surgery. Francis was allowed to observe," he said, and I saw what looked like a glimmer of hope from him.

"Alright, that's something." I wasn't sure whether to be hopeful or not. A tube in the brain didn't seem to be cause for celebration...

We all sat down. The ICU was much calmer today, and this waiting room had been designated as Michael's since he was an international patient. This really was a modern state-of-the-art hospital. It still smelled like cleaning products, but it wasn't as cold and sterile as expected.

"Who's Francis?" Dad asked.

"Francis is a friend of mine. He's a trauma surgeon who flew out with us to be with Michael," David said, as Chris sat with her head on my shoulder. She wasn't coping well today.

"That's very generous of him."

"Yes, it truly is."

"Dad, when Michael returns home, he will need to use one of the Medi planes."

"Of course. Have you told Brad?"

"Not yet; we don't know when he will be ready to return home," I answered with a heavy sigh.

"Still always five steps ahead." My father's encouragement still meant a lot to me.

"I feel useless and helpless. There's nothing to do but think."

As we were speaking in hushed tones, Francis walked into the waiting room and sat down. He seemed tired.

"The procedure went well. He will review him tomorrow and decide whether he will proceed with surgery or not."

"Thank you for being with Michael. This is my father, Ross Kingman."

"It's good to meet you, Ross. Thank you so much for coming to be with Sofia, and to see Michael; they both need you so much."

"Michael is important to our family, and my wife and I love him like he is our very own."

Michael was loved by whoever he met. He needed to get better, for all of us.

"Sofia, shall we go and see Michael now?" Chris said, as she broke out of her trance-like state and spoke quietly to me.

"Sure," I said, following her out of the waiting room.

As we walked into his room, my eyes were met with a now completely bald Michael. He had a thin tube in his head, attached to what looked like a drainage bag. He was worlds away from the Michael I knew. He seemed smaller, frailer, and much younger, as if he was regressing. It brought a fresh wave of tears to my eyes, which I managed to keep at bay.

"Isra told me you washed Michael this morning. Were they not doing it properly?" she asked, holding my arm.

"No, I wanted to. I like to think he would do it for me."

"Were you not afraid to touch him?"

"No, I made sure not to disturb the machines and not to get too close to any of his tubes. Are you afraid of touching him?" I looked at her and saw how torn apart she was.

This was not just about me.

"A little. I've never really been good with hospitals and illness. Even when his brother was sick, I didn't cope very well." Her vivacious and bubbly personality, replaced by a vulnerability, was painful to see.

"No one can ever be good with hospitals. All we can do is try. Will you give me your hand?" I said, holding mine out to her.

Chris gave me her hand, and I held Michael's. I joined their hands together, then I sat down.

"See, it still feels like Michael, only a little weaker."

"You're right. I don't know what I would do if I lost him, too."

"You need to tell him. He can hear you."

"You've been talking to him, too?" she asked in astonishment and mild amusement as she looked intently at him.

"Yes, he can hear us. He just can't talk back."

"You're sure about this?" she asked in disbelief.

"Yes, I am. I read about it somewhere, and that information has always stayed with me."

Chris sat and held Michael's hand for a while. Although she was in turmoil, she got to hold her son's hand. I never got to hold my sons' as they lost their innocent lives. I quickly shook myself out of that self pity mindset. I needed to stay in the present.

"You're just full of surprises. I'll go and get Ross so he can visit with you."

"Ok," I said as I blinked back unshed tears.

Dad came in a few minutes later, and he was at a loss for words. When I mustered the courage to look at him, I burst into tears. He held me while I cried and shook with everything in me. As he held me, I questioned how much more my father could take. Some two years ago, both he and I had been in this exact same position when he had personally flown out to get me and the remains of my family from San Marcos.

Chapter Twenty Nine

Sofia

We left Michael's room after a while, returned to the waiting room, and said our goodbyes. I took Dad to the Long Bar, where we had dinner. After Dad's car dropped me back at the hospital, I made myself comfortable next to Michael's bed. He still seemed so peaceful, and the whoosh and beeping from the machines was morbidly reassuring. It represented life — Michael's life — and the fact that I came so close to losing him, but he was still here with me. While I sat in the company of my own thoughts, I briefly thought about the lack of movement from the baby. I would organise a check during the daytime to make sure everything was well and to put my mind at ease. For tonight, all I wanted to do was focus on Michael.

I held his hand, occasionally drifting in and out of sleep. While sitting at his bedside, I developed some cramps in my stomach. It didn't seem unusual until I stood up to go to the bathroom and noticed the blood on the chair. When I got to the bathroom, I was horrified when I pulled my underwear down, and a gush of blood escaped from me onto the floor. This was when the worst pain suddenly spliced through my lower back and stomach. I gasped and tried to deep breathe, waiting for it to pass. I sat on the toilet seat, doubled over in pain, as I willed myself to be woken up from this nightmare within the original nightmare. The severe pain passed momentarily, and I was able to pull at the call bell in the bathroom. The night nurse arrived immediately, and she took in the pool of blood on the floor.

"What's this!" she exclaimed, looking at me.

"I think I might be losing my baby!" I wailed.

"Right, take some deep breaths and try to stay calm ok," she said reassuringly.

I was dizzy and terrified of passing out. She laid me down on the bathroom floor, put a pillow underneath my head, left the bathroom, and returned with a wheelchair.

"Ms Kingman, I have spoken to the obstetrician on-call, and he can see you straight away. Our orderly, Paul, will escort you to the maternity section. He is waiting outside this door. Is there anyone I can call on your behalf?"

"Thank you, but the person to call is already here laying in that bed," I said. My voice shook and tears streamed down my face.

As Paul wheeled me to the Maternity Department, I knew the baby was gone. There was just too much blood, and common sense told me to prepare myself for the bad news. The obstetrician was patient and very gentle in his manner. He kept calm as he examined me and attempted to school his features while he performed the scan; I wasn't fooled. I could tell he didn't have good news. This time, there was no knob turned up for me to hear the heartbeat and no hand holding with Michael.

He shook his head and told me he had failed to detect a heartbeat; the baby was gone. He asked me if I needed some time alone, which I refused. Time alone with my thoughts was not something I needed. I, as of late, had been having it in abundance.

He went on to offer options to remove what was left of our baby from my body. I opted for the surgery that could be done within the hour. This was so final, and I was devastated. The only link I had to Michael had been severed in the worst way while he was holding on for dear life by a very small thread. I felt so alone, and the hope I was holding onto slowly dwindled.

I was assisted into a hospital room of my own where I got ready for surgery. I made the dreaded phone call to my father, asking him to return to the hospital. When he arrived, and he was directed to my room, he knew what had happened without me needing to say a word. He held me for the second time that day as I cried for the loss of yet another child.

"Would you like me to call Chris and David?" He spoke quietly, shoulders sagged. He was trying to be strong, but I could see his despondency.

"Not now, let them rest. I'll see them in the morning. I don't think I'm ready for them to know about this. I just hope Michael won't hate me when he wakes up," I said, as I sobbed into my hands.

"He would never hate you. That's not who he is, and this wasn't within the realms of your control," he said, with his hand around my shoulder.

When I returned to my room after the surgery, I was a little groggy but relieved to see my father still waiting for me.

"How are you, sweetheart?" He spoke gently.

"A little sore and very sad."

"I'm so sorry, Sofia. I understand how much this hurts."

I then remembered that I was a twin, but my brother had been stillborn. My father walked in my shoes twenty-nine years ago.

"It's seven o'clock, Sofia. I've called Chris and David, and they're on their way in."

"Did you tell them everything?" I asked, my lips quivering and the lump in my throat getting bigger.

"Yes, darling, I did. I spoke to your mother, too. She's broken and upset that she can't be with you." I yearned for my mother, she would understand. I was missing her, and she's the one I was thinking about as my eyes grew heavy. I blinked them closed before they were filled with tears.

"You're here, Dad, and that means so much to me. Could I have some of that water, please? My throat feels so dry." I had to give him something to do, as he didn't know what to do with himself.

As he was pouring some water for me, Chris and David arrived looking quite forlorn.

"I'm so sorry this has happened," Chris said as she walked towards my bed.

I couldn't help the tears. Her kind words made the tears flow endlessly, and I couldn't contain the loud sobs coming from me. I was crying for my baby, for me and for Michael. I was crying for everything I was going through, and for the uncertainty of it all.

My father slipped out of the room. He had been on the brink of tears himself ever since he arrived a few hours before. He had to be strong for me, and I knew wherever he had slipped off to, he was shedding a few tears of his own.

David came closer and hugged me, too. Their pain was etched on both their faces, and the hopelessness of the situation was difficult to ignore.

"I'm sorry. I know you and Michael were so happy and excited about the baby," David said as he held me.

"We were, and Michael told me the day we found out we were expecting was the happiest day of his life. I couldn't even keep our baby safe until he woke up."

"You know this is hardly your fault, and I need you to stop blaming yourself for this. This was not within your control." David's tone took an authoritative note; it was hard to not pay attention.

"David, Sofia is not one of your employees, don't speak to her like that," Chris chided him.

"It's alright, Chris. I'm not offended." I couldn't help but laugh weakly as I dried my tears.

"I'm glad you think he's funny. David can be so bossy sometimes." Chris' mock upset was exactly the diversion I needed, even though it was only for a few minutes.

Dad then returned with the obstetrician behind him. "Good, you are awake. May I speak freely?"

"Yes, these are the grandparents, but I think the granddads need to get some coffee." The two dads had to go. I needed a semblance of privacy when I heard what the doctor had to say. Dad and David quickly left my room.

"The procedure went well, Sofia, but I'm afraid I don't have any answers as to why this happened."

"I understand," I told him as he continued.

"I would suggest you wait for one full monthly cycle before you try again. There is nothing to suggest that this will leave any long-term fertility problems." This was a relief, although it takes two to try again, and the other half of the equation was incapacitated.

"Thank you, for everything. You were so kind to me."

"I won't see you again, but I recommend you stay with us for another six hours for observations. If all is well, your nurse will discharge you. If not, she will give me a call, and I will return to see you." He left, and Chris left too straight afterwards.

After she left, I cried myself to sleep, something that I was becoming accustomed to again.

Chapter Thirty

Sofia

I woke up with a start eight hours later, confused and disoriented, until it all came back to me. Fresh tears rolled down my cheeks as I sat up in the hospital bed, deciding it was time to get up. My overnight bag was next to me. Francis had been right; this hospital was modern and state-of-the-art, with a clean and comfortable private bathroom. I washed away all traces of the surgery from me and got dressed, called for my nurse, and left a piece of my heart at the maternity wing in the American Hospital.

I made my way to Michael, where I would have expected comfort, but there would be none from him. I apologised for leaving him for so long, but I explained I had to have a check-up with a doctor. Even though he was unconscious, and his understanding dubious at best, I didn't have the heart to tell him about the loss of our baby while he was fighting to come back to life. As I was sitting at Michael's bedside, pondering life, David arrived.

"Sofia, it's good to see you up. You look well," he said with a smile.

"Thank you. I feel better after the rest. Are there any updates?" Even though I did my best impression of being upbeat, no one would be fooled.

"Yes, come through to the waiting room."

I followed him, and his neurosurgeon was there with our contingent.

"Hello Sofia, I am so sorry for your loss."

"Thank you. How's Michael today?" The focus needed to be on him. I was very much alive; he was barely holding on.

"The swelling has gone down remarkably, so we will now start to wean him off the sedative we have been administering continuously. This should allow him to start waking up naturally."

"How long will it take for him to wake up?" Chris asked with visible optimism. She had a sparkle in her eyes, which was welcome to see.

"It's difficult to give an exact time frame for that as it varies from patient to patient. I would expect him to start stirring in about six hours."

"When he wakes up, will he be in pain?" I had to know. I couldn't bear it if he was.

"He'll have a headache, some sensitivity to light, but don't worry we will keep the lights in his room dimmed. He will feel dizzy too, and may have some pain from his fractures. We will make sure he has enough pain medication. I must say, however, in the first twenty-four hours after he wakes up, my preference is that there is very little excitement for him. Please keep your questions to a minimum. Don't volunteer too much information to him unless he explicitly asks. Even though the swelling has gone down, his brain still needs to recover. It's best if he thinks for himself. Don't feed him information, so we can also assess what his brain function is like."

"That's a lot to take in, but yes, I think we all understand," David said as he looked around at us.

We all nodded and murmured in acknowledgement, then the neurosurgeon left.

Francis sat next to me. "I'm so sorry about the baby. You will miss this one, but it will get easier." I had heard this before; it doesn't get easier, but one learns to live with the pain.

"Thank you. That means a lot to me." I had to be polite; honesty was not what he was looking for from me.

"I wanted to add on to what the doctor said. When Michael wakes up, follow his lead, with regards to your life and his. Let him ask the questions, and don't be tempted to tell him everything at once. Imagine waking up from a hundred-day sleep on a different planet. I'll tell Chris and Dave the same, because all we want is for him to come back to us."

"I understand."

Would he still be the same man I knew a week ago? I had to stay optimistic. He was still alive.

He went and sat with Chris and David. I suspected to tell them what he had told me. The hundred-day sleep parallel was frightening. Dad came and sat beside me.

"It's good to see you up. Are you okay?"

"Yes, Dad, I feel much better, a little hungry. Have you eaten?"

"Perfect, I could eat."

We said our goodbyes and left the hospital campus.

"Thanks, Dad. It feels great to get out for a while and forget some little troubles."

"I hope you don't feel guilty about leaving Michael's bedside. You need to look after yourself as well. You've been through something difficult."

"I want to be there all the time, but I understand the importance of self-care."

"Good and stay in touch with your therapist. Your mother and I don't want to lose you to grief again." I hadn't spoken to my therapist since all this had happened with Michael. I had been so focused on him. I had forgotten to look after myself.

"You won't lose me, only as an employee. I can't come back to Kingman Air. I've been thinking about it. I used my job there as an emotional crutch for far too long, and it's time to do something I love."

"Like what, sweetheart?" he asked, beaming, as if he could read my mind.

"Photography. I should never have stopped, but I was just too sad to do that after the boys were gone, and I needed something challenging to keep my mind occupied and not think too much. Throwing myself into my job at Kingman did that, but it wasn't healthy. I enjoyed spending time with you and learning from you, but I'm ready to leave now."

"I'm happy you say that with conviction. You've done great work at Kingman, and I know you will do well at whatever you put your mind to."

"So, you're not upset? You were grooming me to be the next you."

He laughed and kissed my hand. "Only in the slightest, because I'm losing the best person I have. All I want is your happiness. Just promise me whatever happens here, you will go through with your photography plan."

"Definitely. I promise," I said, trying to smile through the pain.

After our meal, Dad returned to his hotel suite, and I returned to the hospital. I was looking forward to the next phase of Michael's recovery. When I arrived at the ICU, Chris was with Michael in his room.

"They have started weaning him off the sedative, but I don't see any changes with him yet," she said impatiently.

"I see they've removed the tube from his head?" I liked it. It made him look more like him. I missed him so much.

"Yes, that wasn't needed anymore. The worry was keeping it in for longer than necessary could introduce infection. Thank God you came back. The nurses are so excited for Michael Masterson to finally wake up. I think they want autographs."

I couldn't help the eye roll and the scoff. "Oh dear, whatever for?" Because he was *him*.

"I think you might be the only woman unaffected by Michael." Chris was oblivious. I'm his number one fan.

"I'm affected; he's my whole world," I replied, blinking back tears.

"I know you love him, it's obvious, but there's no swooning and eye fluttering, like he's probably used to. As a teenager, he loved being chased by girls, and he loved chasing them too, but swimming kept him busy. You know, he was a reserve on the Olympic swim team?"

"I know he loves to swim, but he never told me that." I was surprised.

How could he have never mentioned something so significant?

"Yes, he was. He has always been so focused and razor sharp. Everything he's achieved doesn't surprise me. Which is why I know he will come out of this," she said resolutely.

I let her have a moment as we sat in Michael's room for hours as we talked about him from her perspective. They always were close, and Michael was there for his mother when they lost his brother. He had never changed; he was still caring and thoughtful.

After hours of sitting in his room without any change, Chris was tired and decided to go home and get some sleep. I chose to stay, as I didn't want to miss Michael waking up. Morning came, and sixteen hours later, there was still no change in his consciousness, or lack of. His doctor didn't seem too worried when he came to visit on his rounds.

My father came to visit too and apologised as he needed to leave. I was happy for the time he had been able to take to come to Istanbul and to be there for me. Prior to leaving, he arranged for a Medi plane to return Michael home. It was already at an aerodrome close to the hospital on standby. Francis went to meet the crew and to make sure it had everything necessary for Michael's journey once it was confirmed that he was ready for repatriation.

On the fifth day of weaning Michael off his sedation, his arms and legs started moving involuntarily. On the sixth day, he finally opened his eyes momentarily and went back to sleep. On the seventh day, he was awake long enough for the tube to be removed from his throat, and he was breathing all by himself. He had a blank stare and didn't seem to recognise anything or anyone. On the eighth day, he maintained eye contact with Chris and smiled at her. He asked for water; the feeding tube passed through his nose was removed, but he wasn't able to hold the cup of water himself as he sipped through a straw. Not once did he acknowledge me. He wasn't speaking, but he followed Chris' movements with his beautiful eyes which I longed to have look at me, too.

On the tenth day, the neurologist updated us. "We have conducted numerous tests on Michael, and his brain function is normal. We are not sure when he will start to speak or start moving around. This is the stage where we would recommend a rehabilitation centre. However, we know you want to get him back home. I can authorise you to take him home, but straight to an inpatient neuro rehab facility, as he still has a long way to go on his recovery journey."

Chris and David were happy and relieved. This was anticlimactic for me. I pretended to share in this elation, but internally, I was screaming in anger and frustration.

Was I that forgettable? Was what we shared too insignificant to remember that his brain had decided not to bother? If he never remembered me, or us, then would we cease to be?

After waiting days for Michael to wake up, he was awake, but he wasn't Michael; not the one I knew, anyway. He recognised his mother and looked at his father with a glimmer of recognition in his eyes, but he didn't seem to know who I was. I didn't know what my purpose was around him anymore. Francis organised neuro and physical rehabilitation in Seattle. Within twelve hours, we were all on the Medi plane with Michael. The crew on the Medi plane attended to Michael well, and he was whisked off to the neuro rehab facility by a waiting helicopter as soon as we touched down on the tarmac. I went with him to the facility while Chris and David went home. Miles was waiting at the rehab facility. As soon as we arrived, and they saw each other, Michael's eyes lit up and he smiled.

That confirmed what I already knew. Michael didn't know who I was.

Defeated, I went home.

Chapter Thirty One

♥

Sofia

I called my therapist, my parents, and Brad in that order. My mother would be arriving that evening. I hadn't told her about Michael's condition. Then I had to tell Brad I wouldn't be returning to Kingman. I would miss him terribly, as he had become a good friend. After my calls, I took a bath and then went to the baby's room. The cot had arrived, and it was beautiful. I sat on the floor and cried about everything that had gone wrong.

This was where Chris found me when she came to the house a few hours later.

"May I come in?" she asked softly.

"Chris, of course you can." I gasped in surprise, sitting upright.

I had already been caught crying and sobbing in the nursery. There was no use pretending that I had been doing anything else.

"I missed you at the rehab facility." She spoke gently.

"Yes, I was here getting settled back in. How is he?" I asked, my voice shaking.

"He's happy to see Miles and has been quite responsive to him," she answered softly, compassion in her eyes.

"That's very good. It's a relief he has his mind."

"Sofia, talk to me, please. We've gotten to know each other well the last few weeks, and I think I know when something is not right with you."

Nothing had been right for the last few weeks.

"He doesn't know who I am; it hurts, and I'm worried. I don't know if we'll ever get back to us. When I go and see him tomorrow, who am I supposed to be without overwhelming him like his neuro from Türkiye said? When you were there with him, did he seem to notice that I wasn't there?" I sounded like a petulant child, but she had asked.

"No, he didn't seem to. You know, he only woke up a few days ago after a severe head injury." She was trying to make sense of a senseless situation.

"I know, but he knows his parents, and he nearly leapt for joy when we arrived at the facility and he saw Miles. It's not your fault, but I had much greater expectations when I had been talking to him and willing him to wake up and come back to me."

Before she could answer, the shrill gate noise startled me. I looked at my phone and saw my mother had arrived. Chris came downstairs with me, and we greeted my mother together. My emotions overwhelmed me, and I started to cry again. Since I had last seen her, I had lost my baby; I was losing Michael, and I was terrified that I was on the path to losing myself. Again.

"Sofia, what is it, darling?"

"It's everything. He doesn't know me, he doesn't know us, and I don't even know what to do. I also don't know what to do about the baby's room, and all the baby stuff we had bought."

"I'll sort out the baby's room. Will that help, darling?"

"Yes, Mum, it would."

"Tomorrow, you and I will go and see Michael, and then we can figure things out, ok?"

"You're so sensible," I said, relieved my mother was finally back in my life in the way I had longed for, for so long.

"It's only because you're overwhelmed. Have you eaten?"

How I had missed her.

"No. I'm not hungry." Or maybe I was. Food was the least of my worries.

"Well, I am, get dressed and you can take me somewhere."

Mum made everything seem so simple. I left her with Chris while I got dressed.

When I got downstairs, Mum and Chris were having a drink. They were giggling and had snacks on the marble counter in the kitchen, as if they were at a party.

What could they be celebrating?

"Do you want a drink, darling?"

"Not on an empty stomach. I'll get ill otherwise."

How could they be so happy? Couldn't they see I was crying inside.

"Chris and I were talking; what made Michael notice you in the first place?"

"I don't know. What are you getting at?" I sighed, exasperated by her alcohol fuelled good mood.

"Well, make yourself irresistible to him."

"He's not in that frame of mind." She was definitely drunk if she thought Michael was in the mood for seduction.

"He's a man; he's always in that frame of mind." She laughed softly.

"Oh, that's really a bad idea." He had a tube to help him go to the toilet. I doubted anything worked as it should in that department right now.

"I don't mean for you to dress in a lewd manner but try and make him notice you."

"Ok, Mum, you've had enough alcohol. I'm confiscating it." As I was the only adult left in the room.

"Now listen, Sofia, Bianca has a point." Chris spoke, much louder than she needed to.

"Chris, not you, too! You know how Michael is at the moment. I don't think he's even thinking about that."

"Ok, so no jeans. Every time you go to see him, try and dress up, get his attention, even if you don't have it, and flirt."

"What's in this alcohol?" I chuckled. This was becoming hilarious.

"Think about it. You're tall with legs up to your armpits, you're gorgeous, you have the bosom which all these young men seem to stare at, and those come-to-bed brown eyes. Let your hair down. I've always thought you looked sexy that way. Even if he doesn't know you, he'll definitely notice you," Mum said.

I couldn't help but laugh. "I like to think my mind is my best attribute, like you've always told me," I said, pointedly at my mother.

"Yes, it is, and I'm glad you know that, but right now, you need to use all the weapons in your arsenal. Do you think your mind is the first thing he noticed about you?" she said, with a mischievous grin.

The conversation started out as preposterous, but after a while, it became entertaining. Going out to dinner was soon forgotten. After we ordered some food to be delivered, the two mums plied me with alcohol and cheered me up. They shared stories about their younger days before meeting both their husbands. A lot which I had never known about my mother, and some which I knew Chris and I would never have talked about were it not for the situation we found ourselves in. We all needed to laugh. Chris had to call her driver to get her back home as she was in no condition to drive while I helped Mum upstairs to my bedroom. It had been years since I had shared a bed with my mother. Tonight I needed her next to me.

I was up early the next morning, but Mum had already been up. She had emptied out the baby's room, and most items could be returned except the crib. She and Marianne had helped each other wrap up the crib in heavy duty plastic, and it was ready to be taken down to one of the storage rooms. Marianne loaded all the baby stuff into my car and Mum told me she would return them while I was flirting with Michael. When I got dressed, I decided to humour her and wore a fluttering wrap dress. I was overdressed but I would try anything. Mum and I went out to brunch, then made our way to the rehab centre.

"Mum, do you think I should wear my ring?"

"No, remove it. If he's in his right mind, that might be off-putting."

"He's not in his right mind," I said, shaking my head.

Mum laughed, and I couldn't help but laugh too. We made our way to his room, where he was sitting with Miles, talking very slowly. I was surprised he was speaking at all.

Miles stood up to greet us. "Hi Bianca, it's good to see you again. Morning, Sofia."

Mum went closer to Michael and held out her hand.

"Hi Michael, it's so good to see you. I'm glad you're doing so much better."

Slowly, he stretched his hand and shook hers. He didn't say anything, but he was concentrating on her face. Mum didn't offer up any more information. I went and shook his hand, too. There was some silence until Michael turned to Miles.

"Miles, who are these lovely ladies?" He spoke, but his speech was slow.

"Okay, brother, I am saying this once, so pay close attention, as I will be quizzing you tomorrow. This is Sophia Kingman, and this is Bianca Kingman."

Miles didn't say any more, he just answered Michael's question.

"Michael, I'm taking Bianca to get coffee. Would you like some?" Miles asked after more awkward silence.

"Yes, please, one sugar."

When Miles got up with Mum, Michael's eyes followed him until he walked out of the room.

"How are you, Michael?" I asked him once we were alone.

What was I supposed to say to the most important man in my life? How could I show him how much we meant to each other? When in his mind, he was meeting me for the first time?

"I know I'm supposed to say that I am fine, but I have the worst headache, and I can't quite remember a few things and a few people, so excuse me if I offend you." With the slow speech he sounded robotic, as if he had been rehearsing that.

How would I ever get through to him?

"Okay, I won't get offended." I smiled. He had always loved my smile, and it was one of those weapons in my arsenal.

Chris and David then arrived. Chris had a huge smile as she looked at my dress.

"Good morning, Michael, Sofia." His face lit up as he looked towards them.

"Morning. Parents," he said, pointedly. He still had his sense of humour. It made me smile.

"You look good this morning. How are you feeling?" The effervescent Chris was back. Of course she was, her son was back.

"The headache is the worst, and some other aches and pains."

"Who is your gorgeous visitor, Michael?" David asked.

"Oh sorry, this is Bianca Kingman. She came in with Sofia, who is getting coffee with Miles," he answered slowly, but in a matter-of-fact tone.

That was all I could take. I felt the tears welling up.

"It was so good to see you today, Michael. I'll leave you with your parents," I said, forcing a smile.

"It was good to see you, too. Will you visit again another time?"

"I will. Take care, Michael," I said, hurriedly and left.

"I'll just walk her out," Chris said as she followed me.

"I can't believe the difference, Chris. He is speaking now." I was pleased, yet so heartbroken.

"With Miles, he just seems so free. It might be that childhood bond."

"I'm so happy about that, but he mixed my mother and I up."

"I heard that too, but baby steps. Two days ago, he couldn't even speak, and today he is shaking hands and talking. Even attempting to make introductions. Please give him a chance; don't give up on him. Please," she said as she held both my hands in hers.

"I won't." He never gave up on me.

"That dress is lovely, by the way, so tasteful yet so sexy. It would be hard not to notice you in it."

I chuckled, remembering last night's events.

I walked out of the centre, and all I wanted was to go to the home, which Michael had told me was as much mine as it was his. I needed to feel close to him. Mum had my car, so I got into the first taxi I saw, and it took me home.

Chapter Thirty Two

♥

Michael

I had been told I survived a bombing. That in itself was a miracle. I don't remember anything about a bomb, or that I even took a trip to Istanbul. I didn't have any memories of the last few years. I was discombobulated, and it felt like a thousand hangovers all at once. I was not myself, and there was some deficit within my mind, body, and soul.

Miles and my parents had been spending a lot of time with me, but they were walking on eggshells. My doctor didn't want them telling me anything about my life, to see if I would start to remember anything organically. The science experiment he was conducting on my life sounded like he was pulling ideas out of a sack of magic tricks. I never imagined I would be an invalid, and one who didn't have all his faculties. I got irritable, and I couldn't help it.

Was that my persona or would that be the injury?

It seemed being with Miles helped. He was not making light of the situation, but it didn't feel like doomsday when we were together either.

Viv hadn't been here to see me yet. I suspected she might be on a modelling assignment. The last I remembered she had become the spokesmodel of some luxury brand. I just couldn't remember which one. I wouldn't ask about her yet as I didn't want to put anyone on the spot. They have been through too much already. I would be patient and bide my time, although I missed her, and I couldn't wait to hold her in my arms. I was angry and disappointed she hadn't dropped everything to be with me after I survived a near death experience. She always had a way of making everything in my world right. Last I remembered, she had agreed to marry me.

There were some people who had visited that I hadn't recognised. I didn't even try to remember them as it took too much effort, and it hurts my head when I tried to think too hard. I gave them all the same line: I've lost my memory and please don't be offended. They had all been gracious; I felt like a fish in a bowl.

I had finally got the urine tube out and regained some dignity. I would be attending aqua therapy, and I couldn't wait. I might have forgotten some things, but I knew for certain that I was at home in the water, and that was where I did my best thinking. In the water and on dry land with my camera.

I would follow the doctor's orders and let my brain heal. I would avoid the internet and spare my family too many questions. The nights in this place were the most difficult. They were long and lonely. I was sure I used to have someone sit and talk to me while I was asleep in the hospital. She was too kind to have been doing her job and seemed too witty to have been Viv, but I wasn't even sure if that was a memory or a fantasy.

It had been a week since I arrived here, and mornings couldn't come soon enough. I was now getting better with hand movements and not spilling coffee all over myself. I even sounded better when I spoke. I was told I needed to keep working on my manual dexterity. I had been learning to pick up rice grains, marbles, and peanuts, much to Miles' amusement. At least he was having some fun, even though it was at my expense.

My physical therapist, Joe, took me to aquatherapy, and I was pleasantly surprised with how great my movements were. I had a fracture to my shoulder and some broken ribs, but unlike the mental anguish, the physical pain was bearable. He helped me into the water, and instantly I felt alive. He tried to manipulate my arm and move my legs for me, but I was ready to go. I managed to swim two laps until he told me to stop; otherwise, I would tire myself out. As far as I could remember, I swam at least an hour every day. He was adamant that I take it slow, reminding me of the broken ribs and overdoing it in the pool could cause me some pain and shortness of breath. As I was an "invalid" and he was a professional, I had to listen.

As I was coming out of the water, I saw Sofia Kingman sitting out at the bench waiting for me. I sat down and tried to towel myself off while Joe ogled her. I couldn't blame him; she was stunning. I needed to know who she was. I suspected mixing her up with Bianca had upset her a few days ago. She came to see me every day, but she was distant and let me lead the conversations. She tried to put a wall up between us, but sometimes she forgot and became herself, and those were the best moments I shared with her. I wanted to tell her to be herself, but I didn't know what the boundary was with her, although I felt like I knew her on a deeper level. She never stayed long, and her visits always left me wanting more. I didn't want to get too attached, especially with the confusion in my head.

I still needed to see Viv; I had been here for nearly a week, and she still hadn't come to see me. If only I had my phone; I couldn't even remember my fiancée's phone number.

Sofia was wearing yet another dress which just confirmed I still had the other important function in my lower body. In the rare moment my mother hadn't been hovering, and I was alone with my physician, I asked him if everything would ever be normal in my lower body. The urine tube had alarmed me, and never performing again crossed my mind, although this was the least of my worries. The physician laughed it off and said the only way to know for sure was to have a little practice. I wondered when I would ever fit that practice into my hectic, invalid schedule.

Joe finally turned to look at me after he had been staring for a while. "Michael, is she here to see you?"

"She's not here to see you. So today is the last day you gawk at her like that. Do you understand?" I barked at him.

When it came to defending her, how had my speech suddenly improved so much?

"I'm sorry, man. I didn't realise you're together like that." He had the decency to apologise.

I didn't have a response, because I didn't know how to characterise our relationship, or whatever it was we had going. I had sounded proprietary and somewhere inside I had felt it too.

When she walked towards me, Joe left without looking at her again.

"Hi Sofia, how are you today?" She wore what Vivian had once told me was a bodycon dress. Green, and ending right above her knees. It wasn't doing much to hide her long legs. I was now sure; everything in my shorts definitely still worked. The dress clung to her curves like a second skin, and it took everything in me to concentrate on her brown eyes.

"Great. Did you have a good session?" She smiled that smile which churned my insides.

"It was the best. I felt alive, and I think I might come back this afternoon."

"That's wonderful. I'm happy you enjoyed it."

Who was she, and why did seeing her smile make me forget why I was here?

"Sofia, would you like to grab a coffee with me?"

"Are you asking me on a date? Perhaps you could get dressed first?" She giggled.

In my state, she mentioned a date. *Did she know about Vivian?*

"Is this look not working for you?" I smiled at her. I had to know what was going on here, and light humour always went a long way. That, I remembered.

She bit her lower lip. *What did that mean?* I wondered. She might have been flirting with me, I couldn't be sure.

"It's a good look. Only you might get photographed in the cafeteria, and some girls will swoon, then a riot might ensue." I was falling in love with her sense of humour.

"Oh, yeah. I didn't think about that," I said as I winked, which gave me a sharp pain on the left side of my head.

Was this the universe punishing me for flirting behind my fiancée's back?

"Ok, why don't I grab the coffees and I'll see you back in your room?"

"That sounds good. Do you still want me to get dressed?"

She seemed mildly surprised. My feeble attempt at humour fell flat. I suppose I was wrong about the two of us.

She left and instead of using the wheelchair, this time I walked gingerly back to my room, a little deflated after the final exchange with her. I thought I liked her. In fact, I knew I did, but if we weren't together, why would she be here?

Was I seeing two women at the same time? Was that who I had become?

I had too much time on my hands to think about everything, and I still didn't know anything.

As I was thinking some more, she reappeared with coffee. The clicking six inch black heels she wore announcing her arrival. "I got some muffins too. Is that something you like?"

"I love blueberry muffins. How did you know?" I was fishing. This was against the doctor's rules, but I needed to know something, anything.

She gave me that smile again. I could fall in love with it. I just needed to understand us, or if there was an us.

"Sofia, I have to ask, are you and I close? I get the sense we might be."

"If you have to ask, we can't be. Isn't that something you would know, or perhaps feel deep within?" she asked, teasing me. She bit into her muffin, and that action alone made me want to know what else her mouth could do.

"That's not fair. That's a non-answer."

Another smile. She had to be one of the most beautiful women I had ever seen, and I had seen plenty.

"Ok, let's not make this about me. How about I ask you this, are you seeing someone?"

"Do you mean right now?" She was singing from the same hymn sheet as everyone else, keeping me in the dark. At least she flirted with me while doing it.

I laughed out loud. Out of the corner of my eye, I saw my mother approach. I was happy to see her but disappointed my time alone with Sofia had come to an end.

"Hello, son, I heard you laugh all the way from the elevators. You look great."

"I've had a great morning, and I feel good."

"Perfect. How are you, Sofia?" she asked, kissing *her* on the cheek.

"Great. I was just finishing my coffee and about to leave." They were comfortable around each other.

"You don't have to leave on my account. I think you make Michael laugh better than I can."

Was my mother dropping hints? I couldn't concentrate anymore.

Was Sofia blushing? I couldn't tell either. I definitely liked her, but I couldn't read her. I was not intuitive, nor did I feel sharp. The drugs I was on weren't helping either, or it might have been the two laps in the pool, and I was starting to feel tired.

"Son, you're drifting off to sleep. Get some rest now. I'll see you later."

They left, and I had a sweet dream, with Sofia laughing, but Viv was in it too, and we had children. I had to talk to Miles. He would be honest with me.

That evening after he finished work, Miles came to visit as he had done without fail since I arrived at rehab.

"Miles, there's something that's not right, and I hope you can help me."

"Are they treating you okay in here?" he asked with a concerned look.

"Yes, it's not about my care. Why hasn't Vivian come to see me yet?"

He seemed reluctant to start talking. Even in my haze and brain fog, I could tell he was struggling with what he had to say. The normally confident Miles was fidgety. He removed his tie, undid his top button, and broke out into a sweat. This was huge.

"Miles, forget the doctor's rules for a minute, and just tell me."

"Five years ago, just before you got married to her, Vivian left you. She married another man and had two children with him. On a side note, she recently left him, too." He spoke hurriedly, spitting it all out.

"What! That can't be. We were so in love. It seems like yesterday I was engaged to her." She was always gone for work, but I had stopped seeing her campaigns. She must have been seeing the idiot behind my back.

"Now, there's more to this story, and this is the most difficult part to hear."

"What could be worse?" I sat up and waited for another punch to the stomach.

"I'm the man Vivian married." He spoke with regret.

Him. How could I not have seen this, or did I? How could I know when I didn't remember?

"You? Why? How could you?" I yelled. "Were you two running around together behind my back?"

He hung his head and tried to speak. "Michael, I…" I cut him off.

"We've had this conversation before, haven't we? I bet you didn't have a good enough reason then, like you don't have one now. There can't be a reason for what you did."

"We've spoken, and even came to blows. This broke you, and it tore you and I apart. For years, our relationship was strained. The way we were changed, but we've worked hard to get us back to a good place. You are a good uncle to my girls."

"Wait, did you say she left you? The girls?"

"Yes, she's fallen out of love." He sighed in defeat.

"I'm sorry about what happened to your family, but whatever happened between us was your fault. What kind of man would do that, to his brother no less?" Disgust laced my voice.

"You're shocked, and this is news to you, but for what it's worth, I'm sorry. I'm a good man and I want to continue being a good brother and friend like I am now."

"That's your own opinion of yourself. Because of my vulnerability, you'll feed me whatever lies you want to. I can't believe I'm asking this question, but do I even trust you?" I scoffed.

"We work well together. We even work out together sometimes, but when it comes to matters of the heart, you keep me at arm's length. It hurts, but I know I deserve it." He seemed to be telling the truth, but how honest could he be if he could do something like that?

"You hardly look like you've been working out. Am I the one doing all the heavy lifting?" This was heavy, so I decided to let him off the hook.

"And that sense of humour wasn't injured. Thank God." He smiled weakly, his confidence still wavering.

"It's been five years since this Viv issue, and something tells me I'm over it."

"You are, believe me."

What did that mean? Was I with someone else? Sofia?

"If I've become so good at this uncle business, when will I see my nieces?"

"They have been asking to see you since you got back, but we didn't want to disturb your brain."

"They can't disturb it more than it already is." I chuckled at my own joke. "Miles, I need you to work with me on something. It's important I do it this way."

He leaned over attentively, visibly relieved the awkward conversation was over. "I would do anything for you."

You should, after that betrayal.

"I want to go home, wherever that is, and I want to be gone by this time tomorrow," I said in earnest.

"You're asking for the impossible. You need to be in here," he said regretfully.

"I can't stay here. I have no control over my own life. Everyone is lying to me by omission. Whatever I'm doing here, I can afford to do it at home, and I would rather do it there. Make it happen. That's all I ask of you."

He exhaled deeply with his eyes closed. "I'll start with your doctor," he said with steely determination.

"Don't tell Mum and Dad until you absolutely have to. It's time they both start treating me like a man," I said, and I didn't waiver, silently daring him to challenge me.

Chapter Thirty Three

Sofia

Today was a good day with Michael; he wanted to explore what was going on between us, and the fact that he couldn't remember me, and yet still felt there was something between us had to be a good sign. I had been tempted to tell him everything about us when he had asked, and he had seemed ready to hear it, but I had to be patient. Even though his speech and mannerisms were improving every day, as were his movements, he had a long road to recovery ahead. I would wait, and I would tell him everything when he was ready.

I arrived home, and took a long bath, remembering the first time he had made me come undone in this bathroom. I was looking forward to the day Michael and I would be together in every way that mattered. His body had taken a beating from his injuries, but I still wanted to wrap myself around him and remind him of how we made each other's bodies scream. His body recognised mine, and it had hardly been discreet about it after his Aquatherapy.

After the bath, I checked my emails, and I had an email from Great Expedition, a periodical magazine conducting research all over the world. They were inviting me on a six-month trip to take photographs in Antarctica. This had Brad's fingerprints all over it. This was what I had always wanted, a dream come true, but I couldn't leave, not at this crucial time in Michael's recovery. I felt deeply disappointed, but I had to be present for Michael. I wore my ring on a pendant around my neck, and I couldn't wait to put it back on my finger. I was only dreading the day when I had to tell Michael our baby was gone.

When the doorbell rang, Miles was at the door, and I was surprised to see him.

"Is everything okay?" I asked, noticing the worry on his face.

"Michael has chosen to leave rehab against medical advice," he said.

"What! He needs rehab!" I cried.

"He realises that. He made me spend the last few hours arranging for rehab right here at home."

"He made you?" I yelled, full of suspicion. I wasn't conditioned to trust Miles.

He took another deep breath before he spoke again. "He knows about Vivian and I." Michael hadn't lost his mind; he was still sharp and knew how to get what he wanted.

"Oh, so this was penance. You couldn't say no because you want his forgiveness. You did this for yourself!" I retorted.

"I did, but I also did it for him. He's not coping well there. He'll have physical therapy for four hours every day, neuro rehab for another two, he will have nurses available around the clock if he needs them, and his doctors will conduct home visits daily, so he'll still have a full roster of rehab."

"You've got it all figured out, don't you? You didn't think to ask my opinion!" I was now seething.

"From where you're standing, it might not seem like it, but I would do anything for my brother, and this is what he wants. It might even do his memory some good to recover in his own space," he said convincingly.

I took some deep breaths and managed to calm down. "You might be right about being in his own space. I'm not angry about him coming home, just surprised. Here is where he belongs."

What about us? He still didn't know who I was.

"Good, I'm happy about that. I want to be there for him, but I understand you two need your space, but I can be here if he needs me." They seemed to have worked out their issues.

Would we be able to find our way back to each other? For the first time since the incident in Istanbul, Michael and I would be under the same roof. Alone.

Chapter Thirty Four

♥

Michael

I was going home! The irony of it all was I was looking forward to anything that would take my mind *off* my mind. Fortunately, I didn't have any memories of the bombing itself; my psychotherapist called it Post Traumatic Amnesia, a trick my mind was using to protect itself from a bad memory. I called it Self Preservation, as I imagined nothing good would ever come out of remembering the worst day of my life.

Arriving home was a relief. I was happy to be back in my own space. I went around the house, and I liked it. There were two large pools, one indoor and one outside, a well-equipped gym, and an inviting home theatre. I couldn't even remember my own home, but I was already happy in it. It had views of Lake Washington framed by magnificent floor-to-ceiling windows. I imagined they were the reason I bought the place. I also found a princess room with twin beds, which I deduced were for Maxie and Laila.

I decided to take the easy route and go for a swim. I swam for an hour, much needed for my sanity, until Marianne called out to offer me food. I suspected my mother had put her up to this. After giving me a rundown on how to work the microwave and the coffee maker, she was finished for the day and told me Sofia was on her way over. I couldn't help but feel elated.

When she arrived, I couldn't help the breath that left me. She was perfectly formed, and this time, she had her brown hair up in a bun and pouty lips smiling at me. I looked down her long, graceful neck and noticed a pendant that rested between her ample breasts. She wrapped her toned but delicate arms around me as she hugged me. I pulled her closer, flush against my body, and inhaled deeply. She smelled familiar. I had been in hospital for too long and I had to calm my raging hormones.

"Welcome home!" she said shyly.

"This is a great welcome. Do you live here?"

"I do." She didn't offer any other explanations.

We walked into the living room, and I led her to a crescent sofa. A delicate smile danced on her lips for a second. *Why?*

"How long have you lived here?"

"Since before the incident in Istanbul." She was direct.

"I'm sorry, but I don't have any memory of that."

Her answers were straightforward and yet so evasive. She wasn't being honest with me. We had to talk.

"Would you like to eat? Marianne's been cooking." I could finally handle a fork and knife after hours of practice.

"I would love that."

We walked into the kitchen with its enormous central island.

How much input had she had in this house?

This was a chef's kitchen. I didn't try to sit at the island. I still wasn't coordinated enough to perch on the stool. I led her to the plush banquette that looked directly into the backyard and the lake beyond.

A window was open, and the smell of rain was in the air. Seattle was still as rainy today as it was five years ago.

"Sofia, will you tell me about us?" I asked, looking at the gold flecks dancing in her eyes. Unique and unforgettable.

"What do you mean?"

"I don't remember you, but you and I are something more than whatever is happening here."

"What would make you say that?" She smiled. Even though her body looked like it was made for sin, she had the sweetest smile.

"It can't have been my imagination, but we had a connection in the rehab facility." She hesitated. "What are you hesitant to tell me?"

"Since you've been back from Istanbul, what have you learnt about yourself?"

"I don't have memories of the last five years, and I am not sure if I will ever get them back. My doctor wants me to give my brain a chance to heal, something about neuroplasticity and such, so he's discouraged me from finding out any information about myself but wait for my brain to remember."

"So why are you asking me questions?" she asked patiently.

"Because you and I live in the same house, and life's too short, and it's for living. I want to live mine as honestly as I can."

"So do I," she said wistfully.

"Can you give me the answers I need?"

She sighed before she smiled and looked into my eyes, telling me what I had suspected since she came to watch me swim. "Michael, we are everything to each other."

After she had said those words, I got up and pulled her into my arms. My eyes were heavy with unshed tears, as my chest tightened, and I fought hard to swallow down the lump now in my throat. My body shook as I held her close, breathing her in, willing my mind to remember what it couldn't. "Sofia, I'm so sorry."

"Why are you sorry? This isn't your fault."

"I'm not the man you must have fallen in love with." The tears rolled down my face freely.

"Apart from not remembering who I am, and all about us, you are still the same," she said softly as she wiped my tears with her soft fingers, her eyes welling up too.

"You have me at a disadvantage. You have all your memories of us, and all I have is my intuition and flashes of some things I can't make sense of."

"Things like what?" she asked, hopeful.

"A beach, with a lot of blood and it is littered with candles. I've had that memory a lot."

She smiled, a really wide smile. Then she got out her phone and searched through it. "Does it look a little like this?"

She showed me a photograph just as I described, except there was no blood, only red rose petals, blanketing what looked like a beach.

"Yes, that is exactly what it looks like, except those are roses."

"Yes, they are. Sit with me, and I will tell you about that day; although I'm not sure your doctors would approve."

"It will be our secret." This was against the rules, but this was important. *She* was important.

She told me all about a trip we had taken to Bora Bora. She had photographs she told me I had taken, and in the photos we were both happy on that day. As she was talking, I looked down at her pendant. That was when I noticed the engagement ring.

How could I have not seen it?

I was overcome, and I couldn't help the flood of emotion taking over again.

We held each other as we both cried. I cried for the memories I suspected I would never get back, but Sofia's tears were happy tears. She was happy she had me back, but did she? I knew what I needed to do.

I pulled away from her and spoke to her gently. "Sofia, I need time."

"What do you mean?" Shock and confusion were now on her face. She moved closer to me; her body was a distraction, but I had to speak.

"Everything you've told me has made me happy and I want us to be us again. Those photographs you showed me felt like I was being told a story. I want to live my life, and not be told about it through photographs, or even other peoples' memories. I don't know what that means yet, but please give me a chance to figure it out."

"Oh no, this is what your doctor meant! It's information overload." She was panicking.

"That's not the issue."

"What is it then?"

"I want to be able to love you like I do in those photos, and right now I don't feel that way." I died inside, as I told her I didn't love her.

"I understand if you don't love me, Michael. I'm nearly a stranger to you." She held my face in both her hands as she implored my sensibilities.

"I feel a connection to you, but I can't give you what we had on that beach in Bora Bora, not right now," I said as I moved her delicate hands from my face.

She had a horrified look on her face. "What are you saying?" Her voice cracked as her body sagged into the banquette where we both sat.

"I'm saying, please give me some time, and perhaps you can move out of my house."

"Perhaps I can move out of your house! What the hell do you mean? This is my home and you're my fiancé! Where do you expect me to go?" She had become hysterical, and the anguish in her voice tore right through me.

"I'm saying I need to work on myself so that I can be with you. Right now, I can't be with you, not the way you want me to be, or the way you deserve."

"Are you breaking up with me? After everything we've been through. Do you know how difficult it was to get here, Michael?" She was crying. This seemed so wrong.

"Exactly. I don't know what we've been through. That makes me feel like I am half the man I once was, and when I am with you, I want to be the best man that I can be. This version of who I am won't work in a relationship." I was dizzy with emotional exhaustion, but I needed her to understand.

"You're making the biggest mistake of your life. It doesn't have to be this way. We can work this out together. We love each other, don't you see?"

"I see the photographs, but I need to feel this, and right now I don't."

"Is this about Vivian? Are you in love with her? I know you now know about her." She sobbed.

"This has nothing to do with her. This has everything to do with you and me. The you and me that changed after Istanbul."

"Which Istanbul, Michael?" She asked softly, with tears running down her face.

"The only one."

How many were there?

I felt terrible, and I sounded cold, but this had to be done. It might have been a selfish decision, but it was the right one.

"Michael, you have made so many decisions that have never steered you wrong; you use your head and your heart. Why can't you do that now, please? For the second time in our relationship, you are letting your ego get in the way of what we have. Trust the decision you made to be with me, please. It was the best decision for both of us."

She was now wailing, but my mind was made up. "I'm sorry, Sofia. I don't want to hurt you any more than I am, but you need to leave. There's nothing here for you, not right now."

I got up from the banquette, leaving Sofia sobbing, and went upstairs to Laila and Maxie's room. I couldn't bear to look at Sofia again tonight, not after what I had done.

"I love you, Michael. Please let me stay." I had reduced a beautiful, confident woman who was in love with me to a begging, blubbering mess. I would be going to hell on judgement day.

"Please don't beg; it's unbecoming." I even sounded like a cold bastard.

Chapter Thirty Five

♥

Sofia

This was not how I had imagined Michael's homecoming would be. I hadn't expected a reconciliation of epic proportions, but I had imagined we would slowly return to who and what we were before the Istanbul bombing. I never thought Istanbul would mark both the beginning and the end of us.

I felt the ache deeply, but I had been hurt before, and I had lived with hurt for a long time. I wasn't going to return to that place. I was older and wiser, and this heartbreak was light years away from the one I had endured before. I picked myself up from the banquette, promising myself that I had cried all the tears I could for that relationship.

I didn't bother with sleep. Instead, I packed up all I had and organised some movers, while trying to figure out how I would get onto the research team at Great Expedition. As soon as morning came, the movers arrived to take my belongings to my jet. When they left, I did too; though I made my way to see Chris. I had always liked her, and she had been kind to me in Istanbul when I had lost my child.

"Sofia, you're an early riser this morning." Even in the morning, she was still glamorous, dressed in white silk pyjamas and a matching silk robe.

"Yes, I am. I'm sorry I got you out of bed, but I just had to see you before I left."

"Left? Where are you going? Michael has only just returned home." She was just as confused as I was.

"Michael and I haven't worked out like we all hoped we would after he returned, and so he has asked me to leave."

"Impossible. He did that? It's your home too. Let me call him." She made to leave the foyer.

"No, Chris. I'm here to say goodbye, not to get you involved," I said, firmly.

"Sofia, I am so sorry this has happened. You two are so right for each other. Are you sure you can't work things out?"

"I'm in love with him, but this time, my love doesn't seem to be enough."

"His mind's not right. First, he discharges himself from rehab, now he's putting you out of your own home. Come here and stay with us while he throws his tantrum. He will soon realise exactly what you mean to each other." She tried to plead with me.

"I can't stay. It's over between us," I said with conviction.

"My boy has definitely lost his mind. I don't know what to say. I'll miss you. You were there for me when I had lost all hope. Even though he doesn't know it, you were there for him when he needed you most. I'll always love you for that," she said as her voice cracked.

We hugged and both cried silently. I left and made my way to Boeing Field, where my jet was ready to take me to LA. The flight felt longer than its two hours, and the cabin was unusually silent. The flight attendant left me well alone as I cried silent tears, and the jet ascended high into the clouds. Again, I left another piece of my broken heart where I would never get it back.

I called Mum while on the flight and told her I was on my way to LA. When I landed, I went to see her, and I cried as I told her what had happened between Michael and I.

"Will you live here with us?" she asked expectantly.

"No. I still have my apartment." I couldn't live with my parents. That was a vicious cycle I didn't want to start.

"Of course. You'll love again; I know you will. Michael has lost one of the best women I've ever known."

"I don't know about loving again. I've already lost two great loves in this life. It hurts right here," I said as I rubbed the middle of my chest.

I spent the rest of the day with her until I couldn't put off returning to my apartment. When I arrived, the tears, which I was sure I couldn't cry anymore, came back. I wandered aimlessly around my apartment, then I was in the foetal position for another three days, crying and eating all the ice cream I could get delivered. That was until I contacted Great Expedition, who accepted me onto their team straight away. Brad had worked his magic, and somehow, I was accepted without any industry experience, just with a few sample photographs I had taken from my travels in Africa. I bade farewell to my parents yet again, and they both tried to reassure me that I didn't need to run away to Antarctica to make the pain go away.

I needed to, and that was exactly what I did.

Chapter Thirty Six

♥

Michael

From what I could remember, letting go of Sofia was the most difficult thing I had ever done, and even though I didn't know nor remember her, I felt alone and incomplete. I had heard the movers arrive, but I couldn't go downstairs to see her. We had said all we had to say to each other, but I couldn't help the feeling of dread. The photographs she had shown me showed me the life we had, and I yearned for it. I didn't know how we could ever have that life if I didn't know who she was. I guessed I could have tried to get to know her, but I was so afraid I would never live up to the man I used to be.

For the first time since I had arrived from Istanbul, I felt inadequate. The effect of losing my memory was amplified. Not only had I lost my memories of her, but I had also lost Sofia. I reminded myself I had lost some part of who I was, but I still had my life and all four limbs, much more than my contemporaries in that restaurant in Istanbul had, and I promised myself to live life as fully as possible.

The visit from my mother and the ensuing conversation felt like a verbal pummelling. She was in a rage and disappointed. She attributed my break-up with Sofia to my neurological state. She tried to convince my father to stop me from working as she suspected my decision-making center was fractured, inflamed, or both, and returning to work would ruin both my business reputation as well as the company's. I assured my father I was capable of making business decisions, and the decision I had made about Sofia was a personal one. Despite the way I felt, I trusted my judgement and stood by it.

After a gruelling swimming session, I had a revolving door of visitors. Francis was the most significant, and I was happy to see him. He was pleased with my general condition and pleasantly surprised by how I was quite like my usual self. Due to the nature of his work as a trauma surgeon, I had always enjoyed hearing about his work. I talked to him about what had happened in Istanbul, and he showed me a photograph of a kidney-shaped tray full of very small glass shards.

"Michael, these shards of glass to me represent compassion, devotion, and true love. As a doctor, even as old as I am, I always learn from every clinical experience, and from yours, that is what I learnt."

"Francis, that's poetic, yet so very cryptic. What do you mean?" I asked with keen interest.

"I'm talking about your young lady. She sat by your bedside for hours in the ICU and painstakingly removed those shards from all over your body, one by one," he said, as his eyes glazed with unshed tears.

"She never mentioned that."

How could I have been so cruel to her?

"That is perhaps still too painful to talk about, as you were not in a good way. She might not want to relive that yet. She went through a lot too, and if she's not talking to someone, I would recommend you make sure she does, although I think her father has got that in hand."

"He was there too, was he?" I asked, racked with guilt.

"Yes, he was. You are loved, Michael. That once in a lifetime kind of love, hold on to it with everything you are. I've taken up enough of your time, so I'll go, but both of you need to come and visit. Ann can't wait to meet her."

Francis left me after that avalanche of information, and I was suddenly weary.

After some rest, I called my driver and left the house as I had promised Miles I would see the girls. They were with their nanny, and she was pleased to have another adult in the middle of the day as they were so full of energy. It was easy to see that we had spent a lot of time together.

Maxie was very talkative and had to ask straight away. "Uncle Mickey, is your brain better now?"

"Yes, it's better. Sometimes it hurts a little though."

"Do you take a nap like a baby?" They both giggled.

"Yes, just like a baby," I said as I sat them both on my lap.

"Does Sofia nap too or does she shh?" she asked as she put her finger on her lips which Laila immediately did too. I couldn't help but smile. Sofia was definitely embedded in all aspects of my life, and I didn't have any answers for the girls. I was filled with regret and my heart was nearly as heavy as my head. She had left an impression on everyone she had met, and I had ruined it.

"She is not here for now."

"Will she bring my mummy back with her?"

The conversation with Maxie was a minefield. Miles arrived while we were having a tea party and joined us for a while. I got up and motioned for him to join me away from the girls.

"I've enjoyed myself, but my brain now hurts. This has to be the best tea party I've been to in a while."

"I'm glad you're here. I don't know what I would have done if you hadn't returned from Istanbul."

"I love you too, brother." I hugged the girls, and my driver took me home.

Chapter Thirty Seven

♥

Sofia

It was a dream come true to be in Antarctica for a photography assignment. I should have been excited at this opportunity of a lifetime. I wasn't excited, though; I was numb, dazed, and confused. I wasn't experiencing the desolation I had felt after Nolan and the kids had died, but I was in a similar headspace. I felt the loss of my unborn child profoundly, and thoughts of the end of the relationship with Michael were all-consuming all night and day.

I had chosen to escape to the South Pole, covered by an arctic white sheet, a glacial desert, cold and dull, a little like my heart and soul. I had poured my all into the relationship. It had been my second chance at true love, and that, too, had come to an abrupt end.

Coming to Antarctica wouldn't help me get over him, our relationship, and what we had been through. Like the landscape before me, my time here would freeze events and suspend me moving forward with my life alone yet again. My therapist had warned me, but this seemed like the least final nail to our relationship coffin.

My parents suspected that coming to Antarctica after the breakup was another attempt to escape reality. I viewed it as a reset, a new career, and a break from heartbreak and the pain associated with it.

When I returned to LA, I would buy a house, a place right on the beach, and make it my home. I would even have a dedicated space for all things photography. I couldn't return to my penthouse. There were too many memories of my time spent with Michael.

The magazine provided all photography equipment, but I brought the Zfc Michael had given to me in South Africa. It was my favourite camera, and even though I was trying to distance myself from him, I still tried desperately to feel close to him. I brought his jacket and some of his T-shirts from my penthouse.

I didn't want to get over him; I wasn't even trying to.

I had been in love with Nolan, but Michael had consumed me. I had never felt the love and attention he had lavished on me, and I didn't think I could ever feel that way ever again.

Had I married Nolan because he was Mr Right or Mr Right now? Was Mum right, and I had been too young?

Michael was the man of my dreams, and that dream had come to an end. I just needed to convince my head and my heart to learn to move on. Only, I wasn't in a rush to do that.

My colleagues knew that this was my first assignment, and they were accommodating. If any of them knew who I was, they were discreet enough to never ask about my personal life. I was grateful. Occasionally, I fumbled with the equipment, as my movements and handling of the photography equipment had not yet become so fluid and natural. At other times, I found myself distracted and missing very important photo opportunities. In pockets of clarity, I made up for these mistakes by taking amazing shots, proving my worth. I kept to myself and didn't try to get close to anyone. I was still wary of exposure and didn't want to end up as entertainment fodder yet again.

The Research Station in Antarctica was focused on astronomy and astrophysics, but I was drawn to capturing photographs of animals. The wildlife in the South Pole wasn't as varied and as magnificent as in the savanna; however, the white backdrop, the frost, and its sparsity made it quite dramatic. When I was able to pull myself from despondency, I was in awe of the breath-taking scenery and tried to be present. I made sure to go outside the Research Station at least once every day, for some shots as well as exercise. Sometimes a colleague would join me, but mostly I craved the solitude and the silence. The South Pole was serene, almost holy.

After having been on assignment for three months, I had become content in my self-imposed exile to the ice-covered desert. I had been able to communicate with my parents sporadically, and with some friends. Bradley made contact daily, and he alone knew the depths of my unhappiness. He was enjoying working at Kingman and the new challenges his new position presented, but we missed working together. He brought up Michael a few times, and I owned up to missing him.

I didn't own up to how he occupied my thoughts all day and night, how I longed for what we had and still held onto the hope that one day we could be together again.

I didn't own up to how lonely I was, with all thoughts of a family that would never be.

I didn't own up to how I still wore my engagement ring around my neck and held it all night for comfort.

I didn't dare own up to how I looked forward to sleep as I saw Michael in my dreams every night. I knew I could never own up to how

I woke up soaking wet, always on the brink of climax, from dreams of Michael's touch.

How could I ever move on? I was teetering on the very edge of insanity.

Chapter Thirty Eight

♥

Michael

Returning to work wasn't as difficult as I had imagined it would be. The idea that my brain needed to remember the previous five years at its own pace didn't spill into our company ethos. I needed, and received, a crash course from the trusted three — my father, Miles, and my executive assistant — on all that had happened in the company over the last five years. Mergers, acquisitions, and high-level personnel changes. I quickly learned I had been actively involved, if not responsible for, all those changes.

I used all types of cues to remind me, flashcards, photographs, and handwritten notes, and in no time, I was well-informed of all that was happening at the company. The extent of my brain injury was kept a closely guarded secret, as that would have made our shareholders and members of the board uneasy; I would have lost my position at the company, as well as the only purpose I had. Miles had been troubled by the legal ramifications of withholding this information, but after some time passed and I settled back into work, he told me it was like I had never left. The neurological deficit I had didn't affect my work, and I was relieved.

However, it had destroyed my personal life. The most important relationship I had in my life was now a distant memory, which I didn't have. My memory flashes had been intensifying. Some I had been able to make sense of; however, some were still a mystery.

From my dreams and flashbacks, it was clear Sofia and I had spent a significant amount of time in Africa. I had plenty of varied flashes of memory where the unmistakable African landscape was the backdrop. I knew I would have taken her to the game reserve I had spent time as a child and had formed a lifelong friendship with the owner's son, Phil. I would visit Phil once I was cleared for long haul travel by my physician, as he was a good friend, and I enjoyed spending time on his reserve.

When I had these flashbacks, I missed Sofia more, and increasingly, our intimate moments started to return to me. It had been four months since the day I last saw her and dismissed her from my home, and from my heart, as if she never mattered to me. Every day I wasn't with her, I missed her, and lately, I had been longing to have her in my bed. No amount of self-pleasure was enough to relieve me of my need.

By day, to curtail my emotions and curb my urges, I threw myself into work, and by night, I worked myself to exhaustion in my gym and swam for hours afterwards. When I would go to bed at midnight, I'd fall into a fitful sleep. When I wasn't having vivid carnal dreams about Sofia, I was having incomprehensible nightmares.

Over the weekends, both my driver and pilot worked overtime, taking me any and everywhere just so I could get lost in towns and cities I had never been to, attempting to take photographs and trying, unsuccessfully, to erase Sofia from my mind. Then, my interest in photography started to wane; Sofia even owned my hobby.

I spent time with Miles and the girls when I could bear company, and my mother finally forgave me for hurting Sofia, although she would mention her from time to time. Little did she know, Sofia was all I could think about.

After being without her for five months, I had an appointment with my neurologist. He was pleased with my progress. He couldn't give me any answers about my memory loss nor the constant flashbacks I still experienced, but he thought it was progress. He agreed with my psychotherapist about maintaining a journal, suggesting I wrote down my dreams and nightmares to retrieve the lost memories. I drew the line there.

I couldn't document my anguish. It would make it even more real than it already was.

The best news I received was that I could start driving again.

As soon as I arrived home, I got in my Spider with my camera and drove to my favourite beach. I felt like a teenager getting their license for the first time. Finally free and independent for the first time in a long time.

When I pulled up to the beach, the freedom severed. I was sure I came here with her. I had seen it in my dreams, when I saw her smile and heard her laugh. My soul was still shackled to Sofia's.

I forced myself out of the car. Needing to find that freedom again. Clutching my camera, I forced myself to look through the lens, desperate for any happiness to fill the holes in my heart. A couple walked by on the beach, hand-in-hand, oblivious to anything else. Their smiles were a painful reminder of what was missing. I clicked to capture their happiness when my own seemed out of reach.

Did Sofia feel the same? I missed her so much. I had tried contacting her, but after weeks of trying, I realised she didn't want to hear from me.

After searching for the fragments of freedom at the beach, I returned home to prepare for my parents' anniversary party tonight.

I wanted to photograph the event, but I was apprehensive. Not only had Sofia taken away my joy for photography, but I also still suffered from occasional headaches from loud noises and dizziness from bright lights. I didn't want to disappoint my parents if I had to leave early.

I didn't want to continue to be a disappointment.

My mother had been excited about this black-tie party all week and when I arrived, I admired the decorations. She had once again succeeded in creating an elegant and extravagant affair. For a brief moment, the desire to capture this memory for her sparked my need to photograph.

As soon as I arrived, she found me. "Congratulations, Michael. I'm so pleased you are driving again," she said as we embraced.

"Thank you, I had missed it. Congratulations on your anniversary; I'm happy for you both. You look beautiful." She was the lady in red, wearing a floor length gown and dripping in diamonds, which I was sure my father had spent a small fortune on.

"Thank you, darling. You look dashing yourself this evening."

I spoke to her for a while until a guest came to find her. I mingled with the guests as I had known them all my life, and some were also my business associates. As I was talking to my father, a woman approached in my periphery. The long brown hair was unmistakable. When I turned around, I came face to face with Bianca Kingman, and I was disappointed. I had been certain it was Sofia. She congratulated my father, and then she turned to me with outstretched arms.

"Michael, you are more handsome than ever," she said, as I walked into her arms.

I was surprised by the show of affection. I had imagined she harboured some animosity towards me at how I ended things with Sofia.

"Hello, Bianca, you are just as stunning as I remember. It's so good to see you." Taking a step back, I looked her over and all I could see was Sofia.

"I'm happy to see you look so well." She grabbed my bicep, and it didn't seem crude, nor was it unwelcome. It was maternal, and it all felt very natural; it was almost comforting.

My father excused himself and went to find my mother.

"Are you here alone?" I was optimistic, discreetly looking around the room.

"What do you really want to ask me?" she asked gently, with a sad smile.

I was hopeful. *Had she finally decided to return to me?* "Is she here?"

"No, she's not here, nor is she anywhere, really. Despite her father and I begging her, she decided to escape to Antarctica to nurse her broken heart there."

"Antarctica? Why would she go there? I'm sorry, that's my fault." I sighed, crushed and disappointed.

"You win some, you lose some." She shrugged.

"Yes, that makes me the loser. I should never have let her go." I spoke quietly, almost to myself.

"Don't be too harsh on yourself. I'm sure when the time is right, you will sweep another beautiful lady off her feet. If you'll excuse me, your mother appears to be free." She kissed my cheek and walked towards my mother.

Seeing her threw me off kilter; Sofia looked just like her, and even sounded like her. Or was that an auditory illusion? I didn't want or need anyone else. The woman I needed was Sofia, although I didn't understand why she would be in Antarctica. I would call my investigator and he would find out. That was why all my phone calls to her had gone unanswered. I was ready to fight for her and get her back in my life. I only hoped I hadn't lost my chance, and that she hadn't met someone else.

Could that be the reason she had left for Antarctica? Had she found comfort in someone else, and they had decided to make that their hide-away?

My mind raced as I imagined her body entangled with someone else's.

I mingled with the guests for a few more hours after that, but I couldn't get thoughts of Sofia with another man out of my mind, doing all the things I should have been doing with her.

Miles came to find me, but I wouldn't take the drink he offered. I had decided to keep a clear head until I felt more in control of my mind. He was the picture of happiness, as he had a rare night away from his girls.

"Did I see Bianca Kingman?"

"Out of all the ladies here, Miles, is she the only one you noticed?"

"Yes, definitely, didn't you?" He laughed; the alcohol was loosening him up.

"Why don't I drive you home, Miles? I think we've both had enough of partying tonight."

"First night out in months. I'm not leaving yet, but you should go. I know you have one hundred laps to swim to try and avoid the matter at hand," he said as he threw back the amber liquid in his glass.

I looked at him, willing him not to say it out loud and make it true. "What would that matter be, hmm?" I challenged him.

"The glaringly obvious bad decision you made when you let go of the best thing that has ever happened to you. She complemented everything you are, and for reasons I still don't understand, you let her go. She was your own personal platoon and was willing to go to war for you."

"What do you know about that?" I asked, my voice low and laced with anger.

"I know letting her go was your biggest failure in life. I also know you will never move on from her."

Suddenly, he looked sober, and his eyes had become quite clear. He was serious, and he didn't make any attempt to back down from his declarations. For months, he had watched me attempt to drown my sorrows in my pool, in my aimless wanderings, and in my work. He knew I had been dying a thousand deaths every day that she was gone.

I didn't have a response. My brother knew me well, and he knew me best. He had seen through all my thinly veiled attempts at moving on. I was never going to be able to move on from her. I still didn't know her, but I needed her. I had to get her back.

"I'll see you, Miles. My pool beckons," I said, as I left abruptly.

Chapter Thirty Nine

♥

Michael

The valet brought the Spider out, and remembering that I was driving, although short-lived and transitory, brightened my outlook. I was finally independent again. I slid in and I was immediately cocooned by the black aniline leather. I was soon off, listening to the engine roar. The drive was an experience, disrupted only by the red light coming up ahead. While I was waiting at the light, bright lights blinded me as an SUV came barrelling towards me at breakneck speed. I had nowhere to go except into oncoming traffic; I was a sitting duck. I couldn't believe it. I had survived the unsurvivable, only to lose my life at a suburban traffic light. The SUV engaged its breaks, I assumed, as it flipped and flew over the Spider as if in slow motion.

The sonority of metal on metal was horrendous, and the blinding lights were frightening. The smell of rubber burning was suffocating. The shattering of glass was the worst sound, and I had only ever heard once before. This felt like a thousand stabs to the heart. The Spider was crushed, but I was unharmed. My chest was tight, my heart pounded, and tears were streaming down my face. Suddenly, my body felt as if it didn't belong to me, and I couldn't move it. I couldn't understand why, as I didn't seem to be injured. My body was launched into the air, yet still sitting in the Spider, and suddenly, I hit a wall and landed on the back of my head on a marble floor.

How did I get launched into the air with such ferocity? Why were my eyes crying, and why was glass all over me and embedded in me?

As soon as I heard the crunching sound, my shoulder started screaming and throbbing, my chest constricted, and I could barely breathe. The worst was the pounding headache I suddenly had. I could only move my head slightly, and when I did, I saw the worst sight. In addition to bright lights and the stars in my vision, body parts were strewn everywhere, some were burning, and I didn't understand where all the fires had come from.

Where was this hell, and how had I arrived there? I wondered, losing control of my body.

While on the floor, I stretched out my hand to the woman next to me, but she had lost her head. Literally. I didn't have a woman in the Spider when I had left my parents' party. Who could she be? I had seen her in a nightmare I once had.

I heard a loud and piercing scream. Glancing around, I realised it was my scream. How could this be happening? I looked around for Kaan; he would know how to get out of this mess. In the chaos, he was difficult to find. I tried to look around me. All I saw were bodies everywhere, tables and chairs overturned, and remnants of meals splattered on every surface. Nothing was left of the restaurant; it had been razed to the ground. I couldn't control my thoughts. I was in the Spider, but how had I travelled to a war zone?

I had to stay awake, but my head was heavy. I needed to stay awake. My father was expecting me back within three days to attend meetings with him. I had asked Miles if I could get Maxie and Laila a puppy to cheer them up since their mother had left. He told me he was thinking about it, but he would agree to it. He always loved dogs.

I had to stay awake for Sofia. She had agreed to be my wife and she was having our baby.

Would it be a girl who would be as beautiful as her, or would she be a swimmer like me?

I had to stay awake and feel the baby move like she said had happened after I left her at home alone.

How could I have left her home alone with only a stocked fridge for company, to come to a war zone?

Why would I shirk my responsibilities to Sofia and to my father to be here?

Nothing made sense.

I couldn't stay awake. I was fading but, in the distance, I could hear the distinct sound of sirens. They were on their way to rescue us. All of us. The restaurant was so full.

Why are they taking so long?

Breathing was becoming harder, and my head was getting heavier. Oh no, I couldn't fall asleep; I needed to stay awake for Sofia.

"Michael, Michael. Wake up, honey. It's time to wake up." My mother was calling out my name.

I struggled to open my eyes, and as soon as I did, I saw everything. All of it. The worst horrors I had ever seen. I closed my eyes and heard it all. First, the deafening series of explosions followed by the screaming and crying. I could smell the unmistakable putrid stench of burning flesh; it was strong, and I could taste it.

I had to open my eyes; seeing my mother is better than this hell. I opened my eyes, and I tried to speak, but no words came out. Tears streamed down my face as my mother mopped my brow.

"Michael, wake up. You're here with me. It's over now, you're ok."

I couldn't stop crying. *Was that me wailing?* I think I might also be screaming, but why couldn't I stop myself?

"Do you have to give him that again? He needs to wake up."

"Mrs Masterson, we need to keep him sedated. This will help him."

"It's been three days. You don't need to sedate him. I don't consent to this treatment of my son."

Who was my mother arguing with? I needed to wake up. *Why was I being sedated?* My head grew so heavy.

Was it another bomb?

Oh no, it was a bomb!

I heard it, very faint at first, and as I woke up, I realised it was Miles trying to wake me up. My heart sank. I was in the hospital again. It had all happened.

"Michael, wake up, man. You need to drink something."

I opened my eyes, and Miles was next to me.

"Hey man."

"Michael, speak up. I can't hear you."

"Water, please," I said, with an outstretched hand.

"Yes, I can give you water. You need to sit up first. Do you think you can?" He spoke gently.

Was he afraid to break me? Again.

Surprisingly, I was able to sit up and move around. I was groggy, but I was able to control my body.

"See how easy that was? Now sip this."

Miles put a straw to my lips, and I took a long sip.

"Miles, what am I doing here? What's going on, man?" I asked, looking around the unfamiliar painted blue room. It was calming, but all I could feel was the thumping in my chest.

"Easy, Michael. Let's take it slow. You're in hospital, but you're ok. Don't worry. First things first, a shower. Do you think you can stand up?"

"I think so. Was I hurt again?"

"No, Michael. No injuries. The Spider, well, you'll have to see it for yourself."

Miles helped me out of bed and walked me into the shower. I wasn't hurt in the accident, but why was I so weak, and why was it hard to do anything for myself?

"I draw the line at showering you, but if you insist, you know I'll do it." He would have. I lost him for a while, but I had my brother back.

"No, Miles, you only learned to shower yourself a year ago, I'll do it myself." I was even too exhausted to laugh.

"Welcome back, Michael. I knew you would return to me; kisses."

"Get out, Miles."

I stood underneath the rainfall shower head, and it felt glorious. *How did I get here?* I was in the hospital, but I wasn't injured. *What happened to me?* I finished in the shower, and when I caught a glimpse of myself in the mirror, the sight was horrifying. I had grown a week's worth of beard. A shave, food, and water were in order. I painstakingly shaved, and immediately, I felt better. I got dressed in the clothes which Miles had arranged for me.

As I walked out, I could smell food, and then I realised how hungry I was.

"That smells so good, Miles. What is it?"

"I believe they call it hospital food," he said, amusement dancing in his eyes.

"Well, I could eat about a tonne of it."

"That has got to be the first time I have ever heard that being said about this food," he said, looking at it with disdain.

I sat down, ate it all, and drank a bottle of water while Miles sat with me.

"What's going on? How long have I been here?"

"I've had them page your doctor for you. He's on his way. What do you know about anything, Michael?"

"An SUV came at me at a red light and nearly killed me," I said, remembering the night of my parent's anniversary party.

"Yet not a scratch on you. I have the video here if you want to watch it."

"No, I don't need to watch it. I remember it all. I need to know just one thing."

"Sure, what is it?" He leaned in, concerned.

"Did I really send her away? Is Sofia gone?"

He sighed heavily and shook his head. "She's not here. I'm sorry, man."

As we were speaking, a rotund, cheery man walked into my room. "Good afternoon, Michael. My name is Doctor Wilson. I'm your psychiatrist."

I groaned in both exasperation and defeat. "Did I lose my mind? Is this a psychiatric hospital?" That explains the calming blue walls.

"On the contrary, I'm sure you know that not to be true." He rubbed his hands in glee, full of excitement. On a good day, his enthusiasm would be infectious.

As he was speaking, I suddenly realised how clear-headed I was. How I remembered every little thing that had happened a few days ago, as well as everything else before that.

"Doctor Wilson, what's my diagnosis?"

"Mr Masterson, if you would excuse us, please. I would like to speak to Michael."

"Sure, I'll see you later," Miles said as he got up to leave.

"Miles, before you go, did you say it was a yes for the girls' puppy?"

Miles was taken aback. He looked at me with wide eyes brimming with tears, and an even wider grin. "Well, under the circumstances, it's a definite yes; welcome back!"

After he had left the room, Dr Wilson sat down in the chair Miles had just vacated.

"What's going on? How long have I been here?" I pressed.

"We've had you in here for the last five days, but kept you mildly sedated to help your brain process what's been happening. The car accident you had was very minor. You walked with the paramedics to the ambulance, but they were worried about your mental state. Do you remember what was going on?"

"Yes, after the SUV had flipped and flew over my car, it was like I was transplanted, for want of a better word, to an incident I was in a few months ago," I explained, piecing together the events that brought me here.

"What incident would that be?" he asked, in that open-ended way to keep me talking.

"I was in a restaurant in Istanbul when a series of bombs exploded. However, all along I had no memory of that incident as well as the last five years of my life."

"Yes, I have consulted with your neurologist and psychotherapist, and how about now? What's going on in your mind?"

"I have clarity. I remember the bombing and its immediate aftermath, and it was the worst experience of my entire life. I think I also have my lost memories back," I said, as my voice trailed off. For months, this was all I had wanted.

"Everyone has a different experience with Post Traumatic amnesia, and it's important that you explore this. I am available to do this with you, but it's not necessary to do so as an inpatient. You're free to go and continue to process things at home. We've been treating you for Post-Traumatic stress disorder."

"How do I remember everything?" I asked, breaking out of my trance when he told me my diagnosis.

"That is one of the mysteries of the mind. Something in your mind may have been triggered. It's very difficult to be specific."

"Thank you, Doctor Wilson. I most certainly have so many questions which I must ask you, but the most important is if there are any limitations to my travelling straight away?"

"Where were you thinking of going to?"

"Antarctica."

"Antarctica! Now that's a journey, but why do you need to go there immediately?" he asked, wide eyed and intrigued.

"There's someone I need to see to help process things."

"From my perspective, you can travel there. Even better if it will help your mind heal and recover. This recovery is a marathon, not a sprint. I would also recommend you consult your neurologist as well prior to travelling."

"Sure, I will. Thank you for everything."

When Dr Wilson and I finished talking, I sprung into action. I called my driver, whom I had hoped I wouldn't need to see again for a long time. While I waited for him, I called my investigator as I had planned to do before the accident, which had simultaneously derailed my plan to see Sofia but had expedited the return of my memories.

This had to be a miracle. I had started to resign myself to the fact that I had lost all knowledge of the last five years of my life. I asked my investigator to find out everything he could, as I needed to see Sofia. In no time, he had all the information. I was surprised to hear that she was working for the small but mighty Great Expedition magazine. Only a few weeks ago, its parent company had approached Worldwide Media to buy them. This had to be the best coincidence. As I needed this to be done quickly and quietly, I asked Miles to help.

Early the next day, I went in to see my neurologist. After telling him of my urgent need to travel to Antarctica, he was hesitant. He reminded me of the ordeal my mind and body had been through, and the need to take everything as easy as possible. He was reluctant about the trip and referred me for further opinion to my general physician. I spent the rest of the day being poked, prodded, and examined. This was a sacrifice I was willing to make to see Sofia again, as I was missing her deeply. The physician spoke at length about the need to be very careful with my health, and to seek urgent medical attention if I became unwell in Antarctica. He signed me off to travel and insisted I took anticoagulant injections with me, which his nurse taught me how to self-administer. I knew to be careful, as Joe had also repeated the same when he thought I might have been pushing myself too hard in the gym and in the pool. I knew my body well, and I had learned to listen to it from a young age as an elite swimmer.

When I went into work the next day, I found Miles straight away.

"Miles, did you manage to acquire Great Expedition?" I asked impatiently.

"I'm not here for decoration. Of course I did. Now that you are here, care to tell me why we bought them and what the sudden urgency was? It was a good business move, by the way."

"They have a research operation in Antarctica."

"And?" Miles was both fascinated and amused.

"Sofia is on that assignment," I answered gruffly.

"She's in Antarctica! Wow, she really knows how to break up." He slapped his thigh as he laughed.

"We didn't break up. I told her to leave," I offered.

"You didn't break up? Hmm, you might have hit your head harder than we all feared. What's the plan now that you're her boss? You do know about our zero-fraternisation policy, right?" He laughed, clearly amused and enjoying the turn of events a little too much.

"Miles, tell me why you're so familiar with this policy? Oh, yes, I remember now. You wrote it for Zane Dixon's benefit to shake off his little man-crush on you." It was my turn to laugh.

I left and went to my office. I put my assistant to work to get everything she could on Great Expedition and its operation in Antarctica as well as personnel information. She was efficient and had all the information for me in record time. Sofia's position was a photographer. The personnel file on her was sparse, lacking anything of substance. I decided researching her was not the best way. I had to go and see her.

I called the pilot and told him to get the jet ready. My assistant reached out to the magazine and informed them that a representative would be travelling to Antarctica to visit the Research Centre. She also arranged what I hoped wouldn't be a wilting disaster in the eighteen hour flight time.

Chapter Forty

♥

Sofia

The Research Centre was in a frenzy after they heard the news that a representative was arriving to see what we had been working on. I, too, was worried about how my work would be received, although I knew my photographs were phenomenal. I edited and re-edited them, just to be sure. Although this was just a six-month assignment, I needed to do it right so I would get recommendations for more work.

I went back to my bedroom cubicle to prepare for the arrival. The living quarters were spartan at best, and just adequate for sleep, reading and, in my case, to ponder all that had been of my life. I had packed some self-help books, and they were eye opening. Although nothing was better than a real conversation.

I was nervous about this meet and greet. I even washed my hair, and wore something other than the Antarctica drab, as my colleagues dubbed our winter wear. I applied some light makeup. As this initial meeting would be indoors, there was no need for too many layers.

We were to gather in the common room and wait. What took me by surprise as I walked into our usually dull and dreary common room was the burst of yellow colour dotted all around. There were sunflowers, at least a hundred of them in small vases everywhere. My frozen heart melted as tears filled my eyes.

How could these thrive in the chill of Antarctica?

This couldn't be for me, but if it was, this was something truly special. My colleagues thought so, too. The usually serious and reserved scientists were reduced to nothing but excitement and loud chatter over the beautiful sunflowers. Some even held onto them. I suspected to take them and brighten up their own personal spaces.

I suddenly felt hot, and the hairs on the back of my neck stood in awareness as Michael walked into the room. I sighed audibly. I was in awe of how good he looked, how healthy he appeared; my memories and imagination had not done justice to how handsome and captivating he was. He had been working hard on his body. His all black jeans and preppy pullover outfit did not disguise his gym honed physique.

When our eyes met, he smiled at me and visibly exhaled. The kaleidoscope of butterflies residing in my stomach suddenly took flight, and I held my breath. He was here, in the South Pole. Nothing could have prepared me for this rush of emotion.

How could he have remembered the special place sunflowers held in my heart?

He greeted everyone and introduced himself. He reassured everyone that the buyout of Great Expedition wouldn't be putting any of our jobs at risk. There had been talk the magazine had changed hands; challenges of print media and maintaining a research facility. Never had I imagined it would be in Michael's hands. He kept it noticeably light, assured everyone he was only here to observe and to ask a few questions, and he begged everyone to be themselves.

I had never seen him at work with his employees. The sunflowers had stolen the show, but Michael still charmed everyone. I was still sad and had hardly gotten over him. Even before I saw him, I was still irrevocably in love with him. He was in my thoughts all day and in my dreams every night. Seeing him elicited a mix of emotions — the dejection at his rejection, the anger at him not giving us a chance, and the sadness for how alone I had felt over the last five months.

Why would he be here now?

Our group dispersed, and I made to leave the common room with them, but Michael called out my name. I walked towards him with what I hoped was a neutral expression on my face. I had decided he would never know how much I was still in love with him.

"Hello Sofia," he said with that devastating smile I could never forget.

"Hi Michael."

"I am so happy to see you. I have missed you so much."

This was a surprise. *How could he miss someone he didn't know?*

"You have?"

"I have," he said, looking at me appreciatively.

"Why are you here?"

"I needed to see you and to speak to you."

"You said everything you had to say five months ago."

"I shouldn't have said all the things I said. That was the biggest mistake of my life."

Mistake? This moment had only ever existed in my dreams. The fluttering in my stomach had returned.

"Your mistake, yes, but I'm not sure what it has to do with me."

"Sofia, I need you in my life more than any words can say," he said earnestly.

I took a deep breath; when and how had he decided this? "I can't have this conversation with you now. I am at work."

He couldn't waltz in and out of my life whenever he wanted to. There had to be boundaries, even if he waltzed in with a hundred sunflowers to break down my defences.

"I respect that, but can you make an exception just this once? When can we talk?"

"In a month, I'll be finished here." It took everything in me to continue to deny him a chance to talk to me.

"I can't wait that long. I need to speak to you. Is there somewhere where we can talk privately?"

I was tempted to be obstinate and refuse to talk to him. However, the pleading look on his handsome face and the sunflowers surrounding me softened me right up.

"Sure, we can go outside for a while." Our shared history was enough for me to agree to a conversation, but I wouldn't be falling for his lines or any other grand gesture.

I returned to my cubicle, wrapped up warmly, and grabbed my own camera. We met at the exit and walked out.

"How are you here?" I asked him, hoping I was working hard enough to temper the excitement I felt.

"I had to see you again, so I bought this magazine."

That was extravagant, but he had always been generous. I was shocked but not surprised. His father had done the same thing to prevent pictures of an injured Michael from ever seeing the light of day while he was in a coma in Istanbul.

"The last time we spoke, you know when I begged you to give me a chance, and to give us a chance, you sent me packing from my home, so please excuse my confusion." I sounded wounded. *Could I be more pathetic?*

"I regret that every day. Sofia, I remember us. I remember everything."

"Hmm, really. I know you have the best investigator money can buy."

Could the investigator have told him about the sunflowers? That was so personal; how would he find that out?

"Ask me anything that only I would know."

"I won't be playing that game. I am glad you have your memories back, as you say, but that doesn't concern me, not anymore."

"Please give me a chance to explain, please," he begged.

"No, you were very much the big man when you made your choice. Now, man up and live with it. I'm feeling cold and I am going back inside." I strode past him as I went back into the building.

I returned to my workspace where I sat for hours, editing and re-editing already perfect shots. I worked hard to ignore him as he engaged with the scientists at the research station. His sudden appearance was a surprise. He had his memory back, and suddenly he wanted to talk and whatever else. I couldn't have him in and out of my life. That wouldn't be good for my psyche. I remained at my desk until the workspace was deserted and I was truly alone, or so I thought until I heard him speak behind me.

"When I arrived in Istanbul and you told me you had felt our baby move for the first time, I promised myself I would always be present for you and our children. As I lay on the floor, after the explosions with the mayhem and chaos all around me, all I wanted to do was to come back home to you."

I couldn't believe it. He really did have his memory back. This was all I had wanted since the day he had woken up in the American hospital. My heart was racing, and I suddenly felt hot. He had finally acknowledged us and our baby. The tears welled up, and I blinked them away. I didn't spin my chair around to look at him. I couldn't, not when I was about to cry.

"When we lost our baby, all I wanted was for you to wake up and tell me that everything was going to be okay in our world again. When you eventually did wake up, not only had you forgotten me, but you had no idea about all the things we had ever shared."

"I am so sorry, I wasn't there for you." He spoke with sincerity.

I couldn't help the torrent of tears. "I'm sorry. I thought I'd moved past the whole mess. I didn't realise talking about it with you would just bring it all back."

"We don't have to talk about it. I didn't come here to upset you." He spoke so gently. This Michael was so familiar to me.

Was he really back?

"Out of anyone in this world, you're the person who deserves to hear what happened."

"Can you look at me, please, while we talk?"

I spun my chair around to face him, but I couldn't open my eyes to look at him.

"I had felt the baby move while we were on the plane on our way to you, but nothing afterwards, but I didn't think much of it. After we had been in Istanbul for three days, and I was sitting at your bedside, that's when I started to feel the pain. It was mild, but I knew something wasn't right. When I stood up, and then lost so much blood, I just knew it wouldn't be good news."

I opened my eyes and saw the anguish on his face. "My father had arrived in Istanbul, so he came to the hospital to be with me. Chris and David had gone to sleep, as this happened at night."

"Why were you in the hospital at night?" he pressed softly.

"I had left earlier in the day, but I had promised you I would come back and spend the night with you," I explained.

"You had promised me?" he asked, confused.

"Yes, I used to talk to you all the time. Chris secretly thought it was absurd, though."

He chuckled. "She would, but now that you mention it, I'm sure I knew when you were there."

"How?"

"I recognised your voice when you came to see me at the rehab facility."

"You didn't seem to know me at the rehab facility."

Could I have caught him in a lie?

"I didn't, but I had heard your voice. It had been comforting, and then when I moved to rehab, I couldn't sleep at night anymore. I didn't know it then, but that might have been the reason. What did you talk to me about?"

"Every little thing. Except the news at that time — I didn't want to upset you."

He smiled at me, then took his phone out and showed me a picture of the glass shards I had picked from his body.

"Will you tell me about this, please?"

I looked down at his phone, and I started crying again. I couldn't stop until he came closer, pulled me up, held me close, and let me cry in his arms. He smelled just as I remembered, and I couldn't help the arousal blooming deep within my core — how inconvenient. It was selfish, as he had been the injured one, but this was all I had wanted from him since the day he woke up in Istanbul.

"I'm so sorry. I didn't think it would upset you," he said as he reluctantly let go of me.

"It's strange, but these tears are a mix of reliving everything and the pure relief you came out of that situation intact. I can tell you about that." I exhaled as the memories came flooding back.

"At first, I hadn't been allowed to see you without parental supervision — your parents. Hospital rules and, of course, being Mr High Profile and such."

"Really?"

Had he not heard this before?

"Apparently, I was of little consequence. Eventually, I came into your room to see you, and when I touched you, I felt these glass splinters embedded in the skin all over your body."

"That must have been difficult to see."

"Not the glass. It was the size of your head that was most unsettling. You didn't look like you. I asked for some tweezers and removed it all."

"Thank you, for everything you did for me, every little thing."

"Of course, I did everything I could; you were mine then."

"I still want to be yours, Sofia."

I wanted to be his too. This was all I dreamed of all those lonely nights.

"Since you now remember me, how did you remember me, anyway?"

"Even when I didn't remember you, I still wanted to be yours. I just wasn't at my best."

"That was never your choice to make," I said as I sat back in the chair, creating space between us.

"I would have always second guessed myself, wondering if you were with me because of the man I once was, or because of the person I became."

"I am not as superficial as you're making me out to be."

"It's not personal."

"It was very personal; I lost the man I loved."

"Loved, as in past tense?" he asked as he rolled his chair closer to me.

"You sent me packing. How long was I meant to be pining for you?" I was defensive, and my voice became louder.

"Have you met someone?" he asked, holding his breath.

"In the South Pole! I came here to escape. People, reality, the hurt, and the heartbreak. How can I meet anyone when you own me, Michael?" I shouted.

He didn't need to know all this.

"Sofia, we belong together, this is why I am here. I need you."

I needed you when you threw me out like trash.

"Why? You've decreed it, so now it's the directive?"

"I haven't decreed anything. I am here begging you to have me back."

"It's the same thing. You still haven't told me how you even came to remember who I am."

"On the first day I was cleared to drive, I was in a minor car accident."

"Oh no, were you hurt?" Immediately, I was worried. I looked him over and he didn't have obvious injuries.

"No, it was a very minor accident, but when it happened, something — the noise of the metal, or the breaking glass — triggered something in my mind. It took me back to the explosions in Istanbul."

"That must have been frightening," I said as my eyes widened in disbelief.

"In the worst way. Every single detail of that day came back to me in living colour. As well as the events of that day, every emotion I felt returned to me. I also remembered everything else that I had forgotten."

"When did all this happen?"

"Nine days ago."

"Yet you're here now. Are you even well enough to be here?"

"Begrudgingly, my physician said I was. I had to see you. I would give anything to have you back in my life."

"In what capacity?"

"You still have my ring around your neck. Why is that?"

"I'm still learning to let go." I told him, instinctively reaching for it and holding it tight.

"You don't have to let go. Come back home and put it back on your finger."

"I can't do that. I don't trust you, not anymore. You broke my heart, and you could easily do it again, in the same callous way you did before."

"What can't you do?"

"I can't come back to your home."

"Can you come back to me, then?" he asked with pleading eyes.

"I don't know."

"That's not a no."

"My work finishes in a month."

"After that?"

"I'm house hunting and taking a holiday."

"Where are you going? We could go together, and you can decide if you want us to be together or not. You don't need to house hunt. Your home is with me," he pleaded, melting me little by little.

"Come if you will, but I already have my mind made up. Your home, although so beautiful, doesn't have a beach, and I have decided to live closer to the water."

"You love Lake Washington, but I'll live wherever you want to live, as long as I'm with you."

He now wants a home with me, when I lost the home, I had with him.

"I don't trust you anymore."

"Please give me another chance to prove to you that I am worthy of your trust."

"I need to think about that." I was worn out. I was in the toughest negotiations I had ever had.

As I laid in my bed, I couldn't believe the day I had. I had fought hard to avoid falling back into Michael's arms easily. I wasn't fooling him; he knew he had me the minute his jet landed in the South Pole. I didn't trust him with my heart, but I knew I would find myself back in his life and in his bed very soon. I wasn't sure about his mental state and how he would be.

Would he be erratic and push me away again or would he be completely back to who he had been before the Istanbul incident?

I wanted him, and all he had to give, but I needed to make the right decision.

Chapter Forty One

♥

Michael

Seeing Sofia was everything I had imagined. She was still as beautiful, articulate, and as intelligent as I remembered. The short time I had spent with her made me realise why I had fallen in love with her, and that I was still in love with her. I hadn't expected her to come back to me easily, but I didn't realise how difficult it would be. Although she was upset about us, the aura of profound sadness she exuded when we first met wasn't there. This was positive; I didn't have to break down her walls as I had to do in the very beginning. The fact that she wanted to discuss her future plans with me proved she was open to being with me again. I just had to keep trying, but I couldn't stay in Antarctica indefinitely, and I didn't expect Sofia to drop everything to return with me. When she talked about her role here, she was passionate about it. Even though it was her first photography assignment, she had produced good work.

The next day went by very slowly. I was seeing everyone and putting on a show to understand their roles, but what I really wanted to do was to be alone with Sofia. We needed to talk, and I was longing to take her back to my jet and show her how much I missed her.

I found her at her desk and asked her to show me around. She told me to bring my camera and meet her after I had dressed to go outside. She returned and led me outside.

"Have you got everything you need?" she asked me.

"No, not quite. I'm still working on that."

She didn't miss a beat, and she chuckled softly. I longed to hear that again and again. We left the building and got onto snow mobiles. Sofia seemed to know where she was going, so I followed her through the barren, undulating landscape. The snowfall was thick, and it blanketed the landscape as far as the eye could see. I should have been feeling the chill still in the air, but being with Sofia was my dream come true and nothing else mattered. As she whizzed past me, I remembered her zest and energy for life, but naturally she was still guarded, and we could've easily shared the two-person snowmobile. When we arrived at an ice-covered inlet and got off the snowmobiles, she directed me to set up my camera and we waited.

As we waited, I had to ask. "The research your team is here for is astronomy and astrophysics. Why are we waiting for penguins?"

Her vivid brown eyes looked at me appreciatively. She was still affected. That made me hopeful.

"I met a man once, and he taught me how to live and love again, and during some of that time, we shot wildlife in Africa. I fell in love with him then. Shooting wildlife makes me feel close to him, even when he's not there."

She missed me just as much as I missed her.

"He sounds special."

"He is, and a little temperamental, too."

"Do you know why he would be temperamental?"

"He hit his head badly."

"So, he is not himself, then?"

"I think he might finally be. I'm not sure."

"Why don't you give him another chance and find out for sure?"

As we were talking, the penguins started to appear. Behind them, three sea lions clambered onto the snow covered rocky outcrop. It was a beautiful sight, and the lily-white backdrop was beautiful. As we both clicked away silently, I watched her and vowed I would make her mine again, no matter what it took or how long.

"Sofia, I need to leave tomorrow and return to HQ." I had the worst timing, but it was inevitable.

"I see." Her face fell.

Was I messing up the chance of getting back with her by leaving so soon?

"How much longer are you here for?"

"After today, another twenty-two days."

"I want to see you again."

"Maybe," she said playfully.

That was all I needed; I left the next day, optimistic I would have her back.

Chapter Forty Two

♥

Michael

It had been three weeks since we spent time in Antarctica together, and I couldn't wait to see her again. The best time to catch Sofia would be early in the morning. My pilot didn't disappoint, and we landed at Van Nuys at six o'clock. I was at her penthouse within forty minutes, and fortunately, the doorman recognised me and let me up without any announcement. Her private elevator took me straight into her penthouse. I was nervous about the surprise visit as I hadn't told her I would be coming, but I had to win her back, by any means.

When I arrived, she was in her kitchen, making breakfast.

"Don't jump, Sofia; it's me."

She turned around with a look of surprise on her face, which immediately morphed into a smile. "What a pleasant surprise. How did you get up here?"

"I used the elevator."

"Yes, you didn't break that part of your brain in charge of your humour. What's that again?"

"That would be the frontal lobe, and everything works perfectly. I can assure you."

"Everything?" she asked, wide eyed with a mischievous smile.

Could she be serious?

"Yes, I can show you if you like."

"Perhaps, but not right now. Have you eaten?"

She wasn't serious.

"I haven't. I would love to eat."

This was a cordial reception, and it had me hopeful, although she was standing far away, and not making any effort to come any closer to me. As it was in the beginning of our relationship, I was on eggshells, with a pounding heart and sweaty palms. I had to get this right. I wanted her back in my life, and the ring on her finger.

"Would you like some help making breakfast?"

"Yes, please. This is my first breakfast since the South Pole, and I want to make it special."

"What would you like me to do?"

"The coffee and the juice, a cappuccino for me, please. The waffles are just about ready."

We worked quietly, and I loved it. It felt normal, and the confined space was perfect for us to be as close to each other as possible. No chef, no housekeeper, just us. I need this every day. We sat next to each other on the kitchen island.

"These might be the best waffles I've had in months, thank you," I said with a mouthful.

"I missed real food while I was away. We were fed some things I'd rather forget," she said, shaking her head.

"Would you ever go back?"

"Not to the South Pole, or even the North Pole. It was too cold, and I got what I needed from that experience."

"What would that be?"

"Real industry experience, and space."

"Space?"

"Yes, to deal with my heartbreak," she said pointedly, sipping her cappuccino.

"I'm sorry I hurt you. I shouldn't have pushed you away like that. I regret that every day."

"You didn't push me away. Pushing away indicates some creation of a chasm. You ended our relationship," she said as she raised her eyebrows.

"Will you ever forgive me for that?" I would spend the rest of my days begging for her forgiveness if she would have me back.

"We had been through so much together. We were having a baby, engaged to be married, you had been there for me when I needed it, and I had done the same for you. I still wanted to be there for you while you healed, but you never gave me that chance," she said, wholeheartedly.

"I thought I was doing the right thing then."

"The right thing for whom? We were living together; had a life together. You didn't even let us try to get back to what we had. Now that I think about it, I am still so angry at you."

"Do you think you could ever forgive me?" Her forgiveness meant everything to me. We would have a clean slate, and I hoped I would finally stop feeling guilty about how I had treated her.

"I don't know. Maybe. I think I can forgive you. You were in a difficult place with your health, but what hurt the most was that you didn't listen to what I had to say about us. If I remember well, you told me that begging was unbecoming."

"That wasn't my finest hour; I shouldn't have said that." I remembered that vividly, and it crushed me every time I thought about it.

"This history talk is really upsetting me. I am going to take a shower and get dressed. Don't follow."

This was not how I had intended this reunion to go. The fact that there was an open dialogue between us had me hopeful, though. I wanted to follow her into the shower and have a proper reunion, but she needed time. When she had dropped her guard during breakfast, she looked at me hungrily, and it stirred a surge of desire and longing. Although we had argued, the sexual tension between us was palpable.

Chapter Forty Three

♥

Sofia

M ichael still affected me, and there was no doubt that I was still desperately in love with him. I was certain he was my forever. I chose the wrap dress that had brought him to his knees in the rehab facility. It was also one of my favourites. I returned to the kitchen where he was, and I felt his hungry eyes on me.

"Are we going somewhere?" he asked with a smile on his face.

"Yes, house hunting for my beach house."

"Sofia, let's talk about this." He sighed.

"Speak," I said to him, a little too abruptly.

Why was I so riled up?

"I want you back, in my life, in my house, and I want to be back in your heart."

"Your house is not at the beach, and I want to be close to the beach." I sounded like a brat, and that wasn't what I intended.

"Ok, why don't I buy this beach house for us?"

"Do you think I can't afford one?" I was offended. Again, he wanted to throw money at the problem.

"That's not what I'm implying. I want to. All I want to do is make you happy."

"By buying me like a whore?" That was not what he said, but that was how it felt. Buying stuff came too easily to him.

"How did this conversation come to this? I didn't say that either."

"You're welcome to come with me to have a look."

"Ok, I will. That dress has got to be my favourite." He changed tactics and employed flattery instead; it worked.

"I know. You were very happy when I wore it to visit you in rehab."

"Was it obvious?" he asked, walking closer to me. He stopped himself before he came too close. This was familiar, like it was in the beginning.

How long could I manage to keep my defences up? All I wanted was to be wrapped up and cocooned in him.

"Yes, you were too high on whatever they were giving you to try and be discreet about it."

He laughed out loud, the laugh I had last heard from him months and months ago. I had missed it, and I missed him, but I was too heartbroken to let him in.

We went down to the garage, and I expertly manoeuvred the Panamera out towards the coast. It handled like a dream and was worlds away from the snowmobiles I had become used to.

"Are you back to driving again?"

"I am, but the Spider is beyond repair," he said wistfully.

"Oh, was the accident quite serious?"

"No, not enough to cause injury, but both cars involved are total losses."

"I'm sorry. I know that car was your first love."

"Its position was usurped. It had become a very distant second."

I smiled; that made me feel giddy. "Well, I'm just glad you're back to being yourself."

We arrived at the first house we would be viewing. The homeowner's grandson was there to meet us. The house hadn't had any updates in sixty-four years. It was quaint, but no amount of imagination was enough for me to consider buying it. Michael and I left after the obligatory viewing.

"That was a little depressing," Michael said, as we walked towards the car.

"I know. Perhaps the next one will be different."

I was wrong; the next three homes were just as bad as each other, and the romance of a beach house was wearing thin. Michael and I had been together all morning and were enjoying each other's company. *Did I really need a beach house?*

"Let's have lunch, Sofia, and talk about this," he said as we drove towards a small group of eateries right along the beach.

"You're right. I'm hungry, or I want to comfort eat. I'm not sure anymore."

We went inside a beachside bistro, where we both ordered a grilled chicken salad. The outlook from the bistro was beautiful, and I looked out at it until Michael spoke up.

"I'm hopeful that you and I are going to work this out and get back to what we had," he said gently, taking my hand in his and holding it against his cheek. I had missed this.

"Are you trying to make me feel better about this disastrous search?" I asked, suddenly noticing how deliciously he filled out his pullover.

"Yes, and I mean it. But I have one question. If you do take me back and let me be yours, do you see yourself living in Seattle?"

I let out a deep sigh. "If I do take you back, and let you be mine, it would be hard for me to live in your house in Seattle. The last time I was there, I lost my home and I'm terrified that I would learn to love it again, then lose it." I told him truthfully.

"The beach house here; is that where you see us living if you take me back, and let me be yours?" he asked, smiling at me, intertwining our fingers. This moment was ours, and it felt like we were the only two people in the world.

"HQ is in Seattle. That's important to you, so is your family, your friends, and everything you know." Even though he was fully recovered, I wasn't sure what such a big move could do to his mind.

"That's true, but the most important person in my world is right here in LA. I'm not saying this because I'm trying to win you back, but because I want us to make the right decision; where would you feel happiest living?"

"That's an easy answer." I told him immediately.

"It is?"

"Yes."

"Will you tell me the answer?" he asked expectantly.

"Yes, but first I have to see the doctor, but I don't need your company for that."

"Why do you need a doctor?" he asked, brows furrowed in worry. He didn't let my hand go, and I didn't want him to.

"For a check-up. I haven't been able to see one in six months."

"Ok, you can drop me off at the penthouse."

Chapter Forty Four

♥

Michael

I had to work harder to get her back in my life. I would live anywhere in the world, as long as it was with her. She despised the vulgarity of both our individual wealth, and disliked any overt show of it, but I wanted to make her happy. I had taken one home away from her before, and it was my responsibility to return the security she had once known. This would either make us or break us, but I had to try.

Within the hour, my assistant had connected me with a real estate agent who had listings right where she wanted her beach house. She was already waiting; she could meet us as soon as Sofia returned home. When she did, I took the car keys from her and asked her to take a drive with me. Despite the rift between us, we were enjoying being together again, and her letting me hold her hand made me happier than anything had in a long time.

The homes we were shown were light years away from the ones we had seen in the morning. As we walked into each one, Sofia's smile became wider and wider. We told the agent we would be taking one of them and would call her the next day to tell her which one.

"Which one did you like?" I asked her.

"I loved every one of them. How do I choose? They were everything I had imagined and so much more while I was in Antarctica. I didn't think there were houses for sale in Paradise Cove."

"I'm happy that you're happy."

"Let me sleep on it, and I'll know in the morning."

She hugged me and kissed my cheek, and I didn't want to let go, it felt like she didn't want to let go either as she lingered in my arms. Holding her close and smelling her intoxicating scent sent me to battle with my willpower. I wanted to have her in all the ways I couldn't have her yet. It was with difficulty that I let go of her perfectly rounded body and held her hand instead. We went back to the penthouse. She was tired from her flight and the excitement of the day. She went straight to bed after she had reminded me not to follow her. I made myself comfortable in one of the guest rooms. Before I tried to sleep, I went into her rooftop pool and swam until midnight. I was just relieved to be back in the same space as she is, and I knew getting her back in my bed would take even more effort and patience.

"Michael, Michael, you need to wake up."

I couldn't have been asleep for long, as the bedside clock read one thirty; however, my pillow was soaking wet, so was my face. I was sure I had thoroughly dried when I took a shower after swimming.

"Michael, you're screaming and crying in your sleep. Are you having a bad dream?"

"I'm so sorry I woke you up," I said, surprised and embarrassed that she was seeing me like this.

"It sounded like you were having a nightmare. Do you have them often?" she asked, care and concern infusing her tone.

"All the time, since I got my memory back."

Would she still want me despite this?

"What do you dream about?" she probed.

"Mostly about the bombing."

"Would you like a cup of tea?"

"Tea? Yes, please."

Besides my therapist, Sofia was the only other person who now knew about my nightmares. They would wake me up, and I would swim, tire myself out, and return to bed.

"Here you are," she said, handing me a mug as she placed her own on the nightstand next to her.

"Thank you. I don't think I've had tea at one in the morning before."

"Tea is best if you want to get back to sleep, and it will just make you feel better."

I could have done with all this care all this time, if only I hadn't been too blind to see it.

"I'm glad I've got the tea connoisseur with me tonight," I said, relieved she now knew my recovery wasn't as perfect as I had made it out to be.

She smiled weakly. "You mostly dream about the bombing. What else do you dream about?"

"A baby screaming, all alone, and I suspect in my subconscious mind, it's the baby we lost."

"That's difficult. Are you getting help?" she said, moving closer to me, serving only to distract me with the softness of her body against mine.

"I have a therapist, a psychiatrist, a really sarcastic brother, and hovering parents, so I'm engaging in copious amounts of talk therapy."

"Of course, Miles would have a bit of fun with you," she said as she sipped her tea. The soft light cast a shadow of her sexy silhouette on the bedroom wall.

"He's probably the best out of them all," I answered, while I tried focusing on her face and not her body's curves, illuminated by the light.

"Have you finished your tea? I'll take the mugs away and go back to my room."

"Sofia let's try something, only for tonight, please," I begged as I looked into her eyes.

"What's that?" she whispered softly as if she knew what I was about to ask.

"Stay in this bed with me. I know it will help. I won't do anything you don't want to." I didn't want her to leave. Ever.

"Will you stay on your side of the bed?"

"I won't. I don't know how to; not with you next to me, but I won't try anything. Trust me?" Honesty was best, I didn't want to give her another reason to not trust me.

She hesitated, then looked at me and smiled. "Ok, just for tonight."

We fell asleep next to each other with my arms around her, as I had been dreaming about for months. I was going to make her mine again.

I woke up the next morning with her curled into me. This was all I had wanted. This was where we both belonged, in each other's arms. Her body was as soft as I remembered, and her feminine scent was enough to drown in. She moaned softly in her sleep and moved her thigh against me, and my body responded instantly. It hadn't forgotten her either.

She stirred and opened her eyes, looking straight into mine. Before I could move in closer to kiss her, she put some space between us.

"Good morning, beautiful."

"Good morning. Did you eventually get to sleep?" she asked sleepily.

"Thanks to you next to me. I slept better than I have in weeks."

"I'm happy to hear that." She was awake now, awkwardly trying to wrap the sheet around her pyjama clad body.

"I only wish you could be as close to me when you're awake as you were in your sleep," I said sincerely.

"I am close; we're in the same bed," she said, unconvincingly.

"We might have shared a bed, but we're still oceans apart," I answered truthfully.

"I don't trust you with my body or my heart. The last time I did, you broke me," she whispered.

"Give me a chance to show you that you can trust me."

"Did you meet someone while I was in Antarctica?"

"Someone? Like a woman?"

"Yes, a woman." She chuckled, but the burning seriousness of the question lingered in the air.

"I haven't been with anyone else. Is this why you're reluctant to reconnect with me? You're the only one I want, the only one I've longed for the whole time."

"How have you been spending your time while we were apart?"

"In abject misery. After I ended our relationship, it didn't take me long to realise that I had made the biggest mistake of my life, but it was like you had fallen off the face of the earth, and you didn't want to be found."

"So, what did you do with yourself?"

"I worked on my recovery, on my fitness, and getting back to work, but I missed you terribly. I missed all of you. When Bianca told me where you were, I had to get you back, no matter the circumstances."

She chuckled. "Of course, it was my mother. She's loved you from the first time she met you."

I smiled. I felt the same about Bianca. "On my way home, after my parents' anniversary party, I was involved in that car accident."

"You wouldn't have had to go through all that if you had just listened to me."

"I know, and I'm sorry. You know I am."

I didn't give her a chance to respond. We had talked enough, and I needed to kiss her. I kissed her for the first time since I had left her to go to Istanbul, time stood still as I savoured her taste and her smell. The kiss was gentle at first, a tender reunion of souls who had been without each other for too long. As the intensity grew, the kiss became more urgent and desperate. She let me wrap my arms around her soft body, and I pulled her closer, feeling the warmth of her body against mine. She moaned like only she could, but I had to stop. I needed her to know she could trust me, and I didn't want to push her away again.

"I missed you too. You're all I could think about for the last six months. I needed to get over you, but I didn't know how to," she said, catching her breath.

"You don't need to get over me. I'm here; we can get back what we had before."

Chapter Forty Five

♥

Sofia

We eventually got up and ordered some breakfast to be delivered. While we were waiting, he walked towards me, pulled me closer to him, and we kissed over and over. I had missed this. I had missed us. These were the kisses that had melted me in the African wild.

"Was getting closer to me so bad?" he asked as he continued to hold me close.

"No, it wasn't," I said, kissing him again.

He even had sunflowers delivered to the penthouse, then handed me a small red box which surprised me.

"Don't fight me, Sofia; it's a gift. We used to give each other plenty of those, and this is no different."

I opened it and inside the box was a key. When I looked inside the card, there was an address of the second house we had viewed in Paradise Cove.

"Michael, I don't know what to say. Thank you."

"You never did tell me where you would like to live."

"Anywhere you are will always be my home." I was sure about him and about us.

"I vote for Seattle during the week, and weekends at our beach house. How do you feel about that? You have a life here too. Your friends and parents, and I want to be a part of that life just as much as you would be a part of mine in Seattle."

"This is why I never could stop loving you. That's the perfect plan, and I can live with it."

In a daze, I kissed him again. "Can we go and see it again now?"

"If that's what you want."

I drove us to the house, and it was still as I imagined it. I knew I would be happy there.

"I am going to enjoy decorating this place, but I think I might need help, and I already have someone in mind." I was giddy, and I had already become used to having him hold me close.

"It's going to be beautiful. I trust you."

"Thank you. This house is a dream."

"You said you were going on a holiday. Where are you going?"

"Somewhere warm. I need to thoroughly defrost, and there will be a secluded beach."

"I need to be there with you."

"Why?" I asked him playfully.

"I'm insane for you. When are you going?"

"In a week. Once I get this house feeling like home. You can come with me, because I might just be insane for you, too."

We held hands as we continued to walk from room to room. We kissed and it was the best walk through I had ever had in any house I had ever been in. We ate again at the beachside café, then he told me he had to return to work. I couldn't hide my disappointment.

"I'll miss you. I've enjoyed getting to know each other again, and I can't wait to return."

"I'll miss you too."

I had become dejected. How could I have needed him so quickly after our reconciliation? When nighttime came, we shared a bed, but he didn't try to make love to me. Being so close to him was enough. He slept through the night, holding me close. He was at peace, and I was content. I realised once more that Michael and I were meant to be together, and we fit.

In the morning, we ate breakfast before he left.

"Are you worried about the nightmares returning when you return to Seattle?"

"A little, but I'll be back with you soon, so it won't last forever."

He left soon afterwards, and a force of habit had me calling Brad to help me with the surprise I had in mind.

Chapter Forty Six

♥

Michael

Leaving Sofia two days ago wasn't as easy as I thought it would be. Now that I had her back, I never wanted to let her go again. I had to speak to her all the time, and she felt the same way. In order to leave for LA again, and then our trip together, I had to put in long hours at HQ.

After what felt like the longest day at work, I pulled into my driveway. I noticed a car that didn't belong, and as I inched closer, I realised it was a Tributo. I couldn't believe my eyes. My father knew how much the Spider meant to me, but would he replace it?

I parked next to it. When I stepped out, I inspected it and found a box on top of it. When I opened it, there was a key fob and a card. I went underneath the light and was able to read the card; this gift was from Sofia. This was both overwhelming and surprising. I immediately called her.

"Sofia, I've got your gift. I'm speechless."

"Have you taken it for a test drive yet?" she asked me, sounding just as excited as I was.

"Not yet, but I already love it and I love you."

"You need to test it first, before you start declaring your love for it."

"I'm looking at it; it's love at first sight. I wish you were here with me right now."

"Take it for a spin, and then call me and tell me all about it, and be careful," she said pointedly.

When we hung up, I took the car out for a drive, and I enjoyed it immensely. I especially loved that it was a thoughtful gift from Sofia. It was a definite upgrade from the previous one. The engine was superb, the interior a dream, and what it represented had me excited.

Did this mean I was forgiven, and I was back in her life completely and absolutely?

The only way to know was to go and see her in person. I called all three pilots who usually fly me, and none of them were in a condition to fly. I would have to wait until tomorrow.

The next day was long, and I was restless. When my workday was finally over, I arrived at the hangar in record time and soon landed at Van Nuys. I went to the beach house, as Sofia had been looking forward to spending her first night there. When I arrived, I was surprised at the difference a week had made. The interior walls were a lighter colour. I didn't have a chance to see anything else.

As I walked in, I saw Sofia on the beach. The view from the front door past the expansive great room was of a small stretch of private beach. It was the very reason Sofia had chosen this house and I had bought it for her. I dropped my bags where I stood, went barefoot, and made quick strides to the sand. She stilled before she turned around, and when she finally looked my way, she smiled a smile I had missed all those months we had been apart. She walked into my arms, and I held her close.

"I am so happy you're here. I have been counting down the minutes of your return since you left." My heart pounded in my chest as I looked at him and realised he was here, and he was all mine.

"I've missed you too." We kissed endlessly until we were both breathless.

"Thank you for the Tributo; I love it."

"I'm happy you love it. The minute I saw it, I knew it was the one."

"That's exactly what I thought when I saw you too, Sofia."

"And yet, you let me go."

"I'll spend the rest of my life proving to you that you made the right decision coming back to me."

"Come inside, I want you to see the house."

We went inside and I showed Michael every inch that was furnished. The kitchen had been perfect and had only needed some window treatments. The living and dining room were one great room adjacent to the kitchen, and they were the most elegant coastal rooms I had ever seen. The organic textures and white oaks adorning the great house made it cosy and feel like home, despite its size.

Michael was impressed. I led him to the bedroom wing and showed him the master bedroom. I had continued the coastal organic feel of the house, but I was starting to worry it was too feminine with the hint of pistachio colouring in the soft furnishings. My worries were unfounded, as he loved it too.

"Sofia, you have done well in such a short time. We are going to love it here."

"I did get some help, you know."

"You may have, but the place is definitely you. It's us."

"Are you hungry?"

"Yes."

"Excellent, me too."

We ate, and we talked about all we had been doing over the week we had been apart. We still fit, just as we had before the incident in Istanbul. Michael was back completely. He didn't seem to have any lasting problems except his nightmares, and he still didn't favour bright lights. I then started to wonder if all other aspects of him were just as I remembered, and I had to know.

"It's been a day, and I'm ready to sleep," I announced softly, without preamble.

Michael held my hand and led me quietly to the master bedroom. I didn't say much as I removed all I had on. Michael understood the invitation, and he did the same. Unlike the very first time we were together, there was no fervour nor urgency. We were both nervous about what was about to happen, although neither of us had ever talked about it.

"Sofia, I've been looking forward to being with you like this for a very long time." He sounded confident, but there was no mistaking the hint of nerves as his jaw ticked.

"Me too."

"I don't know if anything has changed since my injuries." He tried to explain.

"I'm glad you haven't had any practice, and we'll figure it out together," I reassured him.

"I couldn't imagine practising with anyone else."

He kissed me gently, then with determination, as he had been doing since we decided we would be together again. We both didn't have to wonder any longer if Michael had any residual effects. His body told me immediately that he still loved mine. I couldn't contain my excitement any longer, and I had to have him as close to me, the only way I knew how.

"Sofia, please go really slowly; it's been months." He begged as I lowered myself onto him.

"I'm not sure I can."

"I've never been so nervous in my life."

"Shall we stop?" I teased as I nipped his forearm. I had missed his body, and if it was possible, he seemed fitter.

"No, but don't move just yet. I want this to last. It feels like our first time all over again," he said as he pushed up into me.

I gazed down to where we were joined, and that was enough to make me combust. He was able to shake off his nerves, but the air remained thick with anticipation. When I eventually started moving, I felt a rush of warmth spread through my body as I anticipated the breadths and depths of what only he could give me.

I didn't have to wonder or second guess anymore. He reminded me about every nuance he suspected I might have forgotten. He flipped us over and immediately took control. He was demanding and fierce and his pleasure was on his face, in the tightness of his arms and the way he braced against the bed, giving me everything he had. We explored each other with a hunger that only comes from being apart for so long. Our bodies moved in perfect harmony, our heartbeats in sync and beating as one. He needed to prove to himself, and to me, that he was still the man I fell in love with, and he didn't disappoint.

As he took everything, thoroughly and completely, I exploded all over him, and he fell into his own intense explosion. Afterwards, both of us panting and out of breath, we laid wrapped in each other's arms, where we belonged. As I was about to drift off to sleep, knowing we now had our second chance, Michael nudged me gently.

"Are you alright?" I asked, straddling him as he sat us both up on the edge of the bed.

"I'm more than alright. I don't know how I ever thought I could live without you."

"We're together now."

"Do you want to go out for a walk?"

"Only because you asked so nicely, and you have that look on your face, that if I don't come with you, it might just be the end of life as we know it."

This was why I fell in love with this spot right by the beach, for my own piece of paradise at any time. It was a balmy LA night, and I pulled my light silk robe over my naked body, and he brought his camera. The sun had set, and the exterior lighting was beautiful. Woven pendant lights hung in the tree branches, soft white lights dancing on the walkway. Along with that, the soft lighting surrounding the backyard lit up the water in the pool and illuminated the ocean in a magical way. I couldn't believe this place was ours. I was the happiest I had been in years.

"Sofia, will you look at me, please?"

I looked at Michael, and he looked like he had in Bora Bora. I couldn't help the chuckle coming from my throat.

"What is it? Again, you look a little green around the gills."

"Sofia, please take this ring and marry me, please?"

How did he get the ring off my pendant? I wondered as I touched my now bare neck.

"Hmm, I would need some time to think about that, a really long time," I said, as I blinked back tears.

"Sofia, will you let me be your everything again? Please?" he asked in earnest.

Even though we had been here before, I couldn't help the tears rapidly filling my eyes. All I had wanted when I was in Antarctica was to be with him, and he had wanted the same, only he hadn't wanted to cede control to his mind. I finally had him back, body and mind.

"I will marry you."

"You've made me happy. I want us to be married within the week."

"The week! Are you pregnant? It doesn't work that way, you know?" I asked, as I laughed softly, and I looked up into his eyes.

It was his turn to laugh. "No, I'm not pregnant, at least I don't think so, but I don't want to wait any longer to marry you."

"I'm not going anywhere. I've said yes and I mean it."

"Is there a reason you want to wait?"

"Hmm, no. Just weddings take planning."

"Anyone who needs to be there will drop everything to be there for us."

I paused to take in what he was saying. He was right, and I didn't see any reason to wait, either.

"Ok, within the week, where, how, and whom?"

"It's a yes? I need to take a picture of this moment. Let's get back inside and talk about it. It can't be that hard trying to plan a wedding in a week."

The next few days were a whirlwind. There was no question this wedding would be in Africa. As we were already travelling to the Seychelles on holiday, this became the destination for the wedding. Neither our families, nor our few invited close friends were surprised when we told them what the plan was. They had all been waiting for this to happen. Both sets of parents didn't waste any time planning what they could. My father provided transportation, and David booked out the whole resort for a week.

Within four days, all had been organised. A beautiful ivory dress for me, as well as miniature ones for Maxie and Laila. Michael was right; anyone who was of importance to both of us was present. Our party of thirty arrived in the Seychelles, and I couldn't believe this was happening.

The three days prior to the wedding with our friends and family were bliss. We all enjoyed the activities at the resort. This was more than a celebration of our wedding, but a celebration of all we had overcome as a family over the last few years.

About the Author

Sandy J Mcneill is an avid reader who has turned over nearly half a library in her lifetime. Her early exposure to African folklore, Greek, Norse and Roman mythology as well as American and European literary classics helped to feed her already vivid imagination.

In 2023 she finally penned her debut novel "Remains of our Souls". She is looking forward to publishing the next book in this duo.

After completing her studies, followed by much toil and strife in London for many years she now calls Melbourne, Australia home where she resides with her family.

After reading this book, please remember to leave a review.